The Healing of
Ryne O'Casey

The Healing of
Ryne O'Casey

A Novel

Scott Philip Stewart

FaithWalk
PUBLISHING

Grand Haven, Michigan

Published by FaithWalk Publishing
Grand Haven, Michigan 49417

Scripture quotations are taken from the Holy Bible, King James Version, Cambridge, 1769.

"His Eye is on the Sparrow"
Music: Charles Hutchinson Gabriel
Lyrics: Civilla D. Martin

"Higher Ground"
Music: Charles Hutchinson Gabriel
Lyrics: Johnson Oatman, Jr.

Printed in the United States of America
09 08 07 06 05 04   7 6 5 4 3 2 1

Library of Congress Cataloging-in Publication Data

Stewart, Scott Philip.
  The Healing of Ryne O'Casey : a novel / [Scott Philip Stewart].
    p. cm.
  ISBN 1-932902-42-2 (pbk. : alk. paper)
  1. Terminally ill children—Fiction. 2. Boys—Fiction. I. Title.
PS3619.T53H43 2004
813'.6—dc22
                     2004006809

To the memory of my brothers,
Shannon Wayne (1978–1980),
James David (1952–1989), and
Robert Frederick (1960–1989) Stewart:
Hope

To my mother, Jean, and father, Charles,
whose love and encouragement have
blessed me beyond words:
Blessings

To my wife and best friend, Lena, and my three
cherished sons—Scott, Chace, and Aidan—who
make my life complete:
Joy

To the many friends who have encouraged me
to tell Ryne's story, especially Mary Ann Palmer,
whose comments on an earlier draft
alone made it all worthwhile:
Grace

Wherever God erects a house of prayer,
The Devil always builds a chapel there;
And 't will be found, upon examination,
The latter has the largest congregation.

Daniel DeFoe
The True-Born Englishman
Part i, Line 1

A Bad Cold

NIGHT AFTER NIGHT, Esther Jean O'Casey would hit her knees and pray, "Dear Lord, won't you please just come on and bless us with a little old baby? Me and Olie are doing our part—right regular, in fact—to be fruitful and multiply, as *you* yourself commanded. So please pitch in and do your part, and let us find favor in your eyes and bless us with a darling little baby of our own. Boy or girl, that's up to you. Pretty *pretty* please, O Lord! Amen."

No baby.

Believing as they did that God helps those who help themselves, Esther and her husband Benton Oliver (who went by Olie) took out a second mortgage on their house and had several yard sales a month to pay for expensive—not to mention humiliating—tests at fertility clinics at Emory, Vanderbilt, and Duke. They read enough books on the matter to fill up a Frigidaire box. One writer, a Chinaman by the name of Tao, suggested it was all a matter of angles, so they did *it* in every conceivable way—ways Esther had never even imagined *it* could be done; some even made Olie blush and cut off the porch light, which cast a faint glow through the curtains in their bedroom window.

No baby.

Esther doubled up on the fertility pills they prescribed and once even lost fifty pounds on the outside chance her weight had something to do with it. It hadn't. And in short order she put the weight back on with interest.

But no matter what they did, or where they went, or which expert they consulted, the result was always the same: No baby. Then one cold November day, Dr. Helmut Zuckerweig of Duke University, the world's leading authority on infertility, broke the sad news to Esther and Olie: "Zay is nus-sing else ve can do."

If there was no medical reason, they thought, maybe there was a spiritual one. They worked through a twelve-step program with Olie's brother Heyward, who was staggering up the twelve steps for the fourteenth time. They studied the *AA Big Book* along with the Bible every night and both earned ninety-day chips for attending ninety meetings in ninety days. They spent six weeks on the fourth step, made a searching and fearless inventory of themselves, and ended up calling everybody they had ever harmed (or might have harmed) to discuss how they could make amends. Esther even got more or less used to introducing herself as "Esther, a drug addict and alcoholic," despite the fact that she had never so much as taken a swallow of drink in any form, and Olie's drinking days—which consisted of a having two cans of Schlitz every Friday night after work— were long past. And they had always just said no to drugs, even before Nancy Reagan told them to.

No baby.

They tried, it seemed, every holistic remedy in the history of the Appalachian Mountains. They boiled teas and prepared tonics from just about every species of herb, root, and spice on God's green earth. Once they even drove three hours up to the top of a mountain in North Carolina to see some old woman named Versie Moseley who said she was a hundred and twenty-five years old (and she might have been, to look at her). She gave them a loaf of brown bread and piffled on for an hour or so about her rheumatism and such before she fell asleep, and they went on back home.

Still no baby.

After twelve years of trying and pleading, one night Esther prayed simply: "Thy will be done. Amen."

Then it happened. Precisely two months, three weeks, and twenty-two days after Esther turned thirty, for the first and only time in her life she missed a period. And the very next day, Dr. Colin Howard Reardon, the only general practitioner in their hometown of Tynbee, Tennessee, said, "You're pregnant," and handed Olie a black Cuban cigar the size of a rolling pin and warned, "I wouldn't advise smoking this booger in one sitting."

Esther swooned, then dropped to her knees on the office floor and muttered, "Thank you, thank you, sweet Jesus, thank you." Olie and Doc Reardon stood her back on her feet, and Doc Reardon said, "You're blessing now, Esther Jean; you'll curse later on—I'd say when your little one hits his terrible twos."

Precisely eight months and seventeen days later all those prayers, ten years of prayers, were answered in the form of a beautiful baby boy. They called his name Ryne, after Esther's mother's family, and he was, Esther told everyone, "worth the wait in gold."

OLIE DECIDED *never* to light that big cigar. He said it meant too much to let it go up in smoke. He sealed it in a plastic tube sock canister and tucked it away in his chest of drawers. Other mementos were soon added, and the collection had to be moved to the bureau: Ryne's first pacifier. A plaster cast Olie made of the baby's tiny feet the day he took his first steps.

Esther always told people that whoever said *first we walk, then we run* (she believed it was someone involved in AA) had obviously never met Ryne Oliver O'Casey. He skipped right over the crawling and walking stages, as though, at age eleven months, he just got tired of standing around holding onto the rail of his crib and took off like a shot. He was wobbly when he walked, but when he ran he was steady as could be. Unfortunately, he had inherited the clumsy gene from his mother's people (the Rynes) and could fall over anything, or over nothing at all. Olie likened him to a car with no steering wheel, worn-out brakes, and a throttle stuck wide open. Ryne was forever running into things, falling down and bumping his head, scraping his knees, bruising his elbows.

So Esther and Olie never worried about Ryne's bumps and bruises until one night while undressing Ryne for his bath Esther discovered a large, angry, mulberry-colored bruise on his buttocks. "*O*-lie, get Doc Reardon on the horn!" Esther hollered from the bathroom.

First thing the next morning, they were in Doc Reardon's office on the town square in Tynbee. Esther unfastened Ryne's diaper, and before removing it said, "Now we don't abuse him, Doc."

Doc Reardon put the baby through his paces—poked here, prodded there, thumped on his tummy. Then he turned him over and squinted over the top of his spectacles and studied the bruise. "Ooh-ee, this young'n must have made you right mad, Esther Jean," he said. "Did you inflict this contusion with your hand or your foot, or was it a frying pan?"

"Lord of mercy," said Esther. While dressing Ryne that morning, she had prepared her defense against just such an allegation. She proceeded to tell the doctor flat out that she had not afflicted any such *contusion* on Ryne, would never in a million years do any such awful thing to a little old child, especially not to her own little old child, Ryne, and that she would have expected that he, of all people, knew her better than that.

Doc Reardon laid his hand on her shoulder and said, "Esther Jean, I *do* know you better than that. I was just seeing if I could still get a rise out of you."

"Well, pat your own self on the back then, Doc," Esther said. "You got a rise, all right, and if you'd kept on with it, I might have had to rise up and afflict a *contusion* like that on you with a frying pan, if you got one among your things in that medicine chest."

Olie got a big kick out of the whole caper, and she threatened him, too. After apologizing several times for having upset her so, Doc Reardon referred them to Avery County Hospital to have some tests run.

A few days later they were back in Doc Reardon's office for the results. "Mornin' Esther, Olie, Ryne-o." Doc Reardon greeted them in the small examining room that smelt strong of witch hazel and air freshener. He shook their hands and leaned down and jostled Ryne's arms, then sat down on his little stool on casters, rolled up, and opened the chart, which he referred to as he spoke. "There's the good news and then there's the not-so-good news," he said, keeping his eyes trained on the chart. "But there's not any bad news, so maybe that's the best news."

The color drained from Esther's face. She reached out for Olie, who, notorious for his slouch, sat up straight as an arrow and took hold of her hand. He said, "Give us the not-so-good news first."

"The not-so-good news," Doc Reardon said, "is that the tests show that our little Ryne here has got what they call hemophilia type A. Which means he's what is known as a free-bleeder." He went on to explain—Olie later told Esther, who didn't hear a word Doc Reardon said after "free-bleeder"—that some little something in Ryne's blood, *factor eight* to be exact, which helped the blood to clot, was missing, but (and here was the good news) he would be all right if he got blood transfusions on a regular basis. Not to worry, he told them. The blood supply was screened and reasonably safe, and the bottom line anyway was that they had no choice. Without the transfusions, Ryne had little chance of making it to adulthood.

Thus began the murmuring stage.

"It's all my fault, Olie," Esther told him that night after she tucked Ryne into his crib, which she had rolled into their bedroom. "According to that family medical book in yonder, which I just read, hemophilia like Ryne's got is passed on from *mothers* to sons."

Olie was lying on the sofa in the living room listening to gospel music on the radio. Esther shut off the radio and Olie sat up and said, "Even if that's so, Es', it doesn't mean it's *your* fault, much less *all* your fault."

Esther was not in the mood for another of those silly word games Olie liked to play. "Well, it sure isn't *your* fault, Olie," she said and turned to leave the room. "That medical book in our room doesn't say so much as a word about fathers."

Olie called after her. "Don't they call hemophilia the '*royal* disease,' Es'?"

"Well, I don't know about all that," she said, "but I sure don't feel like no *queen*, Olie."

Doc Reardon was right. Ryne was okay. They took him for his factor-eight transfusions on a regular basis, and Esther had learned, more or less, how not to hover over the child and make of him—as Doc Reardon warned—a "cripple."

And even though she shuddered every time he left the house with his friend Terrence Ford armed with a hatchet and Swiss Army knife on what they called Operation Kudzu Kutback, their mission to save the great trees from their Southeast Asian enemies, Esther had resolved that the good Lord had assigned a guardian angel to watch over Ryne. In time, she had apologized to the Lord for saying—and mainly thinking—that she would like to work Him over from here to yonder in the months just after Doc Reardon had diagnosed the hemophilia.

The years went by, and Esther made peace with the Lord and was sure he had forgiven her blasphemy.

RYNE'S EIGHTH YEAR had been a very good year for the family. There was so much to be thankful for, Esther thought, as she set the Thanksgiving table that snowy evening. She set a dish of cranberries on the table and looked in at the living room and got lost in what she called "one of her moments," and thanked the Lord for all his blessings. If she could have chosen a moment to capture—to hide in her heart and take to heaven for all eternity—it would be a moment just like this.

They had trimmed the Christmas tree the night before, according to their family tradition, and nestled holly garland on the mantel and hung their four stockings—Samson the dog had his own—above the fireplace. They set out the three pieces in Esther's Snow Village collection on a big swath of white felt that extended from the tree to the kitchen door. All the little lights were twinking green and red and white, and Olie had built a fire as only Olie could. He said it was all in the right mix of kindling. It crackled and popped, breathing its warm orange breath on the whole living room. Ryne had tuned in KTYB on the AM radio on the mantelpiece and "O Holy Night" was playing.

There was so much to be thankful for that year. Olie had more work than he could handle and had taken on Early Jackson to help him out roofing houses and screening porches. It was supply and demand, he said, and demand was high, had been high all year long. Ryne was making straight As in school and had not had a single incident with his blood all year, which was amazing considering how active he was. Esther had joined the women's auxiliary at church and had, just that Fall, gone through enough yarn knitting hats and scarves for the colored and unfortunate in the town to carpet their whole house. That, she thought, as she placed the turkey on the center of the table, was a matter of supply and demand, too.

"Lord," she prayed, "bless those dear children of yours. Amen."

She placed this year's two new dishes on the table. Every year she tried two new recipes and got the men (Olie and Ryne and Olie's younger brother Heyward) to vote on them. This year's contestants were a chess pie with a tablespoon of lemon juice added for tartness and an apple brown betty, from a recipe card she found pressed into the old family medical book she had inherited from her mother.

"P.S., Lord," she added, "thank you for letting these new antibiotics work on Ryne." She crossed her fingers the whole time she was praying, and asked the Lord to forgive "O her of little faith" for doing so.

The new antibiotics did seem to be working. Shortly after Halloween, Ryne had come down with a cold so nasty they thought it might be bronchitis or, worse yet, pneumonia. Esther was sure he had caught it on Halloween night, probably bobbing for apples at the party the Gossets threw for all the children of the church. However it had caught him, they did not seem to be equipped to catch it. The cold would clear up, only to return worse a few days or a week later. It was almost, Esther said, as if it was meaner on account of the harm they had done it with penicillin and amoxicillin and every other type of 'cillin they attacked it with. The cold was up in his head and down in his chest and in everything else it could get to. When two weeks of antibiotic treatment had not made it better (and might have made it worse), Esther and Olie took Ryne back to Doc Reardon. He referred them to a clinic in Baldridge, in a neighboring county, rather than to the nearby Avery County Hospital, for the lab work.

A week had passed, and they had not heard a word from Doc Reardon. But Ryne did seem to be responding to the medication. Either that, said Olie, or it was just doing its bob-and-weave routine again.

"And P.S.S., Lord," she added, "bless Heyward, too. He smells of drink."

Lord have mercy, Heyward O'Casey, you're in the soup again.

Hey', as they called him, was a raging alcoholic in Esther's estimation, though he swore he was "only a drunk." Esther suspected from his coloring that he had what she had heard called psoriasis of the liver. The only time they ever saw him anymore was on Thanksgiving. He always showed up three sheets to the wind. This year was no exception. Nobody ever said a word about his drinking, but he would expound in great detail about the difference between a drunk and an alcoholic. The main difference, he told them, was that a drunk was by far the better off of the two. A drunk could control it.

Heyward O'Casey's benders were legendary in Avery County. He had done every fool thing a drunk (which he considered himself) or an alcoholic (which he didn't) could do.

"Allow old Heyward, please," he said, when the four of them had gathered around the Thanksgiving table.

They joined hands and lowered their heads.

"Our dearest heavenly father," Hey' started. "Thanks a million for giving us a family, a *family*—even a family where the mother gives favors to one boy and darkens her face on the other and he ends up drinking—but he's not an alcoholic, praise God …"

Head still bowed, Esther squeezed Olie's hand. *Bless his heart.* Every year Heyward offered to say Thanksgiving grace—it was therapy for him, Olie said, and every year while saying it he broke down crying and slurring and would bend the good Lord's ear about how their mother had always favored Olie who, by the grace of God, had turned out right, over himself who, thanks to the devil, had turned out wrong. On he would go, getting himself more and more worked up and start cussing, until Olie would say "Amen" then either deny he was the favored son or agree it might have been the case or try to change the subject or say nothing at all. It didn't matter what Olie did.

This year—Ryne's eighth year—Olie tried Plan C, changing the subject. Three times. But it always came right back around to Mother O'Casey and Olie and *Heyweird*, the ne'er-do-well-no-count-odd-man-out of that exclusive club.

Ryne, bless his heart, tried his own strategy. "Uncle Hey', I know how you feel. There was this time when they were choosing teams for kickball at school—and I'm no good at kickball, and so I was the last one picked. There was even a few girls that got picked before me. Now *that* is humiliating. Of course, everybody got picked before me. And I ended up making an out every time I was up, so it proved they were right."

For a moment, no one said a word. Esther thought there were a few points in Ryne's story—any one of which would stick, one of which would draw blood. "Pass that dressing, Ryne," she said.

Uncle Heyward said, "Well, just imagine if that was your own momma picking sides, and left you standing there until the end."

Ryne winced. "Ouch."

"Ouch ain't the half of it," said Uncle Heyward.

Heyward stuffed the last bite of his pumpkin pie and whipped cream into his mouth, every bite having been baptized in tears. He got up and staggered toward the front door, saying he had best get on down the road lest they all end up sorry.

"Reckon we might all end up the sorrier if you get behind the wheel of that truck," Olie said.

Esther whispered, "Lord have mercy," then shooed Ryne and Samson the dog back into their room and headed into the kitchen to arm herself with the jumbo rolling pin and two or three of the cat ear biscuits left over from Thanksgiving breakfast, armed herself just in case things got out of hand (which they never did). Virtually the same thing happened every Thanksgiving. Olie always said that Heyward just didn't seem to know how to bow out and make a graceful exit.

Esther stood in the shadows behind the kitchen door to keep an eye on things.

Olie said, "Hand over them keys, Hey'."

Then Heyward, God love him, said, "Well, hot dog if it ain't the big man on campus, Benton Oliver 'Casey. I'll show you!" Then he did the best he could (for a man in his condition) to play keep away from Olie. He ended up falling flat on the floor, and Olie picked up the keys before they came to rest by the end table.

"There now," said Olie. "Let's get back to socializing."

Esther told Ryne and Samson, who had tiptoed back down the hall to peek in on the action, that she would tan both their fannies if they didn't march right back into their room and shut the door until further notice.

Heyward rolled over and staggered to his feet. "Well now, I reckon you still got it, 'Casey." Then he ran straight for the front door again, prefabricating, Esther knew, that he just needed a breath of fresh air, and, when he had made it onto the porch, he shouted, "Yee haw. I'll show you!" and took off down the porch stairs toward his pickup, which he always backed into the driveway so that he could make a quick getaway.

Olie said, "We'll see ya, Heyward. No need to run; it's slick out there. Don't forget to put your headlights on and take her easy."

Esther stood at the front door and called out, "Glad you come, Heyward."

Then Olie turned to Esther and winked and held up the spare set of keys Heyward *always* hid under the left rear wheelwell of his pickup for just such times when people alleged he was not fit to drive. Olie confiscated them every Thanksgiving before dinner, under the pretense of fetching some kindling for the fire.

"Bless his heart," said Esther. "The coast is clear," she told Ryne and Samson, who came back down the hall.

Over the holiday music on the radio they could hear Heyward out front ranting and raving that it was a good thing he was only a drunk and not a real alcoholic or else he would be a real mess.

Before they went to bed, Esther put a blanket, afghan, and feather pillow on the sofa with a note that read, "There's a bag a leftovers on the top shelf of the refridgiator. Get you some tea to. Glad you come." Olie put both sets of Heyward's keys on the coffee table, and Ryne put out an *Incredible Hulk* comic book in case Uncle Hey' sobered up and got bored and needed something fun to read.

By the time they got up the next morning, Heyward was gone, along with the care package of leftovers and Ryne's comic book and, of course, his truck keys. On the back of Esther's note, he had managed to scribble a reply. "Thank you-all for a wonder full even. Ester your cookin beats all. Pray for me. Love, Hey O'Cay."

THE MONDAY AFTER THANKSGIVING, Olie went to work and Ryne's cold had cleared up enough, for the time being, for him to get back to school. Esther was sitting at the kitchen table listening to KTYB—they were calling for a blizzard—and peeling the last of the red potatoes, onions, and carrots for the vegetable beef stew she was making for supper. She put her stew on the stove and checked her spoon bread dough, then stood awhile at the sink looking out at the big snowflakes falling from the white heavens above.

It looked like a picture postcard, she thought, the big wet snowflakes falling in front of the bare-limbed sugar maples and tulip poplars on the yonder side of the creek.

KTYB was saying the storm had arrived sooner than expected, and Esther prayed the roads would not get too bad before Ryne's bus started home. Route 12 was bad enough, if the memorial flower crosses at various turns in the road were any indication, even when the weather was not bad. And Olie—bless his heart, he had not put new tires on his truck since Reagan was in office—he was doing some roof work for Nellie Jean Perkins whose house was set way up in the hills.

At a few minutes before eleven the phone rang. Esther figured it was either the school calling to tell her they were letting out early on account of the weather or Olie calling to ask her to put his tools in the shed before it got much worse.

It was Doc Reardon—or some incarnation of him that Esther had never met. She knew something was wrong—*bad* wrong—when Colin Howard Reardon referred to himself as Doc*tor* Reardon. All and sundry knew him simply as Doc, but that November morning he was, he said, *Doctor Reardon*, and his voice could have been any doctor's, the way they speak at but never to you and always from way far off in the distance—as they do when they're telling you for the hundredth time that there was nothing they could do to make you have a baby.

No small talk: The doctor said he needed to see her and Olie right away. It was urgent. No, it couldn't wait until the storm passed. He had a four-wheel-drive Jeep and would be at their house that afternoon at one o'clock so that they wouldn't have to try to make it up his steep driveway in the snow.

Doctor Reardon hung up before Esther had a chance to say "That would be fine," or "What's the matter?" or "I'm not expecting Olie back before suppertime," or anything else.

It was *urgent*, he said.

Esther walked out onto the back porch and stood there flat-foot with her paring knife in one hand and her glasses in the other. She couldn't later say with any certainty how long she stood out there watching the snow falling—or even if she was watching the snow falling at all. But by the time she made it back into the kitchen, the snow was thick and heavy on the branches of the hardwoods.

She shut off the radio and went to work tracking down Olie. He had left the house before dawn that morning for the lumberyard in Sevierville to buy materials—pressboard, nails, and shingles, he said—for the roof work he was trying to finish up on Nellie Jean Perkins's house before the snowstorm hit Tynbee. She figured he had had ample time to make it back from Pigeon Forge to Nellie Jean's on Scopes Ridge just north of Tynbee.

Nellie Jean said she would get him, and as Esther waited for her to fetch him down from the roof, she felt the beat of her heart in the top of her head.

Esther's tone was matter-of-fact. "Olie, Doc Reardon's paying us a housecall at one o'clock," she told him, "to give us word on Ryne. Head on home as soon as you can." She spared him the word "urgent."

Olie had as many questions for Esther as she herself had for Doc Reardon, but she had no answers to give him. She simply said, "This is no time for fencing around. Just come on home now, Olie, and we'll see about all that."

Then Olie returned to the roof, draped a tarp over the exposed portion, which by the time he left was already collecting snow. He told Nellie Jean he would return as soon as he could, then headed home—wet, cold, and numb—through the driving snow showers in his 1964 Ford with threadbare tires and no heater.

In those tense minutes before the doctor arrived, Esther and Olie exchanged hardly a word. It was better that way, lest they work each other up. Esther stayed in the kitchen tending to her stew and spoon bread and boiling water for hot tea and coffee. Olie built a fire, then went back (on Esther's suggestion) to try to make himself look presentable. He washed up, slicked his hair back with tonic, and put on a pair of tan polyester slacks and a blue button-up dress shirt, which Esther had pressed and laid out on their bed for him.

At precisely 1:00 p.m. Doc Reardon announced his arrival with a honk of the horn. Esther, who had been pacing around the house for ten minutes, headed out onto the porch and helped him up the stairs, now caked with an inch of wet snow. "I'm gettin' a mite old for this," he said quietly, as if to himself. She led him in and placed him on the sofa, but when she offered to take his coat and scarf he waved her off with a gesture of something Esther and Olie had not seen in him before—exasperation, maybe—as though in just a few weeks' time he had become a cantankerous old man.

Bless his heart, thought Esther. Colin Howard Reardon had never looked worse. All Tynbee knew that his broken heart was "a tick from quit" ever since cancer claimed his wife of fifty years the previous Spring. *His hour is drawing nigh*, Esther remembered thinking that day. His face was gray as ash and his hair needed combing; his spectacles were smudged and his clothes didn't match. He refused the coffee, but Esther insisted that he take some tea, though he had the shakes so bad more of it ended up on his knit vest and slacks than anywhere else.

Esther had waited as long as she could. "Is it pneumonia, Doc?"

"How I wish to the good Lord above it was, Esther, Olie," he said, rolling his eyes back. He cleared his throat. "Ryne's got what they call the human immunodeficiency virus, type three, or H-I-V. The virus that causes AIDS."

Olie stood up from the Barcalounger. "What? No," he said, frowning. He staggered toward the kitchen then turned back on tip-toe and started cackling, as if he had heard a joke so bad, so *un*funny, that it was good in a way, even kind of funny. Esther kept rocking in the rocking chair, hands folded in her lap. Olie quit cackling. He stood there still with a dead face. It wasn't possible, he said, couldn't be possible that his own little boy—Ryne Oliver O'Casey, of *all* little boys, who was eight years old and in the third grade at Sam Davis Elementary School in Tynbee, Tennessee, and had never taken drugs or had sex relations or done anything, anything but good in his life—had AIDS.

"Not Ryne," Olie said, as he paced back across the living room, wringing his hands as if his saying *Not Ryne* was the end of the matter. On one pass, he stopped dead in his tracks, cocked his head and looked down at Colin Howard Reardon, M.D., looked him square in the eye, and told him flat out that he was dead wrong. "Nosiree," he said. "Whoever it was run them tests is wrong, Doc. *Wrong.* That's all. So I suggest that you have them run somewhere else and get that man fired, or woman if that was the case."

Doc Reardon sat there pitiful, his head bobbing around with the palsy. He removed his spectacles and fedora and said, "I said the same thing myself, Olie. Believe you me, I did. I called the lab and said there's been a mistake here; this just can't be. The woman at the lab said, 'Well, Doctor Reardon, we ran both tests—the ELISA and the Western Blot—and both were positive.' I said all that means is that whose ever blood got tested has AIDS. But if the vials were mislabeled, well, then you got the right result on the wrong blood. 'I doubt it, Doctor Reardon,' is what she said. 'I doubt it. We have a top-notch staff and a very conscientious protocol with several built-in safeguards.'"

"Safeguards," Olie muttered as he slumped back down into his chair.

Doc Reardon said the more he thought about it, the more he suspected the woman at the lab was right. A mislabeling was unlikely, and a positive result on both blood tests meant that Ryne had *it*, and that his having *it* would account for why that nasty cold he caught wouldn't go away even after all the antibiotics and why he had no appetite and had lost ten pounds in the previous three weeks. "Ryne," he said, "must have gotten it from contaminated blood."

"Contaminated blood?" Olie said. "How could that possibly be the case? Ryne's transfusions—well, every last one was took right over at the County Hospital. And as for safeguards, Doc, I seem to recall you telling us there were safeguards to keep the blood Ryne was getting from being contaminated. Wonder what happened to those safeguards?"

Doc Reardon only shrugged his shoulders and his head started bobbing. The palsy or nervous tic or whatever it was (Esther couldn't say for sure) went berserk and his hands were shaking such that they'd have left a welt on anyone who happened too near. There he sat, Colin Howard Reardon, M.D., who had birthed half the population of Tynbee, Tennessee, with his feeble hands trying to steady his wobbly head breaking the worst news of his fifty-year career. "I fear," he said, "that this AIDS virus is all over the place. The Red Cross has been screening their blood supply for HIV since 1985, years before Ryne was even born. They claim the blood supply is better than ninety-nine percent clean, but there's always that one-percent chance—"

"That one percent chance," Olie whispered.

"—that someone could donate blood in what they call the window period, after they catch the disease but before it can be detected by a blood test."

Esther had been sitting in her rocker the whole time, rocking gently, her eyes trained on the crackling flames in the fireplace.

For a long spell, no one said a word, and the wind beat on the house.

Then, still looking into the fire, Esther said, "Are you quite finished, *Doctor* Reardon?"

"Pardon me?" he said.

"I said, 'Are you quite finished?'"

"Well, yes," he said, trying to straighten up. "I suppose so. We could go over the treatment options if you like."

"I don't *like* anything about this," she said. "Not. One. Thing. About. It."

He nodded and lowered his eyes.

"There's only one thing I want to know, Doctor Reardon."

"Esther," Olie said, straightening up in the Barcalounger.

"I'll thank you not to interrupt me, Benton Oliver O'Casey."

Doc Reardon said, "What's that, Esther?"

"Who gave that blood? That contaminated blood that's give Ryne the AIDS?"

"Well," he said. "Well, I'm sure I don't know."

"Well, I'm sure you'll find out," she told him. "I'll go in yonder and ring the clinic and you can ask that nice top-notch conscientious woman, the one with all the safeguards you said told you about all this, and she can look it up in her records."

"That's not ... That's just not possible," he said.

Olie said, "Now, Esther, I know what you're fixin' to try and do and—"

"Shut up, now Olie," Esther said, eyes still trained on the fire. "I'm handling this."

"I know you are, Esther," he said, rising from his chair and taking a step toward the sofa where Doc Reardon sat, at once, completely still. "But there's a time for saying your piece and a time for holding your peace. I reckon now's one of them times you might ort to hold it."

"The only thing I'm of a mind to hold right now, Olie, is the very life of the prevert who did this to Ryne, right here," she said, clapping her hands together and grinding them with such force that her face contorted into blood-red grimace. "Right here, in the palm of my hands. And I want to wring the wretched, stinkin' life out of him!"

"I know you do, Es'," he said. "I know just exactly how you feel."

"Nobody does," she whispered. "Nobody does." Then it got the better of her, and she was out of the rocker, saying, "Oh, oh, oh." She took the screen door clean off the hinges as she made her way out of the house and stumbled across the porch. By the time Olie made it to the door, Esther was halfway up the driveway to the main road, running through the snow, her scream merging with the shrill wind whistling through the trees.

"I'd best let her go," he said. "She needs some time."

When she returned an hour later, bedraggled but composed, looking much the worse for wear, but seeming and sounding much the better, Esther apologized to Olie and Doc Reardon for the outburst.

Before Doc Reardon left that day, he told them, "Remember: We're fighting a battle on two fronts here. One's the virus inside Ryne; the other's the virus outside of him."

At first Esther thought he was referring, by the *virus outside of Ryne*, to the colds and flus and other germs that Ryne's immune system was not at full power to fight off, as he had explained to them. She quickly realized that he was talking about their neighbors, the very people with whom Esther Jean O'Casey had been born, gone to school, gotten saved, been baptized, grown up, and begun to gray around the temples.

"People don't understand," Doc Reardon said, and a gust of wind nearly blew him off the porch. "I'd hate to be the judge of which does more damage," he added. Then he was gone, and, for a moment, as Esther's thoughts wandered back to the vegetable beef stew that was scorching on the stove in the kitchen and to Heyward's Thanksgiving grace, it was as though Doc Reardon had never even been there at all.

"HMM," RYNE SAID that night after dinner when Esther and Olie sat him and Samson the dog down in the living room and told them Ryne had HIV. "How'd I get it?"

"From some fool-person's nasty old blood," Esther told him, figuring it was no use mincing words.

"Well, that makes sense," Ryne said.

Somehow everything always made sense to Ryne—or maybe Ryne just had a knack for making sense of everything, Esther decided—even things that made absolutely no sense whatsoever to Esther or Olie, for instance that an innocent child like Ryne could be smitten with a dread disease the likes of which the world has never known.

There was absolutely no sense in that at all.

LATER THAT NIGHT, when they thought he was sleeping, Ryne heard his mom and dad lying in their bed condemning whoever had donated the blood that gave Ryne AIDS. "If it wasn't for all them fruity people and drug fiends living in sin," his mom said, "our Ryne in there wouldn't have ever come down with AIDS!"

"Calm yourself, Es'," his dad said. "No sense waking Ryne up."

"Oh, Olie," she said. "I'd love to get my big old hands around the neck of whoever did it."

"I know you would, Esther. But that's not the answer."

"Then you're not asking the right question."

"I won't deny that," he said.

Ryne agreed with his dad on that one. Sometimes things just happen and nobody knows how come, and if you go looking for someone to blame you will only end up hateful, and Jesus was not hateful even after all the terrible stuff they did to him.

Ryne lay awake almost all that night, thinking about it. The way he saw it was that whoever donated the blood that gave him AIDS was trying to do a good thing, because if no one had been willing to donate blood, he would have died from his hemophilia as a baby.

Ryne himself hated needles and shots worse than anything in the world, so he could not imagine himself rushing down to the Red Cross to donate blood even if, as his mother said, you got paid for it with cookies and juice and money. Ryne used to run around the office for dear life when Doc Reardon would enter the room with a lollipop in one hand and a syringe in the other and tell him that if he would just be still it would be over a lot sooner, and Ryne would think, "No duh! Why do you think I'm running?" and keep on running around until at last his mother lost her patience and told him to be still or that little old shot would be the least of his worries.

So Ryne knew that whoever gave that infected blood was pretty brave—no matter what else he might have been—and could not be faulted because his blood turned out to be sick. Besides, he thought, whoever it was did not know that his blood was sick in the first place, or else he would not have ever given it.

Jesus, he thought, had done a good and brave thing in donating his blood for everybody, but some people did not even appreciate that. And whoever gave that blood was sick with AIDS, too, just like Ryne, only worse, because by now he had had it longer. He might even be dead by now. And, as his mom and dad had always taught him, it was not right to go around speaking ill of people who were dead or less fortunate because, but for the grace of God, you yourself could be fat or retarded or homely or crippled or blind. "Those people have feelings, too," they would tell him, "not to mention mothers and fathers and brothers and sisters that love them."

But for the grace of God.

The Gift

THE O'CASEY'S BLACK-AND-WHITE ZENITH went on the blink one winter night the following year as the family huddled around it watching *Unsolved Mysteries*. All day it had been making muffled crackling noises—noises that Ryne said reminded him of the one and only time he had ever seen his mom in dungarees and she bent over to pick a tomato off the vine and they split right in two.

"Ryne, that'll be enough of that talk," she told him. "However, it does sound kind of like the fabric in those cheap jeans did that day."

The TV picture got smaller and smaller, like it does at the end of a "Looney Tunes" cartoon, and the family moved closer and closer, until at last it was but a white dot at the center of the screen.

"Well, at least we can listen to it," Ryne's mom said.

And listen they did, with their heads cocked, for about five minutes. Then Robert Stack's voice faded out just as he was wrapping up the story about some ghost-woman that hitchhiked around small towns outside Chicago in a long flowing dress and bummed rides from handsome commuters.

"Oh fiddlesticks!" Ryne's mom said. She slapped the TV a few times, jiggled it to and fro, worked every button on the front and back, and ended up snapping off one of the rabbit ears trying to adjust it. "I don't imagine we'll ever solve this mystery."

His dad said, "I don't guess *they* ever did either, mother. That's why it's call *Unsolved Mysteries*."

She gave him a look. "Well, aren't you clever, Olie." She would like to know, at least, if that ghost-woman (who she said reminded her of Kate Chancellor from one of her shows) had ever been sighted in the South.

"Maybe she was," his dad said with a wink.

"Probably made it as far south as Tynbee," Ryne added.

"Probably," she said. "Smart alecs." When at last she conceded that the TV was gone, she said, "I imagine lightning ran up on it."

She was *imagining*, all right, Ryne thought: There hadn't been a thunderstorm in the area for months.

Ryne laughed, and she smiled at him. It wasn't that she was lying. Esther Jean O'Casey was a good Christian woman who attended Sunday services every week (or used to, before they quit going to church a few months ago), and she warned Ryne and everybody else about the dangers of bearing false witness.

She was just in the habit of treating facts as if they were things you could just make up as you went along—as though saying something somehow made it true. When anybody else stated a fact, though, whether it was made up or real, Ryne's mom would cock her head and say, "Well, I don't know about all *that*."

Ryne's dad hardly ever disputed his wife's *facts*—directly— and he didn't the day the TV died. He said in his theory the picture tube had blown; his mom insisted that it was on account of lightning; and Ryne, not wanting to take sides, said it just died of old age. It was dead. They could all agree to that. The Lord had called it home.

For a few weeks after the TV died, they all told each other several times a day that it was for the best, that, given the poor reception in the mountains, trying to watch a show on it was more trouble than it was worth anyway. Ryne's mom was the least sorry of the three to see the TV go, or so she said over and over. "Families of today," she told them, "have forgotten how to do anything of an evening but park theirselves in front of the boob tube and vegetate."

"Well," said Ryne's dad, who made no bones about enjoying the news, "I reckon this here's one family that will have to remember how to do *something* else."

Ryne's personal theory was that the only reason families used to sit around of an evening talking and reading and all that other stuff his mom said they used to "have a big time doing" was that there was nothing *better* to do—like park theirselves in front of the boob tube and vegetate. Ryne knew for sure that there was one thing he would have to remember how to do before spring arrived—tune in the station out of Knoxville that broadcasted Atlanta Braves games on his father's old transistor radio.

The dead TV sat dark in the corner of the living room for a few weeks before Ryne's dad said, "Least we can do is give it a proper Christian burial," and hauled it away in the trunk of the car to the county dump.

Ryne knew that, of all of them, his mom missed watching TV most. In the supermarket one day he spied her skimming through the *Soap Opera Digest* as they waited in the checkout line. "I caint imagine why that Victor Newman and Nicki won't lay aside their differences long enough to patch things up," she mumbled to herself. "And that Paul Williams, for another, should just keep to himself and leave Danny's wife alone! The good Lord don't take kindly to people carryin' on—"

Then suddenly she stopped herself, as if it had just dawned on her that soap operas were not for real. Her cheeks turned as blotchy red as strawberries and she sort of stooped down and slipped the magazine behind *The National Enquirer*. Ryne heard her whisper, "Of course, for that matter I don't imagine the good Lord takes too kindly to people looking at them awful shows either. Thank heavens, I gave that vice up."

"Thank heavens," Ryne teased, and she said, "Get you a pack of gum."

Ryne wouldn't have missed the TV so much—or perhaps even at all—if he could still go outside and play or have friends over. Before he got sick, watching TV was a thing to do *after* the sun went down. There were too many other things to do during the day. He would get home from school, wolf down his after-school snack, then rush getting his homework done so he could spend what was left of the day with Terrence Ford and Chimpy Mitchell saving the great mountain forest from the invasion of kudzu or hunting crayfish in the stream out back or—his favorite—surveying the big tectonic faultline that ran just under the ravine on the back edge of the McKeating's cow pasture.

Since he got sick and his friends stopped coming to play and the TV went dead, though, Ryne didn't much care whether it stayed dark all the time. When you are laid up in bed listening to Kris Kristofferson sing "Silver-Tongued Devil," he thought, the last thing you want to see outside your window is a bright sunny day to remind you just how bad off you are.

REVEREND DANIEL NATHAN MCKEE, Interim Pastor of the Historic First Church of Tynbee, Tennessee, sweating in the big burlap minister's robe, stood outside the sanctuary door and listened to the congregation on the third chorus of "Sweet, Sweet Spirit." He had stalled as long as he could. It was 6:10 p.m., time to call the July business meeting to order.

If he had not exactly looked forward to the previous nine church business meetings, Nathan McKee truly dreaded this, his tenth business meeting.

He limped past the empty choir loft, around the corner of the chancel, and up the three steps to the pulpit. He assumed his place in front of the minister's chair and surveyed the crowd. *Heavens.* Folks were wedged into the pews. They lined the walls and flooded out into the vestibule. And the smell: The place stunk to high heaven of Hai Karate, Windsong, and the summertime funk of wellworn drawers and b.o.

The only thing Nathan could liken it to was day-old sweet-and-sour pork, and he couldn't help but recall Isaiah's prophecy about the haughty daughters of Zion: "Instead of sweet smell there shall be stink."

Nathan had never seen most of the multitude crammed into the church. The congregations of Tynbee, which had a devil of a time laying aside their differences long enough for a potluck supper or a Saturday night Gospel singing, were in rare ecumenical form this night. It was the biggest crowd in the town's sacred history, assembled tonight over the decision to spend three hundred dollars for a dying little boy.

The hymn at last petered out. Nathan gathered up his things and limped over to the lectern. The pain in his left buttock, which had started as a dull ache that morning, shot like fiery darts up to shoulder and down to his knee. *His thorn in the flesh.* It always flared up, according to his wife Miriam, when Nathan was especially scared of "blowing it." He himself had never analyzed its pattern—if there was one. In fact, he never talked, much less thought, about the time he blew it, blew it so bad that his little brother ended up dead.

The congregants were shifting about, impatient. "Let's get on with it already, preacher," somebody said.

He reminded himself to stay neutral. He was, after all, the moderator, and moderators do not take sides. If he took sides, he was sure to "blow it." He gripped the sides of the oak lectern. Best he could tell without striking a chalk line from the vestibule to the chancel, he was dead center.

"Welcome to the business meeting," he said. Then with a bang of the same hickory gavel that had called to order a century of business meetings at the Historic First Church of Tynbee, Tennessee, he called the July business meeting to order.

And as soon as he did, a white-haired elder of the church, Mr. Travis T. Gosset, rose from a middle pew right of the center aisle.

"For what purpose," said Nathan, "does Elder Gosset rise?"

"Preacher McKee," said Elder Gosset, in his sleepy mountain drawl, "I've an item of business to propose."

"So ordered, sir. Propose."

"I hereby enter a motion that we set aside three hundred and eighty-seven dollars and sixteen cents from the Samaritan Fund to purchase a color TV set for Ryne O'Casey, a member."

"Motion entered," said Nathan. "Is there a second?"

"I s-second Elder G-Gosset's m-motion," stammered T. K. Kirby, a young man who had risen from the back row on the right side of the church. Most in attendance recognized him—as Nathan did—as a stock clerk at the Tynbee Wal-Mart. "I c-can get an employee d-discount."

Someone hollered, "A-man!" An old woman raised her hands and waved, as if to Nathan, or perhaps to the Lord.

"Not so fast," said Elder Luther Bailey, Chairman of the Board of Elders, and the most powerful member of the church. "First off, you have to be a member of the church to enter or second a motion." He rocked back on his heels. "Now that's according to the constitution and bylaws of the church. And I don't believe that young man from Wal-Mark is a member. So he's not legible to speak up."

T. K. Kirby sat down.

And Buster Jeeves, the town stonemason, stood up. "Well, *I* am a member of this church, Elder Bailey, Preacher, and the lot of you, and in my own name *and* in the name of T. K. Kirby, I second Elder Gosset's motion."

"Well I don't reckon I was finished saying my piece, Buster," said Elder Bailey.

"Yeah, you was," somebody shouted.

"Show the elder some respect, young man," an elderly woman chided.

"He don't own this church," somebody said.

"*Half* of it anyway," a man said. "At last count."

At that, nobody said a thing. It was true. If Elder Luther Bailey did not own the church, he owned the homes of half of its members. His *subjects*, as some in the church referred to his tenants, sat on the left side of the church. If he wasn't *the* Lord, he was a landLord.

"Point of order, Preacher?" said Elder Gosset, who had gotten the whole thing going.

Nathan winced. "The chair recognizes—" His hip was a blaze of pain. He was lost, trying to form a mental picture of Ryne O'Casey. *Were Esther and Olie somewhere in that throng? Whom had he, the chair, recognized?*

Half a dozen people had risen to be recognized. The church was silent—for a long moment.

Then Elder Bailey said, "As I was trying to say, we are called to be good stewards of our resources. And these are hard times, and we cain't afford to be too soft. We're not talking about pocket change here—"

"We're talking," said Elder Gosset, his tone now prickly, "about a little boy, a little boy who is dying—"

"It's hot in here," said Nellie Jean Perkins, without getting up from her seat. She was waving an ornate little hand fan bearing a bust of Jesus holding a baby lamb, and the Lord and the lamb seemed to be shaking their heads as she spoke. "What we need right now is a air condition."

"Air conditioning?"

"Where some of us is headed," a man said, "reckon we might need one."

"Order!" Nathan shouted. He hammered the hickory gavel on the lectern. Splinters flew. "Enough. This body will be in order!"

The church fell silent. They had never seen the strange young pastor, who was mild-mannered and cordial, raise his voice, much less carry on—unlike the preachers they were used to: hell fire and brimstone windsuckers.

Then there was murmuring.

His anger focused him. He said, "A motion was entered and seconded. A point of order was raised. Elder Bailey informed us that only members can vote. So we're going to take a written vote on the matter of buying a TV for Ryne O'Casey with money from the Samaritan Fund. Ushers, please come forward."

Nathan huddled before the altar with the ushers and elders of the church and commissioned them. The ushers were to collect and tally the votes. The elders, who alone had access to the Official Register, were to verify each voter's membership. He sent them off and climbed back onto the pulpit and sat down in the minister's chair to get his weight off that leg.

The ushers passed legal pads around in the offering plates and waited at the end of each pew as members signed their names and wrote either "yes" or "no" to cast their vote. The whole time Nathan's wife Miriam and Elder Luther Bailey's wife Sue Ella played a medley of standards—"Onward Christian Soldiers," "Amazing Grace," and "Power in the Blood" on the piano and organ, respectively.

Thirty minutes later, after the Board of Elders had verified the signatures against the registry and tallied the votes, Elder Gosset handed Nathan a slip of paper. The verdict was in. "Well, it was a close vote," he said, when "Power in the Blood" ended. "By a margin of seventy-three votes opposed to seventy-one votes in favor, the motion to allocate three hundred eighty-seven dollars and sixteen cents from the Samaritan Fund does *not* carry."

Elder Gosset joined Nathan on the pulpit. "Pastor," he whispered, "I've something to say. May I?"

Nathan wanted to tell Elder Gosset *no, that it was a good idea just not a good time, that timing is everything, after all, and that a cooling-off period is advisable in highly charged situations. He wanted most of all to say that he was sorry he couldn't afford to get involved—he really couldn't—because his term was up in a few months and he was resolved to shake the dust of Tynbee, Tennessee, off his feet and move on.*

"Say your piece," he said.

Elder Gosset placed his hands on the big Bible that lay open on the lectern and leaned over close to the microphone. "People, it's a sad day when we that call ourselves Christians can't find it in our heart to do a good deed without a bloodbath. I've seen some pretty sorry things in my time, but none the likes of this. As many of you know—you members anyway—it's something of a tradition here at the Historic First Church to provide our shut-ins with a TV set. Anyone who's spent any time at all flat on his back knows how lonesome it can be. Especially for a little child like Ryne O'Casey. Now, I know that you don't like his disease.

Let me assure you, neither does Olie or Esther or Ryne O'Casey himself. But—"

"A curse is what it is," someone shouted.

"*It* might be," said Elder Gosset. "But Ryne O'Casey is no curse. And you can't just say he's some old evildoer who had it coming and go on about your business without—"

"Travis T. Gosset, quit preaching," an elderly man advised. "We've got us a preacher—a enema preacher anyway—and you up there preaching at us."

"He's not preaching," said a woman with wavy lavender hair. "He's just telling the truth is all. Now you hush up and let him go on."

"Never mind," said Elder Gosset. "The good book says 'God loveth a cheerful giver.' So any cheerful soul here who wants to make a contribution to the Ryne O'Casey TV fund see me afterwards, and we'll see if we can't get up enough money. If not, I've got a Farmall tractor in good working order for sale for three hundred eighty-seven dollars and sixteen cents, and, well, either way ... I'll buy the *darn* TV myself."

"Good Book says a man that can't tame his tongue is in right serious trouble," somebody chided. "You should be ashamed."

"O dear brother," Elder Gosset said, making his way down from the pulpit, "I *am* ashamed. Believe me, I am."

Nathan said a quick benediction that no one cared to hear. He hobbled down from the pulpit, avoiding eye contact with Miriam, who was playing the closing hymn, and ducked out the door. He shut his office door, worked the old robe over his head and used it to dry his face, which was wet with sweat ... or tears.

Then, somehow sooner than she could have possibly been, Miriam was in the office with him. She stood there stone-faced with their infant son Peter Nathaniel in her arms. "Give me the checkbook, Nathan." She was not asking.

"Miriam, we can *not* afford—"

"To what?"

"—to get in the middle of this mess."

"*We* are not going to do anything, Nathan. *I* am." She touched his damp cheek, gently, with her fingertips. "You've been—"

He opened his eyes wide, as wide as he could to keep the tears from rolling down his cheek. "We have two months to go, Miriam."

"—crying?"

"Let it go, Miriam."

"No, you need to let it go, Nathan. You didn't kill Philip. Do you hear me? You don't give life, and you don't take it away."

"I didn't come here for *this*," Nathan stated, matter-of-fact.

"God called you here, Nathan." Her voice was pleading. "Don't you see? Can't you see it?"

"This is a little more than I bargained for."

"Who were you bargaining with?"

"What's that supposed to mean?"

"It means," Miriam said, "that the Lord has been calling you for a long time, Nathan, and, I don't know, I guess I'm just tired of having to screen those calls for you: 'Sorry, Lord, Nathan's not available at the moment; yes, he's working on his thesis, yes, the one on pastoral care; seems he's too busy working to do much of anything else—like pastoral care, or even just plain old *care*'—click."

"We have two months to go, Miriam," he said again, louder this time, colder. "Can you not see that I cannot afford to get involved in this, that I will be damned if I do."

"If you *will* is more like it," said Miriam. "If you leave this behind you, Nathan ... You think the guilt is bad now. Just imagine how bad it's going to be."

He said nothing. Looked at the baby. Tried again to picture Ryne O'Casey.

Miriam said, "You think the way not to get in the middle of this is to stay smack dab in the middle." She handed him the baby, rummaged through her purse, pulled out her wallet, then, before he could say anything, before he could get the checkbook out of his pocket, she was gone.

IN THE SANCTUARY, the cheerful givers came and emptied their billfolds and change purses onto the communion table, whose front edge was engraved with the words of Christ at the Last Supper: *This Do In Remembrance Of Me.* The pile of bills, checks, and change was as high as the Bible on the altar cloth. Elder Gosset counted and Miriam McKee tallied and, when the last three pennies were added, the offering totaled six hundred seventeen dollars and twenty-eight cents—twenty-two dollars and five cents of which had cleaned out Miriam McKee's purse.

Then Elder Gosset, Miriam McKee, and several others managed to do in ten minutes what an appointed committee at the Historic First Church could not have done in as many weeks. They decided how the money would be spent and by whom. T. K. Kirby would purchase a twenty-five-inch RCA color TV and a Super Nintendo game system from Wal-Mart at his employee's discount. Miriam McKee would prepay the first six months of cable television service and make arrangements to have it installed at the O'Caseys' home. Elder Gosset, Buster Jeeves, and T. K. Kirby would deliver the TV, the game system, and the greeting card signed by all who had given or would have, had they been able.

For Ryne O'Casey.

ESTHER JEAN O'CASEY was a "born member" of the Historic First Church of Tynbee, Tennessee. Most members of the Historic First Church were born, not made, and according to Esther's late mother, Miz Ida Bea Porterfield, it was a good thing.

Miz Ida Bea was not one to mince words, and if she said it once she had said it a thousand times: "I swan! If you wasn't borned a member of that church I don't reckon you would become one once you was old enough to know what it meant. Why, they'd carry you straight to the 'sylum."

She had a point, Esther thought.

So when Esther got word that the church was donating a brand new RCA color TV to Ryne she knew that one of two things had happened: Either the wrong half of the church had gotten right, or the other half had bought the TV.

Esther O'Casey believed in miracles, yes—maybe even more than she believed in ordinary events. Lord knew she had seen enough of both. But for the life of her she could not imagine that the wrong half of the church had gotten right. She knew Elder Luther Bailey, knew how beholden those poor people were to him, knew he owned their homes and they had to do his bidding to keep a roof over their heads, knew how much he had hated her mother (and in truth her mother had had very little use for the elder, too).

Esther was tickled pink for Ryne, though, no matter who was giving the TV or who had to get right with the Lord in doing it. Ryne needed it, needed something. Ever since he had started getting really sick the previous May, just about six months after Doc Reardon delivered the diagnosis, he had pretty much taken to his bedroom, if not to his bed, coming out only long enough to eat and bathe and go for an occasional ride in the car. When Esther would tease and tell him that if he didn't come out more often—maybe into the living room once in a while—she was going to have to drag him out kicking and screaming, Ryne would shrug and say, "Nah, Mama. My room's where all the action is."

"Well, I imagine it is," she would tell him.

Ryne's room was more than his castle; it was his whole world. He spent his good days putting together muscle car models and sketching pictures and writing things—things Esther was tempted to read—in the three-subject notebook he had once used for homework. On bad days, it was all he could do to read comic books and baseball cards and listen to her and Olie's warped old eight-track tapes for hours on end.

What a difference a year and a half makes, Esther thought, a year and a half and a nasty little old bug too small for you to get your mitts on and wring the life out of it. The summer before Ryne was diagnosed with AIDS, she rarely saw him at all. Back then all the action was out-of-doors. He would leave at dawn and return at dusk. He was busy being an eight-year-old boy. He hunted crayfish in the stream out back. He went on special missions to save the forest from what he called the evil clutches of kudzu. He tracked black bears (armed with a homemade bow-and-arrow and sling in case he actually did see one). He surveyed the faultline that he predicted would, one day soon, be the epicenter of a massive earthquake that would rock Tynbee and parts south as far as Atlanta. He was never alone back then, and Esther had been glad: There was safety in numbers.

A year later, there was only danger in numbers, Esther told Olie. Ryne had lost almost as many playmates as T-cells since this past May, when he became so ill that she and Olie had to reveal the awful truth about his condition. All Ryne had left was one playmate and thirty-five T-cells—poor on both counts.

It was not so much that Ryne felt like playing; a short walk in the house would quickly leave him tuckered out. But it might have been nice, Esther thought, if someone, anyone, had cared enough to call once in a while or stop by to read comics or trade baseball cards with him.

Please, Lord, Esther prayed, as she pressed a sharp crease in a pair of her husband's gray polyester slacks, please, oh please, let that RCA TV set help keep Ryne company.

"I WISH THEY'D HURRY UP and come on now," she told Olie for the fourth time in as many minutes.

And for the fourth time Olie said, "Quit fretting so, Es'."

It was a few minutes after six o'clock on the third Monday evening in July. It was the hottest July on record. Six weeks had passed without rain, and all Tynbee was suffering, but perhaps none as miserably as Esther, who had to admit that she was, as her younger brother Leroy used to say to torment her when they were children, *four-by-heavy*, but maybe not *corn-fed*, which is what he called her when he was really cruel. And even though she wore as little as modesty allowed—a cotton dress, flip-flops, and underthings, Esther was often heard to say she had poured enough sweat that month to singlehandedly lift the county water ban.

"You're in a tizzy, Esther," said Olie.

"I am," she said.

She had washed and dried the supper dishes, covered the leftover meatloaf, and packed what was left of the creamed potatoes and sweet cream corn in the freezer. She was in the room off the kitchen ironing the laundry she had sent Olie to fetch from the clothesline in the backyard. She would press the arm of a shirt or the leg of a pair of slacks, then take off again through the living room to the front door to see if the men of the church were there yet with Ryne's gift. "I imagine the last time I was this out a sorts was when I went into labor with Ryne."

"I remember it well," Olie said.

He was sprawled across the sofa in the living room eating jellybeans from the bag and listening to what Ryne called his *hillbilly bluegrass gospel* on the old transistor radio they kept on the mantelpiece. The radio's reception was bad enough under the best of circumstances. It was terrible with Esther storming around. Every time she paced across the living room to see if they were pulling in with the TV it buzzed like an airplane on takeoff.

Olie held his peace.

Esther went by again, this time with a can of spray starch in her hand, and stood by the screen door, peering out. "I wonder if this is how the Virgin Mary felt when them magis was coming to bring gold, mirth, and frankensteins, or whatever that stuff was, to baby Jesus?"

"Frankenstein?" he said. "I don't know if he was there."

"You know what I mean, Olie."

"I do," he said.

Olie sat up on the sofa, and Esther went back to her ironing. On her next pass through the living room, she cleared her throat and said, "I said, 'I wonder if this is how Mary felt?'"

"What's that, Es'?" he shouted over Mother Maybelle on the radio who was singing "Will the Circle be Unbroken." Esther wished KTYB would quit playing that morbid number. "By and by, Lord, by and by."

"Olie, I wish you would cut that stuff down," Esther said. "A person can't get a word in edgewise around this house with Mother Maybelle singing that morbid song at the top of her lungs."

"You've been doing a pretty fair job adjusting the volume yourself, Es'," Olie said. "Every time you pass by, the radio near-about shuts off. All that hoofing around like a Tennessee trotter."

"Well, I never," Esther said with a huff. "'A Tennessee trotter.' I'm of a mind to come over there and plant my hoof in your behind if you don't shut that *blasted* thing off." Esther blushed.

"What was that you were saying about baby Jesus, Es'?" Olie asked. "Something about Frankenstein and Mary and horses."

"I should've known you were listening," she said. She curtsied. "And I do beg your pardon, Olie, and baby Jesus's, too.

That wasn't a very Christian thing I threatened to do to you. That song just makes me feel so awful."

"That so? It kinda makes me feel some better, Es'."

It seemed the only way she could get a rise out of Olie recently was to annoy the dickens out of him. It used to be she couldn't get him to shut up when she wanted him to. They would stop off at the market for a gallon of milk on the way home from church, and Olie would strike up a conversation with somebody, an old friend or a perfect stranger, and mill around swapping stories so long that Esther would have to start blowing the horn or sometimes march in with her hand on her hip and remind him not to hurry because it was not as if his wife and little child were out in the car waiting for him in the dead of winter or the heat of summer, as the case may have been.

Then Ryne got sick, and Olie shut up.

"Well now, that's more like it," she said when Mother Maybelle had finally hushed up and the deejay was announcing local church services and funerals and the Red Cross blood drive. "What I was trying to say is I wonder if Virgin Mary was a nervous wreck when those magis were on their way to the manger with that gold and such."

Olie had stood up by then and was hitching his slacks up above his navel. He said no, he didn't think that Mary had any idea the wise men were coming. "They must have come to old Mary right out of the blue, Es'."

"I don't know about that," Esther was quick to tell him. She eyed him over the top of her horn-rims. "But I'd lay you odds Joseph wasn't sprawled out on the sofa eating jellybeans."

"Good Book doesn't say just what old Joseph was up to," Olie said, "so we might not better go filling in the gaps, Esther."

At any rate, Esther thought, even if Mary had known the magis were coming, she could not have been any more anxious about it than Esther was for the men of the church to pull up out front with Ryne's new TV set.

She said, "Lula Gosset said T. K. Kirby's coming along with Elder and Buster to help with the TV set. She said it's a right big old thing."

"*T. K. Kirby*, you say? I don't believe I know him."

"You've seen of him at church, Olie. He sits way back in the back with the little children. He's got a stammering problem, and maybe some other problems, too, I imagine."

"Maybe," Olie said. "Stammers."

"If this isn't the hottest July on record," she said.

"I believe that's about the hundred and tenth time you've said that since supper, Es'."

"Oh, I've done nothing of the sort, Olie," she said. "You and your prefabrications. But if I take a notion I'll say it another hundred and ten times."

On her next pass through the kitchen, Olie grabbed her and planted a kiss on her cheek.

"Don't go trying to buttermouth me like I'm some fool girl, Olie," she warned him. "It'll get you nowhere, this sexual harnessment. So just back off, Buster!" She smiled at him. It was the first time in months Olie had seemed so happy. She bent backwards a bit at her waist and waved the can of starch in front of his face. "Or else I'll be forced to spray this starch in your face. Maybe work out some of them wrinkles."

"Lord knows," he said.

"I'm worried sick they won't get here before Ryne's finished in the tub, Olie. And I'd hate this surprise to get spoiled."

"They'll be along directly. And it won't take but a minute to get the TV set in and hooked up. If Ryne should happen out of the tub too soon you can carry him up town for a frozen custard while we get things squared away here."

"I imagine you're right," she told him, though she had no earthly idea how she would manage to whisk Ryne away for a frozen custard with Buster Jeeves's pickup truck sitting out in the driveway with a big TV set in the back of it. Esther was relieved to hear the water still running into the tub. Ryne always filled it so high that if he so much as batted a lash water would slosh out onto the floor. "For once, poor water pressure's a blessing," she said. "He took a couple Spiderman comics in there with him, so I expect he'll set a spell and soak and read."

Esther had just folded up the ironing board when she heard the familiar rumble of Buster Jeeves's truck. She trotted over to the front door. "Ooh, I hear 'em coming yonder even now," she said, clapping her hands together.

"You don't say," Olie said, joining his wife at the front door.

In the twilight they could make out Buster Jeeves's old blue quarter-ton pickup pulling on to the gravel drive.

"Lord, they're gonna wreck!" Esther said. At the top of the driveway Buster had shut off the engine and headlights and was coasting down toward the O'Casey's Chevy Nova.

"Shhh, Es'. Buster shut off everything so as not to alert Ryne that they're here."

"Well," Esther said, "that Buster's clever as a whip."

Olie went out to help Elder Gosset, Buster Jeeves, and T. K. Kirby unload the big box that lay in the bed of the truck under a yellow vinyl tablecloth battened down with ten yards of fishing line.

"Hey, Elder Gosset, Mr. Buster, T. K.," Esther called out, "and don't you-all look nice." The men were in polyester slacks with a center crease and starched short-sleeve shirts.

Hurry up, Esther silently urged them. She could not help but think, watching the four strong-strapping men wrestling the big box from the back of the truck, that any two of them could have handled the job. "Too many cooks spoil the stew," she mumbled to herself. Then she smiled, a great big smile, and whispered, "Thank you, Lord Jesus." They were just being careful was all, and it would have been a crying shame if the TV got dropped.

Esther followed them down the short hall to Ryne's bedroom. "I made sure the towel rack was empty," she whispered. "Ryne's so bashful he wouldn't dream of marching out in his birthday suit. Much less put his dirty jammies back on."

On "three" the men hoisted the twenty-five-inch RCA color TV onto Ryne's chest-of-drawers. When Esther finally agreed that the TV was centered to her liking—after Olie had twice threatened to fetch his tape measure and chalkbox from the shed out back to make sure it was plumb to within a sixteenth of an inch—they got down to business. Elder Gosset went out to the truck to get the greeting card and candy bars. Esther wedged herself into the small space between the foot of the bed and the chest-of-drawers and bent down—at the knees, so as not to be indecent—and located the wall-jack that a man from the cable company had installed that morning while Olie and Ryne were picking up their carry-out pork plates at *The Bubba-Q* across town. She screwed the cable into the outlet.

Olie put the batteries in the remote control and pressed the power button and a screeching noise came blaring out. Loud. "Oops," Olie said, mashing buttons trying to shut the TV up.

T. K. Kirby hit the power button on the front of the TV, and in the silence, aghast, Esther said, "What on God's green earth are you trying to do, now Olie?"

"Sorry," he said. "I don't know anything about these things."

"Well, there's the living proof," Esther chided him in a whisper. "Mother used to say if you don't know what you're doing you shouldn't do it."

"All right now, Esther, I said I was sorry," Olie said, his face the color of one of the ripe beefsteak tomatoes Esther was always bragging about. "Your carrying on is making more racket than the TV did. You know you couldn't hear a herd of wild buffaloes over that noisy drain."

"Maybe not," she said. "But they don't go about turnin' up TV sets full blast, either, Olie."

Elder Gosset returned with the items from the truck, and he and Esther set the blue bow on top of the TV and fanned out the card and candy bars on the chest-of-drawers in front of it. "Have you ever seen such a TV set in your life?" Esther said. "This chester drawers is about to collapse."

"Mom?" Ryne called through a crack in the bathroom door.

"Yes, angel hair?" she called back.

"Could you get me a towel? There's none in here."

"Oh me!" Esther said. "I'll be right there, darling." She blushed. "In there," she said, directing the three men to wait in her and Olie's bedroom. She handed the greeting card to Elder Gosset and squeezed his arm. "You should be the one to give him this, Elder."

When she had passed a towel and a fresh set of Spiderman pajamas to Ryne, Esther led Olie down the hall to the sofa in the living room. There they sat, holding hands, waiting.

"Mom, Dad," Ryne said calmly. "Maybe you should get in here on the double! There's *something spooky* going on here."

Esther rushed down the hall with Olie in tow. "Ryne, honey, what is it?" Esther asked—for all the world as if she had no idea.

"Look at this," Ryne said. He pointed at the TV. "How—? What in—? Who on—? Where did this thing come from?"

"Come on over here, son," Olie said. He sat down on Ryne's bed. "This here TV set is a gift from the folks at the church."

Ryne sat down beside his dad. "Oh."

Elder Gosset, Buster Jeeves, and T. K. Kirby appeared at the door. "Hey there, champ," Elder Gosset said. "It's awful good to see you." He walked over and handed Ryne a white envelope with "To: Master Ryne O'Casey" written on the front in old lady's handwriting.

Ryne said, "Hi, Elder Gosset," then just sat there blushing with the envelope clutched in his hand. "Uh, thank you very much, sir."

"This is T. K. Kirby, Ryne," his mother was quick to point out. "Maybe you recall seeing him at the church. And why of course you know Mr. Buster here."

T. K. Kirby picked up one of Ryne's comic books. "I have some old cuh-comics you j-just got t-to see. Ah-ma-mazing Stories. Sixty-two. Muh-mint condition."

"Cool," Ryne said, his eyes wide. "Spiderman—*sixty-two mint*?"

"Well, how's about you open up that greeting card, Ryne?" Esther said.

Ryne tore open the envelope. The front of the card was a painting of Jesus sitting on a big rock with one child under each arm and a bunch of them sitting on the ground in a semi-circle around him. Beneath the picture were the words:

Suffer the little children to come unto me, and forbid
them not: for of such is the kingdom of God.
And he took them up in his arms,
put his hands upon them, and blessed them.

Mark 10:14–16

Inside, somebody had written in red ink: "Lord Jesus must have had you in mind when he wrote this, Ryne."

At least a hundred people had signed their names in various hands—large and small, lead and ink, young and old, print and cursive, fine and bubble, black and red. Someone had written

"WE LOVE YOU, Ryne" in big green letters all the way across the bottom edge of the card.

Ryne lowered his head and cradled his cheeks in his hands. He screwed his eyes shut, but tears rolled down his cheeks. Olie hugged him close, shoulder-to-shoulder, and patted his back, and, a little while later, Ryne wiped his eyes on the sleeve of his pajamas and said, "Thanks, everybody."

One by one they told Ryne he was welcome. "We love you, Ryne," Elder Gosset said. "And don't you ever forget that."

Esther handed Ryne the remote control. "This is the thing that works it, Ryne." She winked. "Your daddy there can show you all about how to work it."

"We best be runnin' along," Elder Gosset announced a few minutes later.

But Esther would hear nothing of it. "You're not about to high-tail it out of here before you've broke bread, bread *pudding* with us. And I have some ice tea, and," she added, looking at the men over the tops of her glasses, "if you mind your manners I might even treat you to some of my fresh-picked strawberries and sweet cream."

Olie said, "Come on yonder to the kitchen and set a spell with us. We'll testify if your wives expect you've been up to no good."

And don't you ever forget that.

An Only Gets a Sister

I'*M THE INCREDIBLE SHRINKING RYNE*, he thought. It was
strange how good something so little—so little you couldn't
see it without an electron microscope—was at shrinking things.
AIDS was good at it. It shrunk the size of your body. It shrunk
the number of your friends. It shrunk the time you had left. It
shrunk your whole world. Ryne's world had shrunk to eight feet
by ten, the size of his bedroom, where he spent nearly all of his
time—thanks to AIDS.

Ryne O'Casey spent a lot of time thinking about such things,
deep things, as his mom sometimes called them; other times,
she would give him a look and tell him to quit being so morbid.

It was not that his bedroom was such a bad place—not at
all. It was for all he knew the coolest bedroom in the whole wide
world. He had a gigantic Atlanta Braves team poster on the wall.
He had some really cool muscle car and tank models on his chest-
of-drawers; the GTO was finished and the Panzer tank would
be battle-ready in under a week. He had several big three-ring
binders full of baseball cards and comic books on a card table in
the corner. He even had a new mattress and box springs, which
even made sleeping kind of fun, when his temperature didn't red
line and make him levitate off the bed with the shakes.

Step right up, ladies and gentleman, and see with your very own eyes the Incredible Shrinking Ryne. See him levitate, see him shiver, shiver like Jell-O under three covers when it's one hundred degrees Farenheit outside.

But, cool as it was, the room got boring after a while. The "cabin fever" his mother always brought up when she was trying to get him to come out and spend "time with the family" was beginning to set in. For three months he had been holed up in his one-room cabin rereading comic books he knew by heart and listening to one of the three eight-track tapes he had to choose from—Johnny Cash, Kris Kristofferson, and Charlie Pride. He liked them, all right, but after about a bajillion times even cool songs like "Folsom Prison Blues," "Silver-Tongued Devil," and "Snakes Crawl at Night" become more nerve-racking than anything else. The month before his mom had headed off to Wal-Mart to buy a new "victrola" so they could listen to the stack of old records in the closet but two hours later she came back with a new mattress and box springs strapped on the roof of the car. (Ryne had made the mistake of telling her about his backache just before she left.)

One thing about being stuck in his own little Folsom Prison "just to pass the time," though, was that as time passed and he felt worse, he missed being outside less and less. A weird thing, disease: a weird lonesome shrinking thing that steals your life and, in the end, even your will to get it back.

Why would I want it back now anyway? Ryne was asking himself that Monday evening in July as he finished up his bath. He reached into the towel closet above the toilet and, for the first time in his life, it was empty: not a single solitary towel in the whole closet. It was usually so crammed with towels that the door would not shut all the way. That very morning, in fact, it had been full when Ryne reached in to get a washrag. *This is way weird, he thought.* The washer had not overflowed and no one had spilled anything—especially not anything that would take ten bath towels and a shelfful of washrags to soak up.

The sadder his mom got the harder she worked. So finding the towel closet empty was way weird. But everything was empty and way weird, it seemed, at the end of that day, which everyone—but especially Ryne's mom—had complained about being such a scorcher, a day Ryne had spent the best part of lying in bed shivering under a sheet, two quilts, and a crocheted afghan.

Then he walked into his bedroom and found the new TV on his chest-of-drawers. It was hands down the coolest day of Ryne's life.

Naturally, the first thing Ryne wanted to do was fire up the TV and stretch out in bed with his dog Samson and spend the night exploring. *Please*, he was praying silently as he thanked Elder Gosset and the others for the TV, *O please Lord don't let Mama get on one of her talking jags.*

He thought his prayer was about to be answered when Elder Gosset said, "We'd best be getting on down the highway," and Mr. Jeeves and T. K. Kirby agreed, and they were heading down the hall toward the front door.

Then his mom was struck with one of her famous attacks of *mountain hospitality*, and that was that. Time to settle in.

She invited the men to *set a spell*—she really didn't give them much choice, and, at first anyway, they did not seem all that anxious to go. The word *spell*, as used by Ryne's mom, meant a *lo-o-o-n-g* time, especially when food was involved. So he knew as soon as she revealed her plan to feed the men iced tea and bread pudding and strawberries in sweet cream that it would be at least an hour before he could watch the TV—maybe longer. Turned out they set a very long spell that night—one hour and fifty-six minutes. The four men and Ryne all sat around the kitchen table—his mom always stood a spell instead of sitting one. They swapped stories and had sweet tea and homemade bread pudding and fresh-picked strawberries floating in sweet cream, which Ryne knew was really just a quart of whole milk with about half of a big bag of sugar in it. Most of Ryne's helping of bread pudding ended up in the belly of Samson, who had learned just where to position himself under the table to get his share of food without Ryne's mom seeing it and threatening to skin both their hides.

All in all it could have been a lot worse—for instance, if T. K. Kirby had not been there. T. K. was the neatest grownup Ryne ever met. He was like a big kid. He liked talking about comic books, especially Spiderman and Captain America, and the Atlanta Braves and even told Ryne that one time his grandfather took him to Atlanta-Fulton County Stadium to see the Braves play the Giants in a twilight double-header and that d-during the bottom of the third inning of the s-second game he almost caught a f-foul-tip off the bat of none other than D-Dale Murphy, but just before the b-ball reached his hands a little kid in the row behind them leaned over with a catcher's mitt and snagged it. It was, he said, "th-the story of my l-life."

Every time one of the men would start to get up and say something like, "Well, I know it's not polite to eat and run, Esther Jean, but reckon we best be scooting along," Ryne's mom would cross her arms and cluck her tongue and say, "No, it most certainly is *not* polite, Mr. Buster, so you just set yourself back down and fellowship with us. Besides, aren't you a proud grandpa not to be telling us all about that precious little grandbaby of yours."

Whoever it was would sit back down, and then Ryne's mom would strike up a new conversation: "Well, now Elder Gosset, just how are Lula's knees working out?" Then Ryne would go back to discussing things of interest to him and T. K. Kirby and the grown-ups went back to discussing things of interest to

Ryne's mom, and on it went until, after about two hours, Ryne's dad finally stood up and said, "Es', we got to let these good men go."

Ryne's mom put her hands on her hips, gave him one of her looks, said, "I declare. Benton Oliver O'Casey, it's not polite to go shooing off the company!" Every man in the room—including Ryne and Samson the dog—held his breath. Then, with a huff, she said, "Well, I imagine you're right. These are working men."

Ryne's mom loaded the men down with sealed Tupperware containers full of strawberries and what was left of the bread pudding, which they all agreed was the best they had ever eaten, and they all walked slowly out to Buster's truck. Ryne's mom hugged each of the men, in turn, and whispered something in their ears; his dad shook their hands and seemed like he really did not know what to say; and Ryne thanked them again for the TV and candy and stuff. Buster cranked the truck and began easing it back up the driveway. They all stood—Olie and Esther, with Ryne and Samson between them—by their Chevy Nova at the foot of the driveway and kept waving until Ryne's arm got weak. When the truck pulled out onto the highway Buster honked the horn twice and off they roared.

"If they aren't the sweetest three men on God's green earth," Ryne's mom said, shaking her head. "Lord a mercy. I don't imagine them magis could of been one wit sweeter."

They stood there watching the truck's taillights fade in the dark distance.

Then Ryne's dad said, "Let's carry it on inside."

She said softly, sniffling, "I declare, Olie O'Casey, you can spoil a moment."

It was well past dark by then, and though Ryne could not see the tears he knew his mom was crying. The only time she ever blew her nose with the handkerchief she kept tucked down under the waistband of her apron was when she was trying to hide her crying. She cried a lot. She always blamed it on the pollen or the onions she had chopped for a casserole or early signs of what she called "the change."

They all knew what she was really crying about.

Ryne and Samson led the procession back into the house and down the hall to Ryne's room. His dad lay on the right side of the bed with his hands clasped behind his head and his feet crossed. Ryne sat Indian-style next to him with the remote control in hand. His mom took to straightening up the comic books on the card table. "You're making real good progress on that model hot rod, Ryne," she said, and Ryne said thanks and didn't bother telling her that the *model hot rod* was actually a Panzer tank.

"Sit down here and watch some TV with us, 'Es," his dad told her, patting the bed. "You can study those models later." Ryne's mom made a funny face then did a Cotton Eye Joe step and sat down on the edge of the bed and started fluffing up the pillow and smoothing the bedclothes.

"Lights. Camera. Action!" He pressed the power button and brought the TV to life.

"Oh! Will you just look at *that*?" Ryne's mom said. "Now that's what I call Technicolor."

His dad, and especially his mom, wanted to stop at the first show that came along and watch it until it went off. Not Ryne. No way. If you stop at the first old show that comes along, he explained, you run the risk of missing fifty-five other shows—probably *better* shows—playing on the other channels.

"I wish you'd hold your horses now, Ryne," his mom said. "That was the "Murder, She Wrote" show."

"No, that's the *all*-she-wrote show, Mother," his dad told her.

"Seventy-nine," Ryne said. His parents both glared at him, puzzled.

"What?" his mom asked. "Seventy-nine *what*?"

"Oh, nothing," Ryne told them. For the past year, he had been keeping track of all the *wonders of the world* he came across (such as, "why does old women's hair turn blue but not old men's?"). He had come to the conclusion that whoever said there were seven wonders had seriously miscalculated. Ryne himself had come up with seventy-eight wonders, which he had divided into two categories: "Major Wonders" and "Minor Wonders." So far, he had discovered nineteen major wonders and fifty-nine minor ones. He knew that his mom had quite a list, too, because he had heard her say at least a hundred times, usually to his dad, "Olie O'Casey, it's the eighth wonder of the world how you can lie there on that sofa eating jellybeans at a time like this!" or something like that. His dad's lying on the sofa eating jellybeans would not even have rated a "minor minor wonder" on Ryne's list, if he had had such a category, which he did not. Ryne made a mental note to add "Why dad calls mom (his wife) 'Mother'" to the "provisional" list, under which he put all wonders that might make it in onto the master wonder list, which he recorded in his spiral notebook labeled "Confidential." And if it made it to the master wonder list, it would be wonder number seventy-nine.

His mom again: "Ryne, I'm fixing to seventy-*your*-nine if you don't quit changing the channels with that thing." She always tried to sound seriously mean when she said such things, but Ryne knew better, everyone who knew Esther Jean O'Casey knew better, knew that she did not have a mean bone in her body, much less a seriously mean one. His mom was a lot of things, it was true; but a seriously mean woman she was not. His dad always said that Esther Jean O'Casey was the sweetest candy he had ever met packaged in a pickle barrel.

Ryne's mom went on: "Now Ryne, you know how much I love that Angela Lanisberry, so take us on back to channel o-four before we miss the whole show."

Ryne continued hitting the + button on the remote control. "Next," he said, skipping over the commercials and stopping only long enough on the shows for one or the other of his parents to say, "Wasn't that—? I reckon it could of been. Course now we'll never know."

Channel 52, ketchup commercial; channel 53, a nature show; channel 54, previews of movies showing on premium channels they didn't get; channel 55, nothing; channel 56, black man preaching.

"Ryne!" his mom shouted, slapping her big hands against the sides of her head, skewing her horn-rimmed glasses. "Please!"

Startled by the sudden outburst, his dad said, "Good heavens, Esther Jean, you'd think the house was on fire."

"Well," she said, blushing, "somebody's hindparts are going to be on fire if all this channel-changing keeps going on."

Ryne's dad said, "Channel-surfing, 'Es. I've heard of it. They say it's an awful condition. I guess our Ryne here's afraid he's going to miss a good wave."

"He needn't worry," she said. She winked. "'Cause he's fixing to get wiped out by the biggest old tidal wave ever to hit Tynbee, Tennessee." She raised both arms above her head and made the whooshing sound of a tsunami about to break. She leaned over and rained her wiggling fingers down toward Ryne's face.

"Fine," Ryne said, smiling. "Sorry, mom."

"Nothing to be sorry about, now Ryne," she said tenderly. "Just put that TV on channel o-four and all's forgiven."

Ryne pressed zero then four, laid the remote control down between his parents, and lay down on his stomach facing the TV, his hands propped beneath his chin and his feet dancing about in mid-air. Ryne loved his parents more than anything—except God, of course. But he had some business to take care of, and he could not very well do it with them in there wanting to get into a show. His mom carried on some more about Angela Lanisberry, as she called her, and at last Ryne relaxed. He had all night to finish his business.

They were all together in one place, and he was warm, for once, and there was the gigantic TV, and everything was good.

They watched the second half of *Murder, She Wrote*, his mom sitting there, her left leg crossed over her right, hands folded in her lap, saying the whole time, "I just love that Angela Lanisberry, don't you-all?"

"Mm hmm," they told her.

"She looks right good," Esther remarked. "She has a lot more color in her cheeks than I remember."

"Sure does," Olie said. Ryne and his dad looked at each other and rolled their eyes. Their old Zenith was a black-and-white.

"I hope I look that good when I'm her age."

"You will," they said.

During a commercial, Ryne's dad said, "Well, one good thing about doing without a TV for so long is that all the reruns are new to you."

Ryne had figured all along that his parents would be off to bed as soon as Mrs. Lansbury solved the mystery. It seemed to take her forever. The final minutes of the show went on for hours. Ryne lay there with his chin cradled in his palms thinking, *C'mon, you know he's the one, Mrs. Lansbury; so just nab him and call 911 and have a squad car come out and haul him off.*

"Great day in the mornin', Es', it's late," his dad said as soon as the show went off. "I'm taking it in to the bed."

"I'm not long after you," Ryne's mom said. She straightened out her legs, rocked herself up into a standing position, smoothed the wrinkles from the lap of her dress. "This sure was a nice thing, them giving you this TV set. Now don't you lay so close to the screen, Ryne. Radiology comes out of there and it could kill—log up your nose."

Esther cut her eyes around to see if he had caught her slip of the tongue. He never let on. She was careful about such things. Too careful, Ryne thought. Just because AIDS was going to kill him did not mean that other things—like radiation—could not or would not, too.

They all hugged and kissed and said a prayer, as they always did, and Ryne and his dad told his mom a last time or two that they liked Angela Lansbury, too, and that they were sure she would look as good, at least, as Mrs. Lansbury when she got to be that age. Then, at last, very slowly, the rare excitement of the visit having worn them out, Ryne's parents went across the hall to their bedroom.

"Don't forget to brush your teeth, Ryne," his mom called out.

"I won't," he hollered, and before the echo faded she was back in his room.

She approached the bed and leaned down and kissed him. "I love you, angel hair," she said.

"I love you, too, Mom."

"I know you do. Now don't fritter the whole night away channel-surfing, and don't let me hear any nasty talk coming out of this room. Some of them channels we passed weren't suitable."

"I won't; you won't; they sure aren't," Ryne said, answering all three of her questions.

"What's got you so tongue-tied, Ryne? Are you feeling all right? I imagine all this excitement has taken its toll?"

"Nothing; yes, ma'am; no, ma'am, it hasn't," he responded.

Then she got it. "Aren't you a clever one," she said. "Your daddy in there had more to do with that than me, I imagine." She mussed his hair. "Night."

Ryne smiled. "Night, Mom."

Then she left, pulling the door half to behind her, and Ryne got down to business. He gathered up all the materials he would need: the bag of colored markers from the drawer of his nightstand; the sketch pad in which he traced pictures of Spiderman that was wedged somewhere in the bed-high stack of comic books on the floor; the remote control from the card table. He opened the sketchpad to a clean page and, starting at channel 02, began making his very own color-coded cable TV guide, which was much better than the one the cable man had left.

Ryne wrote the channel numbers in big red script and made notes in smaller blue ink under each.

Under 5, he wrote:
"ESPN: SPORTS all the time
baseball game every night!!!"

Under 9:
"TBS: BRAVES GAMES
Westerns
Beverley Hillbillys"

Under 14:
"VH1: MUSIC all the time
Some rad, some bad"

Under 19:
"C-SPAN
politics (boaring)"

Under 22:
"Home shopping junk
skip it—But they had a TOPPS baseball card set!!!
—you need a credit card to buy things"

Under 34:
"Discovery. Animal shows, National Geographic
—might have earthquake and dinosaur shows on"

Under 39:
"Picture won't come in (nasty language and maybe nekkid
people)"

He put an orange star beside the channels he liked best:
ESPN, TBS, DISCOVERY. Before he fell asleep that night
he would put two orange stars by channel 56—THE WORD
NETWORK.

Making the custom cable guide was a big job that demanded a
lot of energy—not to mention time. It was the stroke of midnight
when Ryne reached the last channel, 56. He pressed the button
marked with a + sign on his remote control and a fluorescent-
green 56 appeared at the top right corner of the screen. A little
see-through box at the bottom of the screen said THE WORD
NETWORK.

Ryne expected it to be a network like PBS that showed
Sesame Street and plays with funny-sounding actors from
England. He scribbled a note about it on his personal cable
guide: "WORD: See PBS" and was about to switch back to ESPN
when a voice called out from the darkness of what looked like a
basketball stadium: "May I have your attention, please?"

Ryne put the remote control down.

The voice spoke again, this time sounding like the ring
announcers who introduced boxers before the fights he and his
dad listened to some Saturday nights on the old transistor radio:
"Ladies and gen-tle-men, chil-dren *of* God, join me in wel-coming
to the stage, Sis-terrr Mir-an-daaa *Stry*-kerrr."

Spotlights slashed wildly through the darkness like
humongous light sabres. The audience went berserk, whooping

and hollering and otherwise carrying on. *You would have guessed*, Ryne thought, *that Chipper Jones had just homered with the bases loaded in the bottom of the ninth against the Yankees in the seventh game of the World Series.* All of a sudden the spotlights homed in on the center of the huge curtains, and out leapt a short round colored woman who high-tailed it across the stage like something was after her. She was wearing an aqua-colored kimono and had a big red sash around her waist and a matching red-and-aqua turban on her head.

The audience really went berserk then. They clapped their hands and stomped their feet and waved their arms up high in the air. Many of the folks in the crowd started dancing a jig in the aisles; others were jumping stiffly in place with their arms tight against their sides as if they were in a potato-sack race. There were even a few people rocking around and clapping hand-over-hand. The band started playing, and Sister Miranda Stryker hopscotched around in time to the music, clapping her hands down by her knees then up above her head. Then she began talking in a foreign language: "Aha la ha, hee-bee o-ta-ka, ho-key-ah," or something like that, the spotlight struggling to keep pace with her. The audience was rocking from side to side with their arms in the air, doing a fast-motion "Wave."

"Glory to God in the high-*est*," Sister Stryker sang into the microphone at the top of her lungs. Then the band started playing what sounded to Ryne like Chinese music and Sister Stryker started singing, "Jehovah Rapha, the God that healeth thee." She planted her feet and gyrated like a Bobo doll after you rared back and socked it with all your might.

"Well bless the Load, child, O my soul, and all *that* is within me," Sister Stryker sang, as she walked back behind the Bible stand. Then, with a hand on her hip she wagged her finger at the audience and warned them: "Don't you set yo'self down now. Up. *Up!* Flat of your feet for the reading of the Word *of* Gawd.

In Exodus chapter fifteen and verse number twenty-sits, God A'mighty, Jehovah Rapha hisself, said, 'If thou wilt diligently hearken to the voice of the LOAD thy God, and wilt do that which is right in his sight, and wilt give ear to his commandments, and keep all his statutes, I will put none of these diseases upon thee, which I have brought upon the Egyptians: for *I am* the LOAD that healeth thee.' The Load that healeth thee *and me*," she said. "Well God be praised forever, world without end, forever and ever, and ever and ever, AMEN! That be the holy truth, and nothing but the truth, child, so help me Gawd. Can I get a witness, Elder Butts?"

Elder Butts, a heavy-set old colored man with nappy gray hair like Uncle Remus, stood up from behind the organ. He raised his left hand and crossed his heart with his right and started screaming bloody murder. "Tell it, Sister!" he screamed, and some other stuff Ryne couldn't make out, then the whole audience joined him, dancing and shadow boxing, potato sack racing, and running around in place.

After she got the audience calmed down enough to lead them in a word of prayer, Sister Stryker stood behind the Bible stand and preached a short message, which, Ryne noted, was not even half as long (and twice as interesting) as the sermons he had heard Preacher McKee deliver at the Historic First Church (the few times Ryne had heard them). He figured that explained why Sister Stryker was preaching at a packed basketball arena on TV instead of at the half-full Historic First Church of Tynbee. They were alike in some ways, though, Sister Stryker and Reverend McKee. They both spoke in a foreign language a lot. Reverend McKee used Greek and sometimes Hebrew, Ryne's dad had told him, and it sounded like Sister Stryker was speaking GreekBrew: "Hi-o hi-ha hee-be a-lah." The difference was that she didn't bore you with long explanations about what every single word meant.

This whole Sister Stryker show was exciting. *You kind of had a feeling that something humongous was about to happen.* Ryne found himself moving closer to the TV screen, until at last he was again on his stomach with his head at the foot of the bed, just inches from Sister Stryker, and not the least bit worried about *radiology* coming out of the TV.

The WORD Network was worth missing ESPN for and whatever else might have been showing on the other fifty-five channels—except maybe a really good show about earthquakes. It would be a toss-up, Ryne decided, and the way Sister Stryker was carrying on might just trigger a seismic event. Her preaching was part talking and part singing. She would say something, then Elder Butts would mimic her on the organ: "I'm telling you, Je-esus," she would say, then the organ would go "Da da-da da, da-da-aa," and then she would say something else and the organ would chime in with its echo.

Sister Stryker told them all about how Jesus washed away leprosy and sin—"and he won't using no fifty-nine-cent bar of the Dial soap neither, I'm here to tell you, honey child," then she sang the jingle, "Don't you wish *everybody* did?" She said Jesus healed the sick "without no four years of medical college" and scared the daylights out of demons and ran them off like a mama bear after a stray cat. Jesus, she said, even raised the dead without using CPR: "Won't nothing artificial about his resuscitation, now honey child."

"Faith sure enough is the key," she told them, and Ryne wondered how that dead little twelve-year-old girl Jesus said "Talitha cumi" to—which Sister Stryker said basically meant "Child, get ya hide up and *walk!*"—could have had much faith. He figured Jesus knew pretty much what people were thinking about and how much faith they had even after they were dead.

When she quit preaching and went to praying, a commercial came on. A colored man who looked like Dr. J in a shimmering black suit and red-and-yellow tam like those Ryne's mom crocheted for him introduced himself as Brother Rastus Jefferson. He was seated on top of a desk in a paneled office with a big bookcase behind him. He rattled off all the cities that Reverend Sister Miranda Stryker would be visiting—Baltimore, Maryland; Roanoke, Virginia; Charlotte, North Carolina. He invited Ryne and everyone who was watching to come to the crusades to receive "a miracle of healing." A toll-free number for the prayer line flashed on and off at the bottom of the screen: "Prayer Counselors Are Standing By 24 Hours A Day." Ryne wrote the number on the back of his sketchpad.

Brother Rastus Jefferson said, "Won't you step out in faith and join us? May God richly bless you." Then the screen faded back into the basketball stadium.

Sister Stryker stood at the center of the stage and was healing people from the audience whom the ushers wheeled or toted up to her. She stuck her fingers in their ears and made them hear, snatched cigarettes out of their pockets and ground them into the floor with her spike heels—saying, "This is what I call a *heel*ing!"—and slung their canes and walkers off the stage. She delivered people who were afflicted with demons of laziness and chocolate, unemployment and orneriness, infirmity and irregularity.

"She must be a black belt in Karate," Ryne said. He recognized one of her moves. He had seen it in a picture in the *Kids' Big Book on Karate*, which his mom had picked up for him at a rummage sale. The move was called *the palm-heel attack*—and now Ryne knew why: Sister Stryker used her palm to heal people and attack their demons. Two ushers would stand behind some man about the size of Ryne's mother and hold him up, and Sister Stryker would say, "Foul demons of chocolate get yo'self out of him!" Then she would haul off and strike him in the forehead with the palm of her hand and knock him down, and sometimes the two men behind him would fall down, too, and they would all lie there on the floor passed out and quivering.

Ryne figured having a black belt in Karate couldn't hurt if you were in the business of fighting demons.

Even some of the old people who got wheeled up there got socked in the face and then sprang up out of their wheelchairs and took off across the stage, shrieking, "Jesus, Jesus." Except for one, who got socked and stayed seated and her chair just started rolling backwards fast as you please toward the edge of the stage, which was a good ten feet above the floor, and would have rolled right off if one of the ushers had not seen it in the nick of time and dived face-first and caught ahold of the front wheels just in time. The old woman then stood up and shouted glory. "Praise God," she said, and Ryne wondered if she were praising God because she just got healed or because he had kept her from rolling off the stage and getting killed.

It was like nothing Ryne had ever seen. Sister Stryker was a lot like Jesus, he thought, going around the country—to Baltimore, Roanoke, and Charlotte—preaching the gospel and healing sick people and casting out their demons.

No sooner had the WORD Network signed off than Ryne's excitement began to grow. He lay there restless, with more energy than he had had in months. *This might just be it,* he thought: *the answer to our prayers.* He wondered if Dr. Scarborough and all the others who apologized to his parents because they could not do anything about AIDS had heard about Sister Miranda Stryker. *They needed to.* Because he had a strange feeling that Sister Stryker could do something about AIDS (with Jesus' help, of course: she was clear about that). She seemed to be able to do something about everything else—even if she had to beat the daylights out of someone to get the job done.

He was too excited to sleep. His heart pounded. He pictured himself on the stage with Sister Stryker, who was commanding the foul demons of AIDS to get the devil out of him and never come back. As big as she was and as small as he was, he could picture himself flying end-over-end twenty rows out into the audience when she laid the hand to him and knocked the foul demon of AIDS right out of him. It might take something like that, maybe even an all-out palm-heal attack or a roundhouse kick to the side of the head, to knock the AIDS out of him.

Whatever it took would be worth it.

When he closed his eyes all he could see was Sister Stryker, standing at the middle of the stage in the packed basketball arena, with tears rolling down her plump brown cheeks, shouting, "Docka Load Jesus, honey child, he be the Great Physician. He's sure enough gonna give you a shot, child! When Docka Trapper John, M.D., say 'NO!' Docka Load Jesus say 'YES! Oh yes, child!'"

Ryne shivered from head to toe, and for once it was not because of the chills. He sat up Indian-style and grabbed the sketchpad. "Ask Reverend McKee about Sister Stryker," he wrote, not knowing when he would have the chance since the family no longer went to church and the church and its pastor never came to them. Maybe he could call Elder Gosset.

He picked up the remote control and clicked back through the channels, though this time he was not paying attention to the shows and commercials he passed. He had one thing on his mind: talking his parents into taking him to Sister Stryker's crusade when it came to Charlotte. He climbed out of bed and pulled the pink felt-covered plastic piggy bank with a blue bow on its head from beneath the dresser where he kept it hidden— not because he feared someone would steal it but rather that someone would *see* it. He dumped it out on the bed and started counting the change, mostly pennies, which he had been saving for over a year to buy a full set of Upper Deck baseball cards.

If only he could raise enough money to buy the gas (Brother Rastus had said admission to the revival meetings was free) then maybe, maybe maybe just maybe, his parents would take him to Charlotte so Sister Stryker could try healing him.

His life savings amounted to seven dollars and twelve cents. It was not enough. His dad said their Chevy Nova was in such bad shape it could drink five dollars worth of gas just getting up to Hiram and back.

Ryne hoisted the stack of comic books and collector albums of trading cards onto the bed and started appraising his collection. In the sketchpad he wrote in red marker: "Get Dad to take me to Barfield's Pawn Shop." He tried to estimate how much his comic books and baseball cards would bring. Terrence Ford once told him that his Willie Mays rookie card in mint condition might be worth a hundred bucks. If Terrence was right, that might be the only card he would have to part with to finance the trip.

Before exhaustion got the better of his excitement Ryne recorded Major Wonder number twenty in his Wonders notebook: "How Sister Stryker knocks cancer and stuff out of people with the palm-heal attack?" As he lay there thumbing through a comic book and feeling the flush in his cheeks that marked the onset of his nightly fever, he could not help but think that it wouldn't make much difference how many of his prized comic books or trading cards he had left if he did not get to Sister Stryker.

In a hurry.

Redeeming the Times

ESTHER COULD NOT GET HERSELF SITUATED to her liking. She lay flat on her back, first with the pillow under her head, then with it under her feet. She lay awhile on her left side, then on her right. She worked herself into the fetal position. She tried lying flat on her stomach. She ended up again flat on her back. It had become a nightly ritual. Esther was bone-tired weary, but her mind was all aflutter and she had learned too well that nothing good could come of that.

If idle hands were the devil's workshop, an idle mind was hell itself.

The air in the little bedroom was muggy and stale. Esther felt every bead of sweat that formed on, trickled down, and gathered in the nooks of her body, and it hardly helped that she was fatter than she had ever been and that their old mattress—the very mattress on which she and Olie had consecrated their marriage and conceived Ryne—was lumpy.

In happier times Olie had been a real cut-up. He used to tell her, "Es', this here mattress is lumpy as them sort-of-mashed potatoes you fed us at supper." She would tell him to hush up or she would be forced to sort-of-mash his lumpy old head. And they would both end up getting a big kick out of it. That was back when the lumpy mattress was their biggest problem, before Tynbee's economy crashed and Olie ran out of work and his brother Heyward pitched out of the wagon for the last time (they feared) and her mother passed and Ryne came down with AIDS.

"This old mattress is so lumpy," she told Olie, who was reading his Bible in the dim glow of the nightlamp. She was trying to bait him into saying something cute about her mashed potatoes or her head or something being lumpy.

He didn't bite. "Sure is, Es'," is all he said.

Then Esther took to counting ceiling panels and came up with only forty-one this time, one shy of the forty-two she had counted the night before. She counted them again, came up with forty-two, then shut her eyes and tried to pray. She started twice, then stopped: *Dear God, I come before you tonight to thank you*—but truth be told she could not find much to thank him for. *Dear Lord, why don't you just take me and let Ryne live. I'm older and have done about as much living as I'm going to do, but he's just a little old boy*—and then she started feeling guilty for meddling in the Lord's business.

Finally: *Dear Heavenly Father, forgive me for all my sins and somehow give me the strength to make it through. I imagine you know what this feels like—losing your only son—but at least you knew the reasons. (Forgive me for bringing Jesus into this, too, Lord.) Please understand that it's just because it hurts so bad, so awful bad. In Jesus' precious name, I pray. Amen. Watch over us, Lord.*

From somewhere a colored man with a rich deep voice that put her in mind of Louis Armstrong was singing "His Eye is On the Sparrow."

> 'Let not your heart be troubled,' his tender word I hear,
> And resting on his goodness, I lose my doubts and fears;
> Though by the path he leadeth, but one step I may see;
> His eye is on the sparrow, and I know he watches me.

"Thank you, Jesus," she said, even after she realized the colored man's voice was not coming from on high but from across the hall. Ryne, bless his sweet little heart, was watching church programs on his new TV set (thank you for that, Jesus). Before coming to bed, she had laid down the law to him against watching nasty shows after she and his Daddy went to sleep. "What channel are *they* on?" Ryne had asked, raising his eyebrows, and then explained, when Esther held out her hand and ordered him to surrender the remote control, that he was just asking so he could be sure to avoid them.

Esther giggled and sang along with the man and the organ:

I sing because I'm happy, I sing because I'm free,
For his eye is on the sparrow, And I know he watches me.

The room was dark except for the faint blue glow from Ryne's TV. Olie lay still and silent on his side of the double bed. Before long, she knew, he would commence snoring, which sometimes lulled her to sleep like a lullaby and sometimes annoyed her something fierce. Meantime, she tried to keep herself occupied. The singing was done, and someone was talking, another colored person she thought, but she could not make out what he was saying. She tried counting the ceiling panels by moonlight, which was possible on all but the darkest nights, but it was no use. A big storm was in the forecast for the following day (thank you for that, too, Jesus), and clouds had already begun rolling in.

Ten minutes passed and Olie was not snoring. Esther wondered if he was still awake, but she did not want to ask for fear she would wake him. It was a work night, and with all the fuss over the new TV set and the hour or so they spent entertaining their company, it had been a late night. Olie needed his sleep.

So, alas, there was nothing to do but think, and thinking led to feeling, and soon she knew she would be weeping. It worked that way. As long as she kept herself occupied, she was fine (or if not fine, at least okay). During the day she had Ryne to look after and her vegetable patch to tend to and the full spate of never-ending tasks called Woman's Work: cooking, cleaning, washing, pressing, and sewing. At night, when her hands and her mind were alike idle there were only hellish thoughts and the devil was all over it. Even during the day, if she sat down for a moment's rest the thoughts would come stealing in and plunder what little peace of mind she had left.

Sometimes, like yesterday evening, she would just be going about her business, breading some pork chops for supper and singing "I'll fly away oh glory I'll fly away in the morning" when all of the sudden the devil was in her: Ryne—*your only son, the only little boy you'll ever have—is dying. So how come you're in here squandering the last few precious moments you have with him breading pork chops and singing spirituals as if everything was just hunky-dory and it was natural for parents to bury their children, when what you should be doing is savoring every minute of every day with him or at least spilling tears until you've none left to spill?*

At that, she had picked up the best piece within reach, which happened to be one of the four remaining plates in the china set she had inherited from her mother, and snapped it like a bean in her hands, then slung each piece against the refrigerator and let fly one swear word after another until she heard Ryne coming down the hall and tried to calm herself. Then she had to tell Ryne a lie about a bee chasing her around the kitchen—said she had swatted at it with the plate and missed … the bee, not the refrigerator.

She pulled at her nightgown and began to weep. "No, God. No. Please, God, please, don't you take him away. I'll do anything. Anything at all. Just spare him and take me instead."

"Esther," Olie said, shaking her shoulder. "Wake up, Es'."

"I can't, Olie," she told him. Then she was sobbing. "And I'm not even asleep."

"Now, now, Es'," Olie consoled her, and she wished that just this once he would hush up and leave her be, let her break down and have a fit if that's what she took a notion to do. She knew he meant well, that he had the best of intentions. They all did. But the road to hell was paved with such, and she was tired of hearing *Now, now, Es'*, as if … as if breaking down on the road to Hades when the only son you will ever have is dying, dying slowly right before your very eyes, was such a silly thing to do.

He took her hand and squeezed it, stroked her bare arm, and hugged her close and just held her in his strong arms. "You still have your glasses on," he said.

"Can't see the ceiling panels too good without them," she told him.

"That a fact? Still forty-two?"

"Most times," she said. "Sometimes there's only forty-one."

Peace, be still. Olie's holding her said it all, said *Fear not* and *It'll be all right even if it's not all right, even if it's all wrong,* and *I love you,* and much more than all the little chapbooks for the bereaved that wellmeaning folks had been giving them as *gifts* since they found out Ryne was ill.

Those gifts got next to Esther. She would accept them as politely as she could, with a pinched smile and a cool, "I thank you, I'm sure." She tried willing herself to remember that it was the thought that counted, to keep herself from having to hurt somebody, or at least their feelings. Later, she would tell Olie: "I know it's the thought that counts, so—What *the devil* are these people thinking?"

Olie would tell her they didn't mean anything by it, not anything but good anyway, that they were just trying to be kind, and Esther would clench her fist and say, "They're kind, all right: kind of stupid. Seems like they could at least wait until we had something to grieve about, *if* that's to be the Lord's will, before they start being so stinkin' kind."

That was her Olie, always making allowances for people. And if she had grounds to gripe, it was not that Olie didn't comfort her but that sometimes he did it too much, tried too hard to kill a pain that was at once as natural as childbearing and as unnatural as could be. He was hurting, too, Lord knows, but he just did not seem to be able to bring himself to believe that what was happening was, in fact, *really* happening—that Ryne was getting sicker by the week; that the balance of his life span was now measured in months, not years or decades; that he really did have AIDS; and that AIDS was going to kill him.

Esther squeezed Olie's hand, traced the pads of her fingers over the familiar callouses on his palm. "I don't imagine you got paid for most of these old rough spots, did you, Olie?"

Olie said nothing, and Esther whispered, "I love you, Olie."

Half an hour later Olie was sound asleep and snoring, and for once his snoring neither comforted nor annoyed her: It had no effect at all. Esther was still chasing sleep. In the darkness she lay awake and picked at her damp cotton nightgown. She tried to think about happy things. Count your many blessings, Esther, name them one by one. *Count your many blessings, see what God hath done.*

She had a real blessing to count: the new TV set that some of the members of the Historic First Church (who, for all Esther knew, might have numbered just three, the three who delivered the TV: Elder Gosset, Buster Jeeves, and T.K. Kirby) had given to Ryne.

With that sweet thought in mind, Esther was nearly asleep when, over muffled voices and background music coming from the TV, she heard Ryne let go a gagging cough, not once but twice, and before he could let go a third, Esther was standing in his doorway with her hand over her heart. It was a false alarm, he told her. A nut from one of the three Snickers bars Elder Gosset and them had brought with the TV set had slid down the wrong way.

Esther was of a mind to ask him how on God's green earth he expected to get to sleep after loading up on all that sugary candy so late. She thought better of it; it didn't really matter.

"I declare. I reckon I like Snickers about as good as any candy—except maybe Butternuts," she told him, as she stepped into his room.

"Here, Mom," he said, holding out a Snickers bar.

"Heavens no, honey, you eat it. I mean, eat it *tomorrow*; it was give to you." Esther gathered up her nightgown—blushing when she realized she had not thought to put on a robe—and skirted around to the side of the bed and laid her heavy hand on his forehead. "Land sakes, you're hot as a horse, Ryne. Let me get you some Tylenols and a cup of juice to wash them down."

She was almost to the door, having made her way over the comic books and other stuff on the floor she could hardly make out in just the dim light of the TV, when Ryne said, "Mom?"

"Yes, angel hair?"

"Just how hot is a horse anyway?"

"Oh, it's just a old expression, Ryne," she told him. "What they call a figurine speech."

"Okay. I was just wondering," said Ryne. "I've never heard *that* figure of speech before."

"And besides that," she said, "in this weather we're having, a horse is bound to be pretty hot just like the rest of us, don't you imagine?"

Esther poured Ryne's orange juice from a blue pitcher into a matching blue cup she had ordered at Nellie Jean Perkins' Tupperware party a couple of years ago. She remembered getting herself all gussied up for the party. *Oh, those were the days.* Back then, folks in Tynbee (well, most of them anyway) had plenty of money, and Olie had plenty of work. There were porches to screen and basements to finish and decks to build. Back then, seventeen dollars hadn't seemed like a whole lot of money to put out on the kitchen, so she had bought that set of blue Tupperware cups and a matching set of storage canisters, which, she always pointed out, was the best investment she had ever made—next to marrying Olie, of course.

How things had changed. Now Tynbee was what Olie called a "classless society," which meant, he said, that nobody had any class and everybody was flat broke. Esther thought that, like as not, most of the people in Tynbee had never really had any class—whether they were rich or poor. But at least they used to have some money.

Now all the O'Caseys had, *Lord willing*, was a few more years and a brand new TV.

Esther returned to Ryne's room, administered the orange juice and Tylenol caplets, then settled down beside him on the bed and watched TV. It was 1:00 a.m. by the time they had polished off the remaining two Snickers bars, which they split, and watched part of a volleyball match on a channel Ryne told her showed only sports.

THE NEXT MORNING at the breakfast table Ryne said, "Mom, Dad, nothing else has worked." He was picking at his food—mainly getting it into chunks that Samson could swallow whole so as not to get them in trouble. "But what about Jesus? I was thinking maybe we could give him a shot. There's this preacher woman name Sister Miranda Stryker who heals cancer and stuff, and I was thinking maybe she could heal my AIDS."

Olie cut his eyes around at Esther, the forkful of scrambled eggs stopped dead on the way to his mouth, and Esther said, "I don't know about all that. She's not one of them Looniemajigs or Moonie people or whatever they are, is she?"

"Looniemajigs?" said Ryne.

"Moonies," said Olie.

"You know," Esther said: "one of them poor old sick people follows Some Young Moon."

Olie said, "Way you say it sounds like a Chinese dish, Es'."

Ryne shrugged. "Sister Stryker didn't say anything about Some Young Moon."

"Well, he was way back before your time, Ryne. In the Moonie-fication Church," said Esther. "Now hush up your laughing. That goes for you, too, Olie. Just because them Orientals has funny names is no cause to poke fun. I imagine them people would get a right big kick out of *Benton Oliver O'Casey*, too, if they was to ever meet you."

They agreed.

"Back to the story, Ryne," said Esther. "Some Young Moon was this big old Chinaman that looked kinda like Confuchsia with short hair that used to go about brainwashing people with the occult and calling them Loonies and making them to live in Volkswagon buses up in New York and shave their heads and stand out in the street in orange bathrobes and sell flowers and use the money for Lord knows what."

Ryne and Olie both just sat there looking at her.

Then Esther said, "Well I don't know about all that healing stuff. We'll have to study about this awhile."

For Lord knows what.

Jonah Sails On

MIRIAM HAD BEEN TELLING NATHAN for years that he had a *B.A. in B.S.*, and if ever there were living proof, Nathan found it on that dreary Wednesday morning after the tenth business meeting. He was trying his best to carry on as though nothing had happened—as though the business about Ryne O'Casey had been settled nicely—as though love truly covered a multitude of sins and all God's people played by the Golden Rule.

It was pretty to think so.

He was in his office at the back of the Historic First Church working on his Sunday sermon. He had been at it since dawn, and now, at eleven o'clock, all he had to show for it was a bad headache and a wastebasket full of false starts—one page after another that he had yanked out of the old Royal typewriter, wadded up, and hurled across the room.

During the nine o'clock hour he had worked on a sermon titled "Ecumenical Unity in Christendom." An hour into that, he decided local unity was a better place to start, so he pursued that topic for half an hour, only to get so bogged down in the meaning of the New Testament Greek word *phronein* ("one mind"; as in Paul's plea for believers to "be of one mind") that

his head starting pounding and his left hip started burning like
hellfire …

And brimstone.

Maybe that was a sign. Miriam would probably think it was.
"Maybe you should try—*just this once*—preaching a real roof-
raiser, Nathan." He had heard that before.

Well, praise God, maybe he should. If there were ever a time
for preaching *a real roof-raiser*, maybe this was it. Maybe he
should just get up there and do some good old mountain glory-
shouting. He pictured himself moon-walking across the pulpit,
Bible in hand, stopping every so often and then only long enough
to jump for Jesus, hoot to high heaven, shout down the glory,
and scream *hay-loo-ya* at the top of his lungs.

Miriam always said he might do better if he tried *speaking*
in tongues rather than preaching in tongues—the tongues he
preached being the biblical languages: Greek and Hebrew. She
asked (nearly every Sunday morning), "Why don't you try—*just
this once*—preaching in English, Nathan?"

Well, by heavens, he might just do it. *Just this once.*

Nathan often played the devil's advocate when Miriam
dispensed her unique blend of pop psychology and pop theology.
He called it *pop psycho-theology* to annoy her, but it never did.
She would just turn it around on him. "You're just projecting
your own insecurity onto me," she would say, or some such.
"See it for what it is, Nathan."

When it came to critiquing his sermons, though, he gave the
devil her due. In seminary, Nathan took a year-long preaching
class. Each week he had to prepare and deliver a sermon during
the Friday class session. So every Thursday night after dinner,
Nathan and Miriam would turn their small student-housing flat
into a church sanctuary. It was a dress rehearsal, so Nathan
would put on a jacket and tie and Miriam would put on a dress.
Miriam would slide a kitchen chair into the tiny living room

because, she said, she wanted "to experience the sermon from the vantage of a wooden church pew."

Suit yourself, Nathan always said, though he hoped to high heaven he would land a job in a church that could at least afford cushioned pews. Even then, he had his sights set a good deal higher than "country parson."

He would stack up a dozen or so of his textbooks and commentaries on the coffee table as a makeshift lectern and lean on it as Miriam opened the service with the first stanza of a hymn of convocation ("All Hail the Power of Jesus' Name" or "Joyful, Joyful, We Adore Thee"), which she played on the little electronic keyboard her parents gave her when she went away to college and left her old Wurlitzer upright behind. Then she would sit down straight-backed in the wooden chair with her Bible open on her lap. And Nathan would deliver his sermon.

Then Miriam would play a hymn of invitation ("Softly and Tenderly, Jesus is Calling" was her favorite) to close the service. She always tried to get Nathan to offer an invitation. Maybe the cat would go forward.

Back then, Nathan always asked her for a critique and never got one. Now he never asked but always got one. By the end of the first month of the semester, Miriam was able to predict with *perfect* accuracy the grade Professor Davison would assign to a given sermon. He would say, "Well, what do you think?"

She would simply say A or B or C or D, depending on which letter grade the professor was going to give the sermon. Which, Miriam was careful to point out, was not to be confused either with the grade she would assign it or with the grade it deserved (which only the Lord himself was in a position to know).

"How do you do it?" Nathan asked one of those Thursday nights as they were turning the sanctuary back into a home.

"Well," Miriam explained. "There are basically two factors in the formula. One: the more Greek and Hebrew words you use, the higher the grade. Two: the more down-to-earth the theme, the lower the grade."

Whatever grade he was shooting to get for the first sermon after the tenth business meeting, he had to come up with something, anything, that would keep the congregation of the Historic First Church from tacking his hide to the wall of the sanctuary or, worse, running him off (even if by a narrow margin of seventy-three to seventy-one). He *had* to complete the final few months of his one-year term at the church, *had* to complete his thesis and land a position not at a church, with or without cushioned pews, but at a university, and not to preach but to teach. Until then, he had nowhere else to go, no other source of income, no parents he could call on.

Two and a half months to go.

Another half-baked sermon, this one on Jesus' approach to conflict resolution, flung at the wastebasket. *Aargh.* Nathan's self-diagnosed claustrophobia pressed in on him. Miriam likened it to a spiritual compression sickness.

He got up and took a few deep breaths, walked over and stood at the single small window in his office, which was sealed tight with more layers of paint than he could cut through with his pocket knife. Nathan used his handkerchief and an old bottle of Windex (that smelled like and, for all he knew, might have *been* moonshine) to clean the window, which was smudged with some sort of oily grit, moth wings, and cobwebs. The stuff in the Windex bottle worked, and outside the day had broken gray.

The heat wave had ebbed that morning—at last—and a swirling breeze was working over the pines and hardwoods. Gray-white clouds loomed low down in the valleys like a burial cloth, and if the Angel of Death had materialized from them at that very moment it would not have surprised Nathan in the least.

Miriam's voice played in his head: "If you leave this behind you, Nathan—You think the guilt is bad now. Just imagine how bad it's going to be."

Truth was, Nathan did not want to be a pastor at all—much less a *reformer*. At some point during his second semester in seminary—six years ago, just after he blew it and got his brother Philip killed, he decided to pursue a career in academics. *I shall be a professor, a professor of Pastoral Care.* He broke the news to Miriam over Chinese takeout: "I'm going to apply to the Ph.D. program, Mir'. If I get accepted—and I think I have a really good chance—it means we'll be here in Boston another three or four years."

"God called you to be a pastor, Nathan—to preach." The whole business of his call gave Miriam fits. "You called *yourself* to teach. It's like you're saying, 'Will this do, Lord?'"

Nathan completed all the coursework for the Ph.D. The only thing left was his thesis. His professors urged him to take a position in a local church while he worked on the thesis so that he would be a more sensitive and credible teacher. After all, as a professor of pastoral care most of his students would be training for careers in local church ministry of one sort or another. "What they say is true," said Miriam. "But that bunch of Ivory Tower wonks talking about getting experience in the *real world* is about as 'credible' as Bill Clinton talking about the virtues of marital fidelity."

Whatever, Nathan said. He thought: *You are—Miriam, professors—all wrong. The reason I chose academics over the pastorate is to* avoid *the "real world."*

But the real world, it seemed, was not to be avoided right then. Miriam was pregnant with Peter Nathaniel; it was a complicated pregnancy. Her blood pressure was dangerously high, and her doctor demanded that she cut back on her hours at the group home for troubled youth where she served as a caseworker. So Nathan went to the student placement office at the seminary and got information on three churches seeking an interim pastor. "Take these information sheets home," the placement officer said, "and discuss them with your significant other."

One of the placements was in Fargo, North Dakota; one was in Oakmont, Texas, a suburb of Houston; and one was in a small, seemingly idyllic town nestled in the Blue Ridge mountains: Tynbee, Tennessee.

Nathan presented the information to his significant other— Miriam. She spent the weekend in prayer, seeking God's will in the matter. Nathan spent the weekend in the seminary library, seeking insider information—fishing holes, monuments, hiking trails—about each of the three locations. Independently, through a very different process and for very different reasons, they ended up agreeing on the Historic First Church of Tynbee, Tennessee.

"I feel," Miriam had said, "that God has some work for us to do there."

"I think," Nathan answered, "that I will be able to get some work done there."

God's answer to Miriam's prayer was that the Historic First Church was the most real world of the three churches. The insider guide's answer to Nathan's research was that Tynbee, Tennessee, was the farthest removed from the real world. It seemed to be the perfect place to write a thesis—and to fly-fish in the great rivers that coursed through the region. If he had to get experience in the *real world*, Nathan decided, what better place than Tynbee?

Lord have mercy. Tynbee turned out to be both more real and more worldly than Nathan could ever have imagined. He once told Miriam that it was part of the Bible Belt that had missed a loop. The little church had a long history, all right: a long history of short-lived pastors—all alike casualties of a war they had not started and could not finish. This was the real world of the Hatfields and McCoys.

And in that real world only one thing stood between Nathan and the Ph.D.: the final third of his thesis (which was already approaching 1,000 pages).

Two and a half months to go. Miriam's voice still played in his head: "If you leave this behind you, Nathan . . . You think the guilt is bad now?—Just imagine how bad it's going to be."

Nathan, still standing at the window, did not flinch at all when the storm hit with a jarring clap of thunder. Huge white lightning bolts sawed through the stormheads, and the heavens opened and the rain came and baptized Tynbee.

He tried, tried hard, to picture himself morphing into a country parson and putting down roots there in Tynbee, Tennessee, he and Miriam and the baby. Here, in the hub of anti-Rockwell America. The softball field beside the church was knee-deep in weeds. The church had not fielded a team for two years following the great melee that arose during the semifinal game of the Tynbee Church League Tournament, in which all of the town's churches but one (the Presbyterians) participated. It happened during the game between the Baptists and Methodists (the winner was going to represent the Protestants against the Catholics, who had beaten the Lutherans in *their* semifinal game). The Methodists, as it was told to Nathan, accused the Baptists of loading bats and the Baptists counteraccused the Methodist pitchers of throwing spitballs—after all, they added the fateful words, they knew just the right way to do it, being ones who "sprinkled" instead of dunked. Things got ugly then, theologically ugly, and twelve players, seven wives, and five children baptized in blood—some dunked, some sprinkled— ended up in the ER at Avery County Hospital. The next night, at the Historic First Church business meeting, the vote to suspend the church's "athletic program" carried by a narrow margin.

Out beyond left field was the parsonage, a brick-faced clapboard shack on a small rocky lot. In the backyard there was one of those corrugated metal kiddie pools that were so popular in the 1970s. It had collapsed (who knew how long ago), and the faded blue liner was in shreds. No one, including Nathan, had bothered to haul it off. The place was such a mess that the kiddie pool would not be the place to start, if one were inclined to start at all. Miriam, worried about lead in the paint, had hounded an interior paint job out of him. So the walls at least were whitewashed. There was an old corncrib that served as a firewood bin. Miriam swore something was living in it, and it did make noise from time to time. On the far side of the house was an old candy-striped swingset, which (a member of the church told Nathan) the previous pastor used to get on and swing like he was three years old, he was so batty.

Nathan could picture himself on that old swing, going higher and higher, swinging for all time, as though he were three years old, loop the loop, going faster, so fast you couldn't even see him, like the blades of a fan, spinning madly. Going batty.

Past the swingset was the sliding-glass door that opened onto the back porch, and through the glass he could make out Miriam's shadowy form, rocking in gentle circles at the old upright piano, practicing hymns for the Sunday service. Beside her, within rocking distance, was Peter Nathaniel's Port-a-Crib.

Miriam, my love. What on earth happened to us? To me?

"Nathan, you Jonah!" she told him the previous night when he had reiterated that he had not come to Tynbee for *this*. "You thought you were coming to Tarshish, didn't you? Ha! It turned out to be Nineveh after all. God called you here for something really big, Nathan. Big things happen in small places."

But there was the matter of Ryne O'Casey.

Ryne O'Casey. Nathan tried to picture the boy. He had seen him half a dozen times, maybe, in the nine months since he had come to Tynbee. *That,* he had to admit to himself, *could be construed as Jonah-like.* One day soon he would be teaching young ministers to do what he himself was apparently not willing to do. *Above all,* he would charge them, *be true to your vocation: Minister. Visit the sick, weep with those who weep, rejoice with those who rejoice. Be Jesus to the lepers and prostitutes and publicans and sinners in your midst. For, whatever else he was,* Nathan could hear himself saying, *Jesus of Nazareth was a champion of the underdog, a Friend of Sinners.*

He turned from the parsonage, turned from Miriam at the piano. On the side table beneath the window lay a card from Ryne O'Casey. It had come in yesterday's mail. He picked it up and read it again. It was a homemade greeting card, handwritten in colored markers on a folded piece of yellow construction paper. Ryne had drawn a television on the front and stick figures depicting himself and, Nathan guessed, his parents and dog lying in bed watching it. He had drawn red hearts around the message on the inside: "Thank you all for the wonderful TV set that you gave me. It sure is nice (AND GREAT BIG TO!!!). I wish there was some way I could tell you how much it means to me. It means ALOT! Maybe I won't be so lonely now. Thank you all!!! Love, Ryne O'Casey (and Olie and Esther O'Casey to). PS: I'm feeling pretty good."

Thank you *all,* Ryne had written.

Nathan stared at the handwritten line a long time.

He looked out on Tynbee, his Nineveh, again, down in the valley, beyond tin-roofed farmhouses with beat-up cars on cinderblocks out front and ramshackle henhouses out back. Farmland long fallow stretched for miles in every direction, and in the center of it all was Tynbee proper, a fifty-acre plot. He saw the carillon-topped City Hall building and the great spire of the First Methodist Church (all the churches in Tynbee were *first* churches—even St. Anna's, which was called simply "First

Catholic," and the Seventh-Day Adventist church, which was called "First Seventh"; there was not a single second church in Tynbee). The other roofs were mostly flat, though a few were gabled and had twin brick chimneys—Western Auto, Cato, Dell & Son Jewelry, Hadley's Second Chance Thrift Shop, the Post Office, McCrory, Barfield's Pawn, IGA, and the new video rental store.

Tynbee, his Nineveh. Back in the day Tynbee unincorporated had led the state in poultry production until an outbreak of the Hong Kong Chicken Flu (Chicken 97-type H5N1, to be precise) left the chicken coops of Avery County desolate. Virtually overnight, the county's economy crashed. Most of the younger (third and fourth generation) farmers decided not to rebuild their farms. Instead, they tried to get on at the EastTenn Slacks Company, which manufactured men's double-knit polyester slacks and insulated flannel shirts. It seemed like a good move, a wise move. EastTenn offered a retirement plan, insurance benefits, and regular shift work. All went well until the previous February when EastTenn Slacks became what Tynbee folks referred to scornfully as *FarEastTenn* slacks, closing without notice and moving to Taiwan.

Them chicken farmers, according to Elder Luther Bailey who had disclosed the moral of the FarEastTenn story to Nathan, *was found to have put all their nest eggs in one double-knit polyester basket.* Elder Bailey could afford to laugh: He depended neither on chickens nor slacks for his living.

Elder Luther Eli Bailey. The business meeting: "He don't own this church," somebody said.

"*Half* of it anyway," a man said. "At last count."

That was true. Saint Paul warned Timothy, in King James English, of the perils of "filthy lucre," the love of which is the root of all evil. A member of the Historic First Church had warned Nathan during his first month at the church, warned him of the dangers of "Filthy Luther." *Beware the greed of filthy Luther*, the man had warned Nathan in a lowered voice. *He's the root of all evil in Avery County*, Tennessee. Luther Eli Bailey was a powerful man—"Don't buck *him*," the man had said. Bailey was chairman of the Tynbee city council and was far and away the wealthiest man in the town, and maybe in all of Avery County, which could not be guessed from the miserly manner in which he and his wife, Sue Ella, lived. Bailey, they said, was tight as a drum and had the first dime he had ever earned working as a furnace repairman.

Hardly a soul in Avery County was not indebted to Luther Bailey in one way or another. He was landlord, that is, *lord of the land*, to more than half the members of the Historic First Church. "How did that happen?" Nathan had asked his informant.

"Well, he's a con-man, Preacher. He was doing furnace repair work, which everybody knew he didn't need to do in the first place because he had inherited most of the fortune his grandfather made leasing land to strip-miners. Well, when he'd get a call from a old lady saying her furnace was quit, old Luther would go out and say it was shot—even if it only needed a belt or such. It's shot, he'd say. A new one'll run you a thousand dollars. Well, these poor old people didn't most of them have a hundred dollars, much less a thousand.

"So old Luther'd say, 'What I sometimes do to help people out is front the money for a new furnace. I can finance it like this: I'll buy your house and lot from you, put in a new furnace, and give you a place to live free of charge as long as you need it. If anything breaks, not to worry, I'll fix it and keep the place up. Course I don't have but about three or four thousand dollars, but like I said, you'll have a warm place as long as you need it and a little mad money in your billfold. And with winter coming and all it's going to be mighty cold in a few weeks' time.' Preacher, I can't even begin to tell you how many of them poor old people took him up on that offer."

So although he was the Appalachian equivalent of a slumlord, Luther Bailey's tenants were beholden to him for the simple reason that they had no place to go if he evicted them from his tenements and tarpaper shanties. Another man warned Nathan: *Filthy Luther's well-nigh their God, and when they hit their knees at night … well, he giveth and he taketh away, Preacher … homes and pastors alike.*

Nathan unlocked the metal utility cabinet in his office and pulled out the church directory, an antique burgundy ledger book with the names of all members (past and present) of the Historic First Church of Tynbee. An index card was taped on the front with a warning inscribed in red ink: "For Office Use Only! Pastor, Chairman Elder." Cryptic notations were scribbled in the margins beside each member's entry: "N.T." or "T.," "Al.," "Tob.," "Ad.," and the like. Nathan looked for a legend for the codes. There was none. But he couldn't help but wonder if the "N.T." stood for non-tither (it sure didn't stand for New Testament), the "Al." for alcohol-user, the "Tob." for tobacco-user, the "Ad." for adulterer, and so on.

Beside the O'Caseys' entry was a single code that required no legend to decipher: "AIDS." Other codes had been blotted out with a black marker. He wrote down the O'Caseys' address, located Sevier Mill Road on the wall map, pulled his rain slicker and gray fedora off the coat tree, and left the building.

Nathan fired up the Ford Taurus and headed through the gravel toward Route 4. Jonah or not, he had a call to make.

A pastoral call.

A Historic First

WAS ESTHER EVER SURPRISED on that stormy afternoon in August when the drought ended and, out of the blue, the young preacher washed up on her doorstep. "Great day in the morning, it's Preacher McKee!" Esther exclaimed to no one. She was home alone. Through the living room window she got a fix on him struggling to get his umbrella up against the driving rain and gusting wind before getting out of his navy blue Ford.

She set her glasses on the coffee table, wiped her hands on the soiled KISS THE CHEF apron Ryne and Olie had given her last Mother's Day, and tried to make herself presentable, which, on such short notice, consisted of removing the scarf she was wearing like a babushka and fluffing up the drooping curls of her permanent. Permanent, *my foot*. A temporary *was more like it*. Not three weeks had passed since she frittered away the better part of a Tuesday evening at the House of Hair getting her hair permed by chain-smoking Mary Barry Gunter, who shared gossip about everyone they knew (and as the owner of the only salon in Tynbee, she knew everything about everyone).

"Lord of mercy, now Mary Barry, hush your mouth," Esther told her, when Mary Barry said she had it from a reliable source that the site of the old EastTenn Slacks plant was going to be converted into a three-story brothel, pay-as-you-go. "Keep on with that talk and you won't need to use no perm'nent wave solution to curl my hair."

Before she left Esther had told Mary Barry Gunter, as delicately as she knew how, that her last permanent had been about as permanent as a ghost. Mary Barry said, "What? A ghost? Oh, that, honey. Well, we run short on juice a while back, and Leroy and his big ideas, he said vinegar might do just as good 'til the order come. I used the juice, honey, so I expect your hair'll be curly as Shirley Temple's until Thanksgiving—*at least*."

Thanksgiving my foot, Esther thought. Her hair was a stringy mess; from the looks of it she might have passed a stormy night out on the deck of the Good Ship Lollipop, and it was not even Labor Day. *Thanksgiving*.

Oh, fiddlesticks, Esther thought. Her hair was no use, and it was the least of her worries. She studied her image in the little mirror on the mantelpiece and picked through the limp waves above her forehead. She had not wanted bangs; she had wanted ringlets. *This heat we've had would take the curl out of Bertha Snowden's hair*, she thought, then chuckled as she pictured the big old kinky bush on her colored friend's head. She could not picture Bertha Snowden with long straight hair.

Nothing, not even a permanent, is permanent. If the preacher had had the good sense—not to mention the good manners—to ring her first, she thought, watching the man skirt his way around the puddles like a clumsy Fred Astaire, she might have taken a notion to whip up a batch of molasses cookies or run the carpet sweeper or at least powder her face.

Preacher McKee was favoring his left leg. He always had as far as she could recall—sometimes more than others, like today. Ginger-stepping like a bear with a hurt paw. She was of a mind to inquire about it but decided it would be in bad taste: Some people were touchy about their flaws. By the time he got to the foot of the steps, Esther had decided he needed a shave, too, and a good meal to put some meat on his bones and color in his cheeks. He was thin as Cooter Brown and pale as a ghost.

Suddenly—it always happened suddenly—*the Holy Ghost moved her.* She shuddered. *Lord have mercy.* Preachers and policeman at the door rarely meant anything good—especially, she thought, on a rainy day when you are home alone. Olie and Ryne had taken off for Pigeon Forge shortly after breakfast to pick up the Nintendo, which the Wal-Mart of Tynbee no longer stocked. That was hours ago, plenty of time to get there and back twice, even in the rain.

She called the thing that moved her the Holy Ghost. Ryne and Olie called it cold or fear. Sometimes it was. But sometimes it was a good old stirring of the Spirit. Esther had heard all that superstitious piffle about a chill indicating that somebody was walking across your grave. She seriously doubted that anybody was out wandering around on such a nasty day on their plot in the graveyard behind the Historic First Church where both her and Olie's people were. Piffle. She set them straight: People were all too quick to bring the Lord down to earth.

Please, Lord Jesus, don't let this be bad news, she prayed all the way to the front door. She held the screen door open at arm's length. "Hey, Preacher McKee," she said, her voice hopeful. "Everything's all right, I trust?"

"Yes," he said, hollering to be heard over the wind and rain. "Everything's all right. I'm sorry, Mrs. O'Casey, I should have called first." He did not sound either sorry or as though everything were all right. He closed his black umbrella, shook the rain from it, then propped it against the house just outside the front door. "I was just out, oh, just out this way," he said, "and thought I'd stop in."

"I don't know about all that," Esther said. "But get on in here, Preacher McKee, before you catch your death." At best he was stretching the truth. He was lying. Why on earth would he, who had never paid them a visit, have just happened to be out that way—way out in the boondocks on such a day.

He took off his hat and was in the process of stamping and wiping his feet on the worn straw welcome mat when Esther grabbed his arm and pulled him inside.

"Lord a mercy, Preacher McKee, don't be silly: This is not exactly the Biltmore House. We put that mat there so you can shake the filth off your hoofs on the way out of this pig sty." She steered him by the elbow over to the sofa, which was covered with an old pink afghan she had crocheted when Ryne was in the crib, and sat him down. "I'll fetch some ice tea," she said. She took his rain slicker with her and hung it over a chair in the kitchen. "Sweet or unsweet, Preacher?"

"Unsweet—if it's convenient; sweet, if it's not."

Convenient. Lord. What on earth is convenient? She adjusted her glasses. "I always keep a pitcher a each on hand," she said. "Olie likes it unsweet, too, but like Ryne always says, what's the use? It's like eating cake without the frosting. Course you might be one of them that does."

"No," he said. "I like my frosting."

"Had dinner yet, Preacher McKee?" Esther asked and continued before he had a chance to answer: "Let me fix you a sandwich to eat with your ice tea. Maybe a BLT—without the L. I need to pick up a head of lettuce at the market."

"No, thank you, just the same," he said. "I think I'll have lunch at home today with Miriam and the baby."

"Ohhh," Esther cooed, appearing in the doorway gripping a full pitcher of unsweet tea in her left hand and crossing her heart with her right. "How is that precious little cherub?" She remembered that he was precious, though that was about it.

"He's still precious," the preacher said.

"And beautiful, too, I imagine."

"We were blessd that he got his mother's looks."

"And your brains, no doubt," Esther said. "Course all that's not to say that you're not handsome or, for that matter, that your wife—bless her heart—is short on brains. Lord knows she can play that piano better than I ever heard."

"Well, thank you, Mrs. O'Casey, " he said.

Esther nodded. She set a blue Tupperware platter with a pitcher of unsweet tea, salt and pepper shakers, and a plate of sliced tomatoes on the coffee table. She wiped her hands on her apron and sat down, as daintily as her weight allowed, in Olie's barcalounger next to the sofa, said, "And if you don't quit calling me *Missus O'Casey*, I'll have your hide." She blushed. "And that was rude of me to say. I do beg your pardon."

"No offense taken," he said. His smile was awkward. "*Esther.*"

"Well now, that's better, Preacher McKee," she said, "and don't even ask me to call you by *your* first name. Because I won't do it. Nosiree, I won't. My mother used to say, 'A preacher man is bigger than his first name. Find one that's not, he shouldn't be no preacher a-tall.'"

A long pause, awkward pause. Preacher McKee cut his eyes around the room, looking at their things—studying them—as if he were trying to get to know them through their things. Most of the preachers they had invited over to Sunday supper had looked at their things with a completely different aim in mind—to find something of the Devil that they could preach a message on. Esther sipped her sweet tea and listened to the rolling thunder in the distance and wondered where on God's green earth Olie and Ryne were and what on God's green earth the preacher was doing there. Trying to get to know them through their things.

Now.

"Ryne's thank you card came in the mail yesterday morning," he said. "I thought I'd drop by and let him know that we got it."

"Well that was right sweet of you, Preacher," Esther said. She salted a wedge of tomato.

"I didn't think to call first to see if it was a good time, which was rude. I'm sorry."

"Oh, hush your mouth now, Preacher," said Esther. "There's no such thing as a good time." Or a bad time, either, for that matter, she thought. But with my hair looking like the wrath of God and Ryne and Olie Lord knew where, maybe there was a better and a worse time—this not being a better time. But, then again, that very morning Ryne had asked her and Olie if they would carry him to a crusade somewhere so some colored preacher woman could heal him of AIDS. So maybe the Lord had called Preacher McKee to the house to answer their question.

If that was the case, it was a good enough time to suit her.

"Good tea," he said, though she suspected he would have been happier with a Coca-Cola.

"Thank you kindly. I don't keep Coke-cola on hand anymore. Got to the point it would just go flat … I expect Ryne and his daddy'll be back before long. Fact is, I expected them back by now, but in this big old storm I don't imagine they're making very good time. They went down to Pigeon Forge, to Wal-Mart, to pick up that Super Ningtendo thing that goes with the RCA TV you-all gave him." She slipped the tomato wedge into her mouth and held the plate out to him. "Try one. You won't find the likes of these at the Piggly Wiggly."

Preacher McKee picked up an oozing wedge of the blood-red tomato like it was a slug. He salted it lightly, then gnawed a little bite off. He was not used to eating tomatoes that way. "Mmm," he said, chewing it, "you grow these yourself. Tasty."

Esther nodded in thanks. "Ryne sure was proud to get that RCA TV set. Why, in just a few days' time, it's like he's a whole different person. He's excited about something again, Preacher McKee," she said. "I just wish you could of seen the look on his little face when he got out of the bathtub and found that big old thing on his chester drawers. It liked to have tore me and his daddy up."

The preacher nodded. He took a little sip of his tea, trying to wash down the *tasty* tomato. "There's something you should know about that," he said. He leaned back and poked his fingers into the pillow nets Esther had crocheted to cover her ill-matching throw pillows. "It wasn't a simple matter."

"I don't imagine it was," Esther said, matter of fact. It was as if he had a confession to make.

Esther was determined not to make it a mite easier—though she would never have admitted it. He had not seemed much interested in stepping in anything (dust or worse) that he could not easily shake off his feet when he left Tynbee at year's end. So Esther had not been too surprised, and neither had Olie, that Preacher McKee had avoided Ryne and their situation. Maybe he had come to explain why his wife and baby—but not he—had signed the card Elder Gosset brought along with the TV. That was no news: The names she expected to see on the card were there.

Whatever he had come to do, he needn't worry that she was going to throw a tizzy about it—unless she took a notion to. She knew good and doggone well that giving that TV to Ryne had not been a *simple matter* at the Historic First Church. There was no such thing at the Historic First Church.

"It was, uh, not a ... *not* simple," he said.

"I don't imagine it was," she said again. She crossed her hands over her belly.

Then suddenly Esther felt anger churning with the tomato acid in her gut. It burned. It was nice enough of him to come, indeed, but she had a sense that his visit was more for his sake than for anybody else's, and if there was one thing Esther O'Casey could not stand it was waffling. Preacher McKee was being polite. Fine. She knew that. And they were, after all, strangers, seeing as how he had not bothered—stop-gap preacher or not—to come and visit Ryne in all the months he had been at the church. He had, she told Olie, avoided Ryne like the plague. The plague. *There's only two things to do with phlegm*, Esther's mother used to say: S*pit it out or swallow it.* Just as Esther feared that the first tremors of a Holy Ghost chill of righteous indignation might rear up and erupt like Mount Vesuvius into a full-blown tizzy and force her to get him told, told but good, he cleared his throat.

NATHAN HOPED TO GOD he did not look and sound as awkward as he felt. "It was, uh, not a … *not* simple," he had told Esther O'Casey, bumbling around trying to avoid coming right out and saying that the church had made a hateful scene over the TV.

Nathan needed to say something, wanted to say something, something that would mean something. Beads of sweat gathered on his chest. His heart pounded. He could not swallow for the lump in his throat, a lump as big as that tomato wedge that had not quite gone down.

I'm unraveling. Miriam had always warned him that if he did not somehow resolve his grief, it would, a little at a time or all at once, resolve *him, dissolve* him. *Your defense mechanisms are failing.*

It's your Judgment Day, Daniel Nathan McKee. There was no escaping it. *No one stands completely straight; we all of us have our leanings. Which way will you lean, Nathan? Which way? There's no such thing as neutrality. You said it yourself—Remember? Remember? Remember?—muster the courage of conviction and own your biases.*

Nathan set his glass of ice tea on the coffee table and excused himself. He staggered down the darkened hall, oblivious to the mess Esther was warning him about. The second door on the right. He closed the door and fastened the lock, as though the thing that was after him were lurking out there in the hall and not in his own heart, as though he could simply slide a lock and keep it out. He took off his glasses and splashed cold water on his face.

There is no such thing as neutrality. Remember? Yes, yes he had said it himself in a seminary class years ago. The professor had extolled the virtue of *de-biasing* oneself, by which he meant, Miriam said, that you should make lukewarmth a way of life. Near the end of the semester, after thirteen weeks of being encouraged to de-bias himself, Nathan had come out of his chair with a start: "With all due respect, Professor, Jesus himself had biases, did he not? Say, against people who thought they could curry God's favor by observing the Law without love, mercy, and justice? And what about Paul? Ha! He was anything but a *de-biased* man. Bias means a leaning toward something— and you can't lean *toward* one thing without leaning *against* something else. Bias is the wellspring of passion, of conviction, and without passion and conviction a person has no business doing ministry!"

The professor crossed his arms and stepped down beside the lectern. "My dear Mr. McKee, is it possible that you have, for nearly a semester now, mistaken the first premise of my argument?"

"How do you even *have* a premise, much less an argument without biases? I have a bias against people who think they have to come to a complete stop before making a right turn on a green light. I have a bias against *Manhattan* clam chowder. I have a bias against people who would deprive me of my right to have biases. And, apparently, *you* have biases against people who have biases."

"My point," the professor told him, "is that biases alienate, Mr. McKee. If you have strong biases, it is probably best to keep them to yourself lest you alienate about half of your congregants."

"If they alienate, they unite," Nathan said. "How would we have a church at all if we were not united by a *bias* that Jesus Christ is Lord. God is biased; *Jacob have I loved; Esau have I hated.* You yourself are biased *against* bias, Professor; I am biased *for* it. The question is not: to have bias or not to have bias? But: Which biases will we have? None of us can say anything— anything at all—without expressing some bias. *Can we?*"

On the last page of Nathan's final exam that semester, the professor scribbled: "Nathan: You have a keen intellect, strong passions, conviction and courage—the makings for great evil or great good. I have a <u>bias</u> for the latter. And <u>you</u>? All the best— Professor LDL." Beside the comment was a circled A.

He had forgotten all that after he killed Philip—killed Philip because (could this be true, Miriam?) because he had leaned. He had leaned, and Philip had died. Nathan's left thigh burned from his groin to his hip and down to his knee.

You couldn't have saved Philip.

Like hell I couldn't have.

I could have.

I didn't.

He dried his hands on the hand towel that hung on a rack beside the sink. The towel was old and faded, but that trademark red and blue could mean only one thing: Spiderman. Nathan pulled it gently off the rack, unfolded it, and held it out at arms' length and studied the image of Spiderman suspended from a skyscraper by a single strand of silk. The picture was identical to the picture on the front of the T-shirt his brother Philip had worn on that last day—that last day when he could have saved him, but didn't.

Nathan glanced at his pale face a final time, realized that he had forgotten to shave. He placed the folded hand towel back on the rack and went back to the living room.

"YOU FEELING OKAY, Preacher McKee?" said Esther. "You look a little peaked, a little green behind the ears. Have you some tea."

Nathan nodded and took a sip of his ice tea. He seemed more at ease after his bathroom break. Poor thing must have been fidgeting around so because he needed to make water and was too shy to say so until nature was not so much calling as screaming.

"I think you and Mr. O'Casey have a right to know," he said, "that some members of the church were opposed to giving Ryne the TV. They argued the money could be put to better use, and, well, the temper of the proceedings at the business meeting was not cordial."

"Cordial?" Esther asked. "Lord of mercy. We're talking about the Historic First Church, not the *Crystal Cathedral*, Preacher. 'Cordial' has nothing to do with the temper of any proceedings at that church. It never has." Esther feared she might have come on too strong in setting the preacher straight—she always preferred spitting it out to swallowing it. But she was not surprised one whit, much less all tore up, to hear that a big stink was raised about giving Ryne his TV set. In fact, her own temper was quite cordial at the moment—though it might erupt in a tantrum any minute.

Maybe, Esther thought, *just maybe, this was the first time he had seen such a thing in church.* The first time you saw it—*really* saw it for what it was—was the most shocking, Esther decided. You were in Sunday school singing "Jesus Loves Me, This I Know" and assuming that the church was filled with people who played the game of life by the Golden Rule and loved one another as they loved themselves, when one day you came across two of the elders or old ladies squaring off out in the vestibule, with raised voices and sometimes raised fists, blessing each other out about the color of toilet paper to put in the church powder room, and it hit you like a ton of Sunday school quarterlies that when it came to real-life matters—like toilet paper—the church was not a whole lot different from the world after all. And that image of elders feuding in the vestibule, which you saw with your own eyes and heard with your own ears, was a lot more vivid than the Sunday School image of Jesus sitting up high on a boulder in a big old white gown and a blue sash suffering the little children to come unto him.

Esther said, "There's no use mincing words about it: There's hell-a-hootin' at the Historic First Church, Preacher McKee. Now don't get me wrong. There's some good folks—awful good folks—that goes there. I think of Elder and Lula Gosset—bless their heart—and Buster Jeeves and Mabel Morton. But some of the others, not the ones beholden to Luther Bailey—and I'm not about to go naming names—are just plain awful folks, more like them old Pharaohs the Lord Jesus was always lighting into." Esther fondled the big buttons on her dress as if they were knobs she was adjusting to turn down her volume. "And here I sit in judgment," she said, almost whispering, "like some old Pharaoh myself; as if I'm any better in Lord Jesus's eyes than Luther Bailey and Nellie Jean Perkins and Jimmy Joe Cole."

Nathan smiled. "Well," he said, "let's just say that the church is a … a … *what*?" He groped at the air as if to snag the best word—or the least obscene—to describe the Historic First Church of Tynbee, Tennessee. "A mess."

"'Mess,'" she said, "is a good word for it." She chuckled.

He smiled, then said: "I was going to say something else."

"I imagine the Lord'll forgive you if you do, Preacher. He don't mind the truth, and Mother always said Historic First Church was enough to make a preacher cuss." For the first time, their eyes locked.

Esther O'Casey's mother also used to say, "What they need to do is take and hang a revolving door on the front of

Historic First yonder." The revolving door Esther's mother had in mind was not for the convenience of the congregation but to accommodate its revolving preachers, who came and went at a pace that would make your head spin. Esther had to admit, when she was honest about it, that her dearly departed mother, Miz Ida Bea Porterfield, had as much to do with the need for a revolving door as anyone in the twentieth century.

The church was founded way back when Davy Crockett, "king of the wild frontier," was representing Tennessee in Congress. In the one hundred and seventy or so years since, the church had succeeded in voting in and out three times as many preachers as the country had presidents during the same time period. And, unlike the nation, Historic First Church had no qualms about impeaching its leader.

During his one-year term on the Board of Elders, Olie had access to records dating back to the church's founding in 1825. Olie said he had calculated that the average term for a pastor at Historic First was one year and eight months.

Esther found that so hard to believe that she twice requested that he refigure them. She asked him if he was sure. She had expected the average term to be much lower—perhaps, all-totalled, six months. There were times during her childhood when it seemed as though someone different was in the pulpit every Sunday.

Every new preacher was greeted with high hopes and low expectations (which, without fail, they lived down to). In an unprecedented move, the Board of Elders had decided to devote a full year to the search for a new preacher—during which time a student intern would fill the gap. Esther knew that it didn't really matter who they hired. The problem was not the preacher but the church. And by long tradition the church would heap all its sins on the preacher, then shoo him off like a bothersome fly. Even if they could somehow get Billy Graham to come be their preacher (and Ruth Bell with him), those dear saints would surely end up in the midst of a big old upscuddle and end up getting run off.

Esther could not decide just what to make of Preacher McKee. He had a right nasty habit of using two-dollar words and then explaining what they meant—which only added insult to injury. Big words, Esther decided, were useful when you wanted to avoid being straight with someone. Like that time way back when that Olie came in late from work reeking to high heaven of some French perfume (she later learned it was turpentine) and she asked him if he was engaging in fornification and he said he didn't even know what that meant, and she said, I didn't think you was, but I was just checking.

Olie once said of Preacher McKee's sermons: "Half his messages are spent explaining the other half. If he would just use plain old English words, I reckon most of us folk would take him at his word about what them Greeks and Hebrews meant by saying thus and such. That way, he could either say a lot more in the same amount of time or say the same amount in half the time and get us home to dinner sooner."

It was not as if a soul in all of Tynbee, Tennessee, had ever so much as met a Greek or Hebrew, Esther thought, much less gave a hoot about learning the language they spoke. The only foreign language they had offered at Reid Cain High School when Esther and Olie attended was Latin, and only the kids on the college-bound track took it. And they never stayed around to afflict it on the townfolk because, as Olie once remarked, the college-bound track only ran one way: Those who took it out of Tynbee never came back.

Preacher McKee was a Yankee, too, from Maryland or Missouri or somewhere up North that started with a M. And that might explain why he was the only preacher at the Historic First Church in Esther's memory who was not a windsucker.

Her mother used to say you could pretty well gauge how good a preacher was by whether he lost his wind and passed out by the end of the message. Esther remembered Preacher Lee Jay Fortner. Lord, could that man suck wind—sometimes even when he was making the announcements before the offering plate was passed: "Blesh God—HA!, thus saith the Lord—HA!, glory to God—HA!, we need a bag or two of cookies—HA! and a firkin or so of juice—HA!, for the young'n's nursery—HA!" Esther would bust out laughing sometimes and then end up feeling like people thought she was retarded or something.

Preacher McKee stood still as a totem when he delivered the Sunday sermon, and he read his sermons instead of preached them, which didn't bother Esther one bit, though some folks in the church thought that a true man of God should just speak as Holy Ghost gave him utterance (those same people thought the Holy Ghost ought to quit uttering right at ten before noon). But Esther figured that if the Lord ever called her to preach, she would ask him to make the Holy Ghost give her utterance the night before so she could write it all down. She hated public speaking—even when it was only to say a prayer out loud in her Sunday school class.

Unlike Preacher McKee, Lee Jay Fortner never used a note, claiming he spoke as Holy Ghost gave *him* utterance, and on occasion he ended up uttering some out-of-the-way things from the pulpit that Holy Ghost had no part in. Esther's mother had been willing to overlook an occasional out-of-the-way statement, but she refused to stand for Lee Jay Fortner or anybody else preaching his own notions as if it was the Bible. Preacher Fortner made the mistake of touching on the evils of dipping snuff one Sunday morning, and it didn't sit well with Esther's mother, who rolled her wheelchair up and confronted him in the vestibule as he was seeing people out. She told him she was seventy-and-four-years-old and had been reading the Bible since before his mother had give birth to him and, in all that time, she had never so much as seen the word *snuff* mentioned in the Bible. Preacher Fortner said, "Dear Lady, the body is the temple of the Holy Ghost," and Esther's mother said that may be, but for all she knew Saint Paul had never so much as heard of *W. E. Garrett & Sons' Sweet, Mild Snuff,* and that maybe the good preacher would do better if he just stuck to preaching the Bible and not his own notions. That was the last time anyone had mentioned the word snuff from the pulpit of the Historic First Church.

Then there was Preacher Otis McDaniel—poor devil was old as Methusaleh. One Sunday, back during the hair wig craze in the 1970s, he got preaching on the evils of women wearing wigs. (He didn't have the first wisp of hair left on his own head, he was so old and bald.) "Wigs, bless God," he said, pointing his shaky finger, "is of the Devil! Why in today's society women has got more hair in their drawers than they got on their head."

That was it. Esther's mother nearly fell slap out of her wheelchair. "I've never in my life heard the likes of this filthy talk," she said.

"Not *them* kind of drawers," old Preacher McDaniel tried to explain. "Not *under*drawers."

"Well I have *never*!" said Esther's mother.

Preacher McDaniel, red-faced and shaking, said: "The drawers like you got in your bedroom dresser where you keep your—"

"I *know* where I keep *my* belongin's," she said. "And, preacher or no, I'm not fixin' to sit here and listen to no bedroom talk neither." That said, she turned and rolled herself on out of the church.

A few weeks later Preacher McDaniel and his poor old wife got run off.

Preaching *against* things did not seem to be Preacher

McKee's style, Esther recalled (though she could not say for sure whether he preached *for* things either). He never railed against the vices, such as imbibing drink or contorting with women of easy virtue you aren't married to. He stuck mainly to explaining the way things were back in Bible times. He sometimes tried to tell a joke, but nobody got it, and he ended up red-faced, feeling like maybe people thought *he* was retarded or something. He always closed his sermons with a reminder about how important it is for the members of the church to love one another. Boy, that fell on deaf ears. Of the two or three things Esther missed since they stopped going to church three months before (when Esther caught wind that some people refused to let their children attend Sunday school with Ryne) Preacher McKee's preaching was not one of them.

"What was that you was saying, Preacher McKee," she asked. "My mind wonders something awful lately."

"It went to a vote," Preacher McKee said. "It was seventy-one for and—"

"Seventy-two against," said Esther.

"Seventy-three."

Esther's face flushed. She got the familiar urge to wrap her hands around somebody's neck. "Well, I reckon those seventy-three people voted their conscience," she said. "Such as it is." She wondered who that seventy-third person was.

"I'm afraid they did," said Preacher McKee. "*Such as it is.* It was hateful, shall we say."

"It don't much matter how we shall say it, Preacher McKee. But I'll tell you this much: If they was hateful, they was honest."

They sat silent for a while. Then Esther said: "I don't know if it's right of me to ask this or not, Preacher, but what are your ideas about faith healing?"

He cleared his throat, said, "Faith healing," and for a moment Esther thought he was going to give her a straight answer that might settle the matter, but he didn't say anything else.

"Reason I ask is Ryne apparently came across some healer on the TV set last night and, well, at breakfast this morning, he asked me and his Daddy if we could carry him up to her crusade to get healed. Olie said it might have been Katherine Kuhlmann, but I heard she was dead. And not colored."

Bless Ryne's little heart, she thought.

"I see," said Preacher McKee. A moment passed. Then he said, "Well, tell me about Ryne."

If at times Preacher McKee had struck Esther as a hurried man, anxious to serve out his sentence at the Historic First Church, the sooner to be done with Tynbee, he did not seem the least bit hurried then. Or anxious. He sat back and crossed his legs and folded his hands neatly in his lap and listened closely, carefully, as she told him all about her son Ryne.

When she finished, his eyes were damp, and he kept swallowing—very tightly, and his shoulders were twitching just a little.

AFTER SHOWING PREACHER MCKEE OUT, at a little after two o'clock that stormy afternoon, Esther went back to her work. She stood at the kitchen sink with her arms elbow-deep in cool dishwater and scrubbed the breakfast dishes. And fretted a while about Ryne and Olie. And thought a while about Preacher McKee.

There was something about that strange man she liked. Despite those silly round spectacles he wore that made his eyes always look like you had just walked in on him in the midst of sitting on the commode, and all those big words he hid behind like Adam's fig leaf, and his big city ways (he did not know how to eat a tomato right, for crying out loud), despite all that, he was charming in his own way and, for a man with so much school learning, he didn't seem interested in putting on too many airs. And, well, somehow—today at least——he had taken down the

Do Not Disturb sign he might as well have hung around his neck like a sandwich board and actually did seem to care, really care—maybe because he was being paid to care. Though she couldn't imagine that. Historic First hardly paid their preachers a starvation wage—which is why most of them had to hold other jobs, mainly auto sales.

Preacher McKee had said he would come back and visit with all of them, but especially Ryne, and Esther was proud to hear it. He apologized for having not come sooner, and the sheepish way he said it led Esther to imagine there was a pretty good reason why he had not done so before. After he had walked out to his car—and Esther couldn't help but notice that his gimp was not nearly so bad—he hollered to be heard over the rain, "I'm standing with you on this."

Esther felt woozy; her head was swimming. She looked out the screen window above the sink at their land. It looked like a scene from one of those coffee table books with pictures of land and seascapes that always made you feel a little blue. A cool mist settled on her face and arms. "Lord," she said. She looked at the great old beech tree on the creek bank. The tire swing hung from its thickest bough was still there. The begonia blossoms were red as blood, the partridge peas yellower than she had ever seen them, and the air was heavy with the smell of earth and mint.

She wondered if it all would look the same, smell the same, move her so after.

After.

"I'm standing with you on this," the preacher's voice echoed in her mind.

Esther snapped to. It was time to put supper on, and there she stood idle. "They must have had to go to China to pick up the Ningtendo at the factory," she told Samson, who lay at her feet. She breaded four pork chops (Ryne and the dog always split the first; she and Olie always split the fourth) and began snapping green beans and tossing them into a pot of water on the stove. She was just thinking that her two men had better have a pretty doggone good excuse for being gone so long and worrying her so or she would have their hides, when she heard the Nova— muffler roaring—crunching down the gravel driveway.

She knew they had no such doggone good reason when, after they closed the front door and were padding across the living room, she heard Ryne's little voice, barely more than a whisper, tell Olie, "Well, Dad, it's been nice knowing you."

"Let me handle this," Olie said in a whisper.

Olie poked his head into the kitchen and said, "Well, look a-here, won't you? If it ain't Dolly Parton with her hair dyed black! Who'd a guessed she was a gourmet cook, too? Something smells mighty appetizing. Esther you look like you've fallen off a bit."

"Fallen off, my foot," said Esther.

"That diet you're on is working out, Es'. Working out nice."

"I ain't on no diet, Olie. If I was, I'd get the law after whoever came up with it."

"You're looking just about right."

"You're looking for something you ain't gonna get right now."

"Well, Esther, you know what's down yonder in Pigeon Forge."

"Benton Oliver O'Casey," she said, without turning around. "Something tells me you'd better fetch that young'n of yours and work your way back in here—nice and easy like. Well, I have *never*. Butter-mouthing me so can only mean one thing about Pigeon Forge. The worse you been the better you talk."

Olie bumbled his way through a long drawn-out explanation: The Wal-Mart in Pigeon Forge had sold their last Super Nintendo minutes before he and Ryne got there. The manager was awful sorry, Olie said, and to compensate for their inconvenience he offered to take an extra ten percent off T. K. Kirby's employee discount price and said he would call as soon as the new shipment came in.

Wasted breath.

"That's all fine and dandy, Olie, and I'm glad you-all made it home safe," Esther said, glancing up at the horn-of-plenty wall clock, "but the way I figure it, the tale you told still leaves about six hours unaccounted for."

"I'll be in my room if you need me," Ryne said, from about halfway down the hall.

Olie sat down at the kitchen table and accounted for the lost six hours: After they left the Wal-Mart, they had lunch at McDonald's. Ryne, he was happy to tell her and she was happy to hear, well Ryne gobbled down the whole cheeseburger that came in his Happy Meal. Then, they got in the car and, with every intention of heading straight home, started out toward the highway. Then Ryne saw the big old billboard for Dollywood.

"Benton Oliver O'Casey!" Esther said. She drew back the frying pan in both hands as if it were a baseball bat. "*Shut your mouth!* You *know* you didn't!"

"Yes, Esther, I'm afraid I did, uh, we did," he admitted with a grimace.

"Don't go blaming your indecision on Ryne."

"Indiscretion."

"Yes it was," she agreed. "It most certainly was."

Then it all came out. Before he knew it, Olie said, he was standing in line at the ticket window at Dollywood buying admission passes, and then they were taking in shows and riding rides and seeing attractions and eating cotton candy and—

"Oh, spare me the gory details," Esther said. "I could just snatch you bald-headed right about now, Benton Oliver O'Casey."

After all, Esther was heard to say time and again that evening and for several days to come, it was not as if everybody didn't know that Dolly Parton was her favorite singing star and that she had always yearned to go to Dollywood (and, more importantly, she thought, Ryne had had a great time).

The time of his life.

Esther Had Heard Enough

THAT NIGHT AS ESTHER WAS TUCKING RYNE into bed, she lowered her voice and said, "If I keep carrying on about Dollywood, I lay you dollars to donuts your Daddy'll end up carrying us over there on Saturday."

They exchanged winks. Ryne suggested that she mention, to herself out loud whenever his dad was around, what an amazing time Ryne had at Dollywood. Esther said, "We're a genius."

So carry on she did. She ranted and raved about how her two menfolk seemed to have forgotten—and how *could* they have forgotten?—while they were having the time of their life at Dollywood, had forgotten that she—Esther O'Casey, their loving wife and doting mother, whose favorite singing star just happened to be, well, Dolly Parton, had never, not even once, been to Dollywood, but had always yearned to, yearned to so badly, as Olie well knew—was home slaving over a hot stove frying porkchops and taking care of some right serious spiritual business with the preacher.

How could they?

Their ingenious scheme worked like a charm. Only once did Olie say, "If I didn't know you any better, and know that you weren't that kind of devious person, I'd swear you were trying to play me like a fiddle, Es'."

Esther told him flatly that she most certainly was not a deviant kind of person and didn't know the first thing about playing a fiddle, and how dare he even suggest such an awful thing of her, the wife of his youth, who *after all* was the one who had gotten the raw end of the Dollywood deal. "Take it back, Olie. You know in your heart I'm not the kind of person that goes about deviating."

"Of course you aren't," Olie said.

Esther always said you could set your clock by Olie, he was so predictable. By bedtime on Thursday, every time they heard her grumbling to herself about Dollywood, Olie and Ryne would break into the chorus of one of Dolly Parton's hit songs, which they changed to suit the circumstances: "Here she goes again, looking better than a body has a right to, and shaking us up so, that all we really know, is here she goes again, and here we go-o-o-o-!"

To Dollywood, that is.

She had Olie dead to rights. Friday afternoon Olie said, "Esther, I believe I've heard about all of this I can take."

"Let's see if you can't take a little more," she said.

And Olie said, "Enough." He broke down and said he would take her and Ryne to Dollywood on that very Saturday morning just one week to the day after he and Ryne wound up there they knew not how. We might as well make a day of it, Olie said. The manager of the Wal-Mart in Pigeon Forge had said they were expecting the next shipment of Nintendos to arrive on Friday evening. Make a day of it—even if they broke the bank in doing so.

ESTHER HAD SLEPT maybe an hour. For once, her insomnia had nothing to do with looking back and everything to do with looking forward. Forward to Dollywood. She got out of bed as soon as the eastern sky pinkened above the dark ridges of the

Great Smoky Mountains. She slipped into her flannel bathrobe and woolly house shoes and headed off to work in the kitchen. It was a special day, and everything had to be perfect. Esther fried a whole chicken, which had spent the night thawing in the kitchen sink, and baked a pan each of buttermilk biscuits and molasses cookies (from scratch, of course). She whipped up a big batch of potato salad in a Tupperware bowl and set it in the refrigerator to chill. She mixed two pitchers of ice tea—one sweet, for Ryne and herself, and one unsweet, for Olie. She wrapped the whole mess of victuals in tin foil and packed them, along with cups, napkins, paper plates, and eating utensils, on ice in the big white Igloo cooler Olie carried to work.

Then she took a bath. She soaked a long time in the cool sudsy water. She was beside herself with excitement. She could not help but wonder if they would catch a glimpse of Dolly Parton herself and maybe even Kenny Rogers with her or at least that truck-driving husband she kept. Olie said he thought it was very unlikely that they would see hide nor hair of Dolly at the park. Esther said, "I don't know about all that." Ryne said he thought he had heard that Dolly lived way out in Hollywood, California; and Esther said, "Well you can't believe everything you hear, Ryne. I think you heard *Dolly*wood, not Hollywood. They sound alike. Besides, I imagine we stand a better chance of seeing Miss Dolly at Dollywood than anywhere else."

She washed her hair, which she had decided to put up in a tight bun. If she didn't, she knew that with all the moisture in the air it would be a wreck before she rode the first ride at Dollywood. And it would be embarrassing—if they *did* happen to run into Dolly Parton—if Esther's hair were a nasty, stringy, sweaty mess, and Esther would end up having to hurt Mary Barry for using vinegar again, or whatever *juice* she had used this time (smelled kind of like wine and, Esther remembering it, whispered a prayer for poor Mary Barry, that she had not gone back to drink).

Esther took special care in applying her makeup, too: She put on extra blush and shaped an arch over each eye with her eyebrow pencil, which she had not done since they last attended Sunday service. She slipped into her least-faded cotton sundress, which had big orange and yellow zinnia blooms all over it, and a pair of white pumps. The shoes were tight and her feet were bound to swell up in the heat and it would not do to get sausage feet and ruin the day, so Esther packed a pair of orange flip-flops in the canvas bag along with sunblock and Ryne's pill bottles. She wished, as she clipped on her silver cross earrings, that she weren't so durn heavy. But some things cannot be helped.

Then she went back to the kitchen and fixed breakfast: scrambled eggs with cheese, bacon, and grits.

It was—Esther pointed out several times as they were loading the picnic basket into the trunk of the old gray Nova at a little after ten that Saturday morning—"a picture perfect day for going to Dollywood. Thank you, Jesus!" The sky was so blue, the low-hanging clouds so white and fluffy and utterly still that for a moment Esther could not move at all. She just stood there, eyes fixed on the blue, lost in one of her moments that would constitute heaven if it never passed for all eternity, thinking of nothing—not a single thing.

"We'd best hit the road," Olie said.

Esther came to, and after they were settled in the car and Olie fired the engine, she said, "Dollywood, here we come!"

Olie and she were in the front seat; Ryne and Kaitlyn Main, Elder and Lula Gosset's eleven-year-old granddaughter who lived over in Union Grove, were in the back. Elder and Lula Gosset, bless their hearts, had caught wind of how much Ryne enjoyed himself at Dollywood. They stopped by Friday night and said they had been meaning to take Kaitlyn to Dollywood all summer and surely would have but for Lula's arthritic knees. They said they would be happy to foot the bill for everybody if Olie and

Esther could manage to take Kaitlyn along with them. "No, don't feel funny about nothing," they told Olie when he protested. They owed *him*, they said, and reminded him about the lean-to he had built for them at cost a few months back. Elder Gosset handed Olie a bank envelope with a one-hundred-dollar bill in it and said he would not take no for an answer. Esther had prayed silently that Olie's pride would not get the better of him.

"Better stop right quick for gas," Olie said as they pulled out of the driveway onto Sevier Mill Road. He could get gas cheaper at the Starvin Marvin in town than at the old filling stations on U.S. Highway 321, he said. Esther said she didn't know whether ice was cheaper at the Starvin Marvin in town or not, but they needed another bag or two to keep the lunch she had packed in the ice chest fresh. They headed into town on Loudon Boulevard, which became Tynbee's Main Street. Esther tuned in an AM station that played hillbilly music, hoping to hear Dolly Parton on the way down to Pigeon Forge. "I wonder will we catch a glimpse of her?" Esther asked. "And Kenny Rogers, too?"

"You never know," they said.

She heard Ryne and Kaitlyn giggling in the back seat.

"Does my hair look funny?" said Esther. "This permanent's anything but, and I'm gonna tell Mary Barry so, too."

"It's not *that*, Mom," Ryne said.

Esther was about to ask what it was then, when Olie said, "What in the world's going on up yonder?"

Just before Hamlin Street, where they needed to turn to get gas and ice at Starvin Marvin, a uniformed police officer was stationed in front of three orange-and-black-striped sawhorses. He was directing traffic away from downtown Tynbee. Olie pulled up next to the county patrolman, whom he did not recognize, and was told, "No, there's no trouble, just a Klan rally of some sort. From the looks of it, everybody in the county's showed up for it." They had closed Main Street to thru traffic. Olie would have to take Warren Avenue over to Starvin Marvin.

Behind the patrolman, about a quarter of a mile back, they could see a great commotion. Someone was hollering through a bullhorn. "What are they hootin and hollerin about?" Esther asked. She stuck her head out the window and inclined her left ear toward the canopy of a hundred Confederate flags flown at arms' length by a bunch of white folks decked out in bright-colored clothes.

"Don't pay them silly old people no mind, Es'," said Olie.

"Shagnasties," she muttered.

"What are they doing, Dad?" Ryne scooted up and rested his chin on the back of the front seat.

"Well, there's a couple ways of looking at it, Ryne," said Olie. "They're exercising their constitutional right to share their ignorance with everybody else."

"The Klu Klux Klan is of the Devil, Ryne," said Esther.

"That's another way of looking at it."

"I said 'of *the* Devil,' Ryne," said Esther. "And I wish they'd just … just go on to blazes where they belong!"

"My Lord, Esther," said Olie. He turned the car on to Warren Street, steering the car with his left hand and patting Esther's arm with his right. "That talk's not becoming of a fine Christian lady like yourself. There's no need you getting all worked up. These people hardly need you to let everybody know how vile they are. They've been practicing that routine for a hundred and some years now."

"Well," said Esther, crossing her arms over her bosom, "it's not like Avery County has the money to protect them devils from the crowd. Last time they come, I heard it cost the county a million or two dollars."

Olie nodded, though he had heard from the Sheriff himself that it cost the county about fifty thousand dollars. Still too much, he knew, but he did not say a single word for fear that whatever he said would only stoke the fire that was kindling in his wife's heart. The color of her face was as good as any test at gauging Esther's blood pressure, and a reddish-purple tint meant it was critically high. Olie said, "Calm yourself, Es'. We'll be out of here in no time. And while we're in Wal-Mart picking up the Nintendo, why don't you mosey on over to the pharmacy and check your blood pressure on the machine they have in there. All this ballyhoo about Dollywood's got you red as a ruby. Then, before you know it, we'll be in Pigeon Forge hobnobbing around with the likes of Dolly Parton and Kenny Rogers, and it wouldn't do very well for you to be beside yourself, now would it?"

"You're humoring me, Olie," Esther said.

"There's nothing funny about this," Olie said, mostly to himself. He turned up the radio and sang along, something he rarely did, with Roger Miller on "Dang Me. "

Olie sang: *"Woman, would you weep for me? Duh-ba ba do do ba ba do do do."*

"Olie, please Lord, hush! Or we'll all be a-weepin'," Esther said. "No sense you rur'nin a perfect day."

Esther might have been able to contain her anger, and avoid making a big scene and being arrested, if they had started off toward Dollywood directly, as Olie promised. They didn't. They gassed up the Nova and dumped two bags of ice in the cooler, and as they were exiting Starvin Marvin, Olie said, "I think we can hit U.S. 321 farther down the road a piece toward Dollywood if we take Elmwood over to Langley Street. Lord knows what'll be going on at the end of Warren by now if we try to get back out to Loudon Boulevard."

For a few minutes it seemed like a good idea. Olie careened the Nova around the oak-lined bends of Elmwood Avenue, which ran parallel to Main Street, and turned up the radio another notch or two to drown out the bullhorn and clamor over on Main Street. Olie knew that the worst thing that could happen would be for Esther to hear just exactly what those Klansmen were carrying on about. He shouted over the blaring radio, "This station usually plays Dolly Parton right after they play Merle Haggard." Merle had gotten to the part of "Okie from Muscogee" about not wearing *our hair down long and shaggy, like the hippies out in San Francisco do,*" when they came to a dead stop at the intersection of Elmwood Avenue and Oak Street.

A short round man in aviator sunglasses and a blue poplin jacket with the letters TBI, for Tennessee Bureau of Investigation, raised his stubby arms to halt them. He stepped around beside Olie's window and informed them they would have to stay put. He said, through the side of his mouth: "Parade's heading down Main Street to Oak, to get to the pavilion on the town square.

"So what you're saying is, we're hemmed in here."

The TBI officer nodded. "Shouldn't take but a hour or so for them to pass."

Olie shut off the engine. "Me and my big ideas. Pop used to say, 'Beware the shortcuts, son. If they was that short, everybody would take them.'"

When the heat in the car became unbearable, they got out, the four of them, and stood in front of the car. People were milling around all over the place. Residents of Elmwood Avenue, most of whose faces were familiar to Olie and Esther, had pulled lawn chairs out onto the overgrown sidewalk; some were grilling franks and burgers and drinking beer. Children clad in bathing suits and cut-off shorts played under lawn sprinklers, for all the world as if it were the Fourth of July. Two rows of county men armed with riot gear—one on each side of the street—marched in lockstep about five feet apart. They rounded the corner from Main onto Oak, ahead of the paraders.

"Lord of Mercy," Esther said, her face red as blood, "every lawman in the country's out here. There's the TBI, Avery County, State Patrol, Sheriff's Department. I'm surprised the National Guard's not here."

"They might be," said Olie.

"This is *sick* is what it is, Olie. All for them bunch of ignoramuses."

Olie shrugged and shook his head. He said, "Esther, now, just go on over to Maudie's and see if you and the kids can go in and sit a spell and cool down. This is not the kind of thing they need to be exposed to."

Esther Jean O'Casey was not to be stilled. "This is of the Devil, Olie, that's what it is. And I've a good mind to let them people know." It didn't help that the day had broken hot and her feet had already begun to swell and hurt. She fetched her orange flip-flops from the trunk and put them on.

"I know, Esther," Olie said. "I know. But Ryne don't need to get all upset, or see you getting all upset, and they're bound to say something's gonna get your goat."

"Look, Mom," Ryne said.

They turned and saw, rumbling slowly around the corner, an old Carpenter school bus packed full of people—mostly children. The bus was painted a camouflage pattern, dull shades of green, brown, and black, like a pair of faded combat fatigues. A flag stuck up from each side of the front bumper: on the left, the Confederate Flag; on the right, a white flag with a red-white-and-blue swastika in the middle, which Olie told Ryne he thought was the emblem of the American Nazi Party. Two Nazi security guards wearing blue jeans, black berets, long-sleeved black shirts, and red-and-white swastika armbands marched on either side of the bus.

Esther fanned her cheeks with a paper plate. She tried not to look at the hateful hoodlums passing by the O'Casey's Nova. "That bus was built for carrying little children to school, *not* to go rolling around Tynbee learning hate. I don't reckon I can stand much more of this," she warned Olie. Olie and Ryne were busy explaining to Kaitlyn what Nazis were and how Olie's father had lost an arm battling them in World War II.

"Esther," he said. He gave her a long look.

Some of the Klanfolk, as residents of Tynbee called them, were draped with robes and pointed hats fashioned of hairpins and shoddy old bedsheets; others had on fancy embroidered robes made of red and green satin, with matching sashes and headpieces like the professors wore at Esther's niece Julie Anne's graduation ceremony at Vanderbilt in June of 1989. Some held round pressboard shields bearing a white cross and a red flame; others proudly waved Confederate flags. They carried banners of all sorts:

KNIGHTS OF THE INVISIBLE EMPIRE
KNIGHTS OF THE KU KLUX KLAN
AVERY COUNTY KLAVERN
FIGHTING FOR YOUR RIGHT NOT TO HAVE TO
ASSOCIRATE WITH NIGROES

Several little tow-headed, blue-eyed boys and girls were among their number, holding up banners their parents had obviously made for them: GOD MADE THEM BROWN FOR A REASON!!! and CHRIST-KILLER JEW-BOY JUDGES AND MEDIA MOGULS RULE AMERICA!!! and GOD HATES FAGOTS!!! But it was the banner at the end of the procession, and the loud-mouthed man who was toting it, that would eventually send Esther O'Casey over the edge.

Ryne asked Olie what a "fag-o" was, and Olie said, "Just someone else these people hate." Then he opened the trunk and rummaged through the ice chest. He filled four paper cups with ice and, seeing Esther edging her way closer to the procession, said, "Which is which, Es'?"

"Which is which *what*, Olie?" she answered, without taking her eyes off the procession.

"Which pitcher's sweet tea and which is unsweet?"

"The one with a 'U' on the lid is unsweet, Olie," she told him, her voice sharp. "The 'U' there on top stands for unsweet."

Olie went on about his business of pouring tea in the cups and keeping a wary eye on his wife, who had again begun grumbling: "These sorry baboons need to be brained."

"Well, now," Olie said, "we don't need any gorilla warfare today, Esther Jean, so how's about you just leave dealing with these folks to the police and the good Lord." Olie served them each a cup of iced tea, then sat down sideways in the driver's seat of the Nova with his legs hanging out the door. Ryne, who had gotten tired, was sitting on his knee, and Kaitlyn was on the hood of the car, using Esther's purse as a cushion against the heat. Esther was pacing around in front of the car, wringing her hands, which, she told Olie, was better than wringing somebody's neck, which is exactly what she was of a good mind to do. They watched as the American Nazis passed by, wearing police-like uniforms, with light-blue long-sleeved shirts and navy caps, slacks, and ties. Then came a dozen or so skinheads, mostly teenaged boys who looked, said Esther, like they needed to have their hindparts tore up but good with a hickory switch. Hoodlums. They had close-cropped sideburns and pimply faces, and their dungarees were rolled up to the tops of their shiny black jackboots.

It came as little surprise to Esther that some of the paraders' faces were familiar. The Klan was no *secret society* in Tynbee. "I bet you anything that Luther Bailey's behind all this." Rumor had it that Elder Luther Bailey himself was a Klansman—and for all she knew he was behind this whole shebang. Lord knows he hated her mother, hated Esther, too, and had been mean as a snake after he found out Ryne had AIDS.

"He might be," said Olie. "He might be."

She looked at Olie, who had turned his head away from the parade, and asked, "Isn't Tennessee where the Klan all got started in the first place?"

"Yes, Esther," he said, "way back in 1866, if memory serves. Claimed they was the ghosts of the rebel dead come back to haunt colored people. They were ghouls, all right. But Georgia's where a lot of this new Klan mania started … "

On he went, and if Olie was trying to get her attention off the parade by giving a long answer to a short question, it was not working. Esther was studying the parade and nodding as he went on with a story she and Ryne had heard a hundred times (a story that Ryne at least never seemed to tire of hearing): the one about how his one-armed father had made the scene in the nick of time and put a would-be lynch mob to flight with a scattergun for wrongly accusing Isaiah Snowden, a colored friend, of poaching chickens. "You should of seen Pop handle that shotgun with one arm," Olie told Ryne, "using his stump as a kind of table for the barrel. Of course, friend or not, colored or white, it didn't make no never mind to Pop. Right is right."

"Think how he would of hated this," said Esther, "seeing all these Nazis and shagnasties he gave his arm to put down de-fouling our town square." Then she lowered her voice to a whisper: "Speaking of the Snowdens, I hope to high heavens Bertha and them kids don't catch wind of this." Esther was not so much worried about Bertha—Bertha would flat get them told—as she was about Bertha's four little children, who if they saw this might have suspected there was something wrong with them rather than with these hate-mongering devils. Esther would not have traded one of those precious Snowdens for the whole bunch of white trash stinking up the streets of Tynbee just then.

None of the colored folks who lived in Tynbee were up there, fortunately, but the whites made a pretty good showing. The ones who were not marching in the parade stood on the sidelines, some waving little rebel flags in a show of support, just as they waved little American flags at the Fourth of July parade. Others screamed at the procession, "Get on out of here, you bunch of godless po-white-trash Nazis!" Some screamed worse things. Most stood by in silence, so it was hard to tell which side they were on. Maybe most were in the middle—none of it making much difference to them—because they were not colored, Jewish, or gay.

The White Aryan Race marchers, in their black shirts and red swastika armbands, made the Nazi salute, thrusting their hands outward, and chanting, "Heil Zigfried! Heil Hitler! White Power!"

Near the end of the procession that was snaking its way toward the gazebo, which Olie and Lawayne Perkins had built the summer before on the town green in front of City Hall, marched the preacher—the Grand Wizard, the Grand Pooh-Bah, the High Hum Yonka. He was, Esther would describe him as she was giving her statement to the Avery County Police, an oily-looking little ignoramus with black hair greased back into a pompadour and bushy mutton-chop sideburns that had gone out of style with hula hoops.

"We are the white patriots of Amurica!" he shouted through the bullhorn. "A way back in Genesis it says that God put a curse on Cain with a mark, turned his skin the color of mud, so ever'one who seen of him would know that he was accursed! God is a-doing for us the job we should of finished for ourself back in the War for Southern Independence!"

Ryne said, "He sounds like Gomer Pyle."

"Lord of Mercy," Esther cried out, "and this man has no more business trying to preach a message than Gomer Pyle, either, Ryne. At least Gomer Pyle had a good heart."

Under the preacher's right arm—the one he was holding the bullhorn with—was a big black leather Bible. With his left hand he was holding up one side of a long banner that stretched nearly the width of Oak Street. Esther edged a little closer to the street to see if she could make out what the banner said.

"Why don't you come on back here, Es'?" Olie called out, "so we can get on down to Dollywood soon as this big shebang is over. Looks like this is the grand finale."

The preacher had taken to sucking a little wind and, but for his message, might have been one of a long-line of windsucking sermonizers who had occupied the pulpit of the Historic First Church of Tynbee. He said: "Yesh—HA!—what we should of done—HA!—is wipe out these accursed—HA!—these colored nigroes—HA!—and sodomites—HA! But no—HA! We let 'em share our land—HA!—and our school houses—HA!—and our turlets—HA!—and our women-folk—HA! But now God—HA!, the Almighty—HA!, is wipin' 'em out for us—HA! Ay-man— HA!"

Olie said, "Don't you worry none about him, Es'. Old boy's fixing to give hisself a stroke."

It was just then that the message on the banner came into Esther's view: "I'm going to beat the mess out of him!" she rumbled, and Olie and Ryne would later say it sounded like the buzzing of a jumbo jet when the engines were first fired.

"There goes Mom," Ryne said.

Olie shot his head around and watched, stunned. "Esther!" he bellowed. It was for all Tynbee as if Esther Jean O'Casey had flat lost her mind right there on the town square.

"Stay right here!" Olie instructed Ryne and Kaitlyn, who, as soon as he had said it, climbed up and stood on the hood of the Nova for a better view. Olie pursued his wife, who was off on a rip-and-tear and had a thirty-yard lead on him. For a big woman, she was surprisingly light on her feet. For a big woman in flip-flops, it was nothing short of amazing. "Lord, Lord," he said, "that old boy don't know what he's in for."

Esther was at a full gallop. Her flip-flops clicked like hoofbeats of the Four Horsemen on the blistering August asphalt. What little slack there was of the zinnia-covered sundress she was wearing blew back behind her like the tail of a racehorse.

Indignation spurring her on, her arms flailed. She moved low to the ground and, without breaking stride, maneuvered her way through the column of policemen lining Oak Street, over the curb and across the sidewalk, past beer-sotted spectators sprawled across lawn chairs and flaming grills and groups of children quietly playing jacks. Olie couldn't keep up, couldn't catch up, couldn't do much of anything but jog along in the aftermath and watch people scurrying to make room for his wife. He moved as fast as he could, but like the Red Sea closing on the Egyptians, the holes Esther made in the crowd closed back up as soon as she had passed through.

It was too late. With her elbows raised out beside her at shoulder height—like the wings of a pteradactyl—and the knuckles of her fists touching in front, Esther plowed into the windsucker's chest just below the arm he had raised up to hold the bullhorn to his mouth. The sheer force of the impact blew the preacher sideways into the long banner and down hard onto the pavement. The bullhorn soared a good ten feet in the air and crumpled when it hit the ground. The banner the preacher had been holding in his left hand entangled three of the KKK Special Security Forces men who were bringing up the rear of the parade, and they, too, went down.

By the time the police and Olie and the press of the crowd got to them, Esther was straddling the bony little man, raising his limp, frightened form off the ground by the lapels of his brown leisure suit. "Don't you ever say such things again, you wicked little wretch!" she was screaming at him. Hovering over his limp form, she squeezed his pale cheeks in her big hand, as though he were a little boy who had smarted off. She said, "Preaching this hateful filth in the name of God. Praise God for *this*!" She drew back her right hand to smack his face.

Before she had the chance, half a dozen law enforcement officers were on the scene. They hauled Esther off of the man and, most of them trying to keep from laughing out loud as they cuffed her, read her her Miranda rights and ducked her into the back of an Avery County Police cruiser. Meanwhile, paramedics examined the fallen preacher, whom they had laid crosswise on the long banner that read:

PRAISE GOD FOR AIDS!!!
DIVINE JUDGEMENT ON NIGROES AND SODOMITES!!!

All in all, it could have been worse for the man. He had a bad headache and possibly a mild concussion, a few bruised ribs, a dislocated shoulder, and he could not talk. "He was white as the sheets them fools with him was wearing," one of the paramedics later told Olie. "She scared both the devil *and the color* right out of him."

For her part, Esther's flip-flops would never be the same. She had sustained a rip in one of the side-seams of her sun dress and a skinned right knee, which the paramedics bandaged before the police closed the door and hauled her away, alone and crying in the back seat of the police cruiser with blue lights flashing and sirens screaming, to the Avery County police station. The onlookers, when they realized what had happened, voiced their sentiments as the police car crept through the throngs: Some booed and hissed and raised clenched fists; others clapped and cheered and hooted.

The circus went on without its ringmaster, who was transported by ambulance to the Avery County Hospital for X-rays and observation.

Olie returned to the Nova, oblivious to the jeers and cheers of those he passed on his way. "Dollywood's going have to wait, kids," he told Ryne and Kaitlyn. He turned the car around and headed south on Elmwood. By God, they *would* let them pass through at the other end this time. "Mom's doing hard time in the county pokey," he told Ryne who asked where his mom was.

A little later, as they neared the police station, Olie said, "Ryne, I do hope you know how much your Mama loves you."

Ryne looked down at his black high-top sneakers. He knew what had happened even without being told. Tears ran down his cheeks, shadowed under the bill of his Atlanta Braves cap. He nodded; yes, he knew his Mama loved him and he knew how much.

By the time Olie, Ryne, and Kaitlyn got there they had booked Esther on charges of assault-and-battery and public disorderliness, though a clerk, an old friend of the O'Casey's, said he heard they could have charged her with a hate crime or even attempted murder. The magistrate set bail at two hundred and sixty dollars. Olie had the hundred-dollar bill Elder and Lula Gosset had given them, the one hundred and twenty dollars from the church for the Super Nintendo, and fourteen dollars of his own. "I'm twenty-six bucks short," he told the indifferent desk clerk, who simply shrugged.

Olie felt a hand on his shoulder, turned and saw his boyhood friend, Sheriff's Deputy Hal Jackson. Jackson winked. "I hear she could get tarred-and-feathered for this awful crime."

"You know Esther, Hal," whispered Olie. "She just flat refused to let it pass the way you have to let a bad cold pass because there's no cure for it."

Hal Jackson nodded and removed his ten-gallon hat. "Yeah, I hear you, Olie. But you can't really fault her. If you had a cold and that bug was big enough for you to get your hands around its neck, wouldn't you be tempted to beat the fire out of it? Boy, I know I would. Especially if it was to mock you like that little yahoo was. For ten cents I would have shed this badge and worn him out myself, Olie, and half his posse with him."

"He *was* carrying on," Olie said.

Hal Jackson said, "I saw Ryne out in the car." His tone was more serious then. He put his right hand over his heart as if to pledge allegiance, asked, "How is he, Olie, really?"

Olie just stood there in the hall of the Avery County police station with a handful of too little cash in his right hand and a pink carbon copy of Esther's summons in his left, silenced by that question. He nodded his head, not the way you do when you agree with something but the way you nod when you simply cannot think of anything to say. Direct questions about Ryne always made denial a dangerous refuge. Olie wanted to say that Ryne was better, or at least not worse, but he wasn't, wasn't at all, and maybe if anyone other than Haliburton Jackson had put the question to him he would have looked him in the eye and lied—lied and let it be.

"Slipping," he said, and his voice broke. "Slipping away. Just in the last month or two I've seen him go down, Hal." Olie's eyes closed slowly, slowly as the curtain falls on the final act. "My boy is slipping away."

Hal Jackson just nodded, said nothing, thank God. There was nothing to say. They stood, the two men, humbled before the question and its awful answer for a long while before Hal Jackson passed his hat around and collected the twenty-six dollars that stood between Esther O'Casey and freedom.

They processed her out and, but for an occasional sniffle, Esther rode home in silence. They could tell she was upset, though, from the way she trembled. Later that night, as she and Olie lay in bed, when she was fairly certain that Ryne's TV would drown her out, she cut loose and carried on. "The Lord'll deal with me for that shine I cut up town today, Olie, won't he? And don't you say he won't because he will," she told him. "I should of turned the other cheek and not taken a notion to beat that wretched little fink to a pulp, Olie: It was wrong. For 're-vengeance is mine, saith the Lord.'"

She had gone and ruined everything, she said: the trip to Dollywood, the Super Nintendo, their reputation and standing, such as they were, and everything else. "Them people will probably end up coming over here this night and burning a cross on the lawn out front."

"No," Olie said, "I think they've done about as much dancing as they want to with Esther Jean O'Casey. They'll sit out the next Tennessee waltz."

"Well that may be," she said, "but still I should of just turned the other cheeks."

Olie hugged her close. "Turning your own cheek's one thing, Es'. When they start striking Ryne's cheek, well, that's a different matter altogether."

It was, Esther explained, as if she were having an out-of-body experience of some sort. "Olie, it was like I was a big Zaccheus up in one of them great big old sycamore trees watching this big old stranger woman in a flower dress cutting a tear up town to get to that little ignoramus. See," she said, "I'm still not right about this." Turning her gaze heavenward, she said, "Lord God, forgive me for all of this sin. Not that I'm making excuses, Lord, but I'd just heard enough is all."

All of the feelings she had tried so hard for so long to beat back erupted like a volcano on the town square that day. She broke the silence and let out the secret, and, in some strange way, though she felt bad she felt better. "I hope that preacher lives, Olie, and that all those others with him I laid out on Oak Street are all right. But I don't give two hoots whether that hateful flag they were toting was torn."

Torn to shreds.

Dam Break

THE EVENING OF THE KLAN RALLY, Nathan was in the second bedroom of the parsonage—the *Thesis Room*—putting the finishing touches on his sermon, entitled "And a Little Child Shall Lead Them." He wondered if it would be the last sermon he would ever deliver to the congregation of the Historic First Church of Tynbee, Tennessee. Wondered if old Professor Davison would assign it an F.

"I might as well leave the real world with a bang," he told Miriam, "not a whimper."

"Oh, really?" she asked, brow arched. She set the glass of ice water and bowl of wheat crackers she brought him on the writing leaf of the rickety secretary she had dickered out of an old man at a rummage sale for seven dollars and twenty-five cents. "This poor thing is about to break."

"I am about to break," he said.

"You *need* a break," said Miriam. "I thought you could use a little refreshment. Here, drink some water. You haven't eaten anything since breakfast, Nathan. The sun is setting."

"I said, I'm on the verge of a break," he told her again.

"A break? A break*through* or a break*down*?"

"What's the difference?" he said. "A break is a break is a break."

"Your hands are shaking, Nathan." She touched her fingers to his forehead. "You're clammy. Come lie down."

He waved her off. "Spiderman," he said.

The Spiderman hand towel he came across in the O'Casey's bathroom the previous Wednesday had started it all. He couldn't shake that image of Spiderman scaling the skyscraper on the front of the iron-on T-shirt Philip had made in his art class. For seven years Nathan had beat back that memory, all those memories.

"Spiderman," Miriam whispered. "I see."

"Do you believe in faith healing, Miriam?"

"Where did *that* come from?" She scratched her neck. "Spiderman. Faith healing."

"Do you believe in it?"

"Spiderman?"

"Faith healing."

"Well, sure. I guess," she said. "You see, it depends on what you mean by 'faith healing,' If you mean do I believe that faith can make us whole, then—"

"That's *not* exactly what I mean," he said. "I mean faith-healers. Ernest Angley. Oral Roberts. That televangelist you said uses an earpiece."

"You're the one said that, Nathan."

"No, I said he wears a *hair*piece."

"Benny Hinn?" said Miriam. "I think that's his real hair."

"I know a hairpiece when I see one."

"You'll know one soon enough," she said. She patted the thin hair on the crown of his head, and he shook her off.

"My question was about faith healing, not my hair."

"Yes," she said without hesitation. "Of course I believe in faith healing. Don't you?"

"Well, I don't disbelieve in it," he said.

"That's a start," she said. "Why are you asking?"

"Esther O'Casey asked me about it."

"She wanted to know if *you* do faith healings?"

"No, Miriam, she did not want to know if *I* do faith healings. She said Ryne saw some faith-healer on TV, an African-American woman named Sister … something or other. He asked her and Olie to take him to one of her crusades in Nashville so that she could heal him."

"Well, maybe she can."

"Miriam, you mean to tell me that you believe, *really* believe, that—"

"Sure I do. Besides, it doesn't *really* matter what *I* believe about it, Nathan. That's the Lord's business."

"It's a *business*, all right," said Nathan. "I'm just not sure it's the Lord's."

"So what did you tell her?"

"To be honest," he said. "I don't remember." He picked up the glass of water Miriam had brought to him and took a sip, but his hand was so unsteady that when he went to set it down he ended up spilling it all over his sermon. The edits he had made in red ink streaked the first page like fresh blood. "This past week has been a blur."

"You're shaking, Nathan," she said, "I think maybe you had better come lie down and rest."

"I need a few more minutes to wrap things up."

"That's what you said two hours ago." She helped him mop up the spilt water. "A few minutes," she said. "I mean it, Nathan." Then she left to tend to the baby.

Nathan's eyes fixed on a line on the the first page of his sermon—"And that little child is you." The spilt water had turned the red ink into streaks and smears the color of blood, the color of Spiderman's mask, and from them emerged the image of his brother Philip in his Spiderman T-shirt, looking up at the cleft rock face of Skyler Heights, his voice saying, "You've always been my favorite superhero, Nathan."

"Shut up," Nathan told the image.

For six years Nathan had done, in Miriam's words, his "dammed"-est to repress his memories of that December day, to blot out not only that last day but all the days that went before it—because it was the days that went before it that made what happened on that last day too painful to remember, to look at.

And now it was staring him down.

His dull headache sharpened, stabbing with every heartbeat. Miriam called it his "tell-tale brain," saying it was guilt he refused to resolve.

He got up, steadied himself, and left the thesis room. Halfway down the hall, he said, "I'm going out for a walk." Miriam, who was tending to the baby in their bedroom, said something. Or maybe she was talking to the baby. He hoped so. He moved faster, moved close to the wall to keep from falling, and went out the front door.

The night was moonless and cool, and the air smelled strong of onion grass and wet dirt. Nathan trudged through the thick column of broom sedge that separated the parsonage lot from the churchyard. The broom sedge was heavy, sludgy with dew and rain, and to make it through he had to lunge forward and push on, chest first, in a breaststroke. He had to keep going, keep moving, though he did not know where he was going and his legs were weak. When they finally gave out he fell flat, clipping his shoulder on a tombstone in the graveyard behind the church. Dew seeped through his T-shirt and chilled him. And beyond the *chi-chi-chi* sawing of the katydids the tell-tale brain beat on.

First the chill, then the stupor, then the letting go.

You couldn't save Philip ... I'll be back, Esther O'Casey, you bet I will, and give Ryne my best ... I'm standing with you-all on this ... and the love of many shall wax cold.

As he lay amidst the green glowing foxfires in the graveyard, the dam broke and the onrushing memories carried Nathan back to the watershed of his life.

Nathan and Miriam, then married eighteen months, were living in Boston. Nathan was in his second year of seminary, and in addition to his academic work he was interning as a hospital chaplain an hour west of Boston. Miriam was working with disturbed teens at a group home as part of her own Master's program in counseling and also working part-time at a daycare center to help them get by. They were exhausted in every way at the end of that Fall semester. Nathan had finals the week after Christmas, but he was, he told Miriam, as prepared as he was going to get.

There was no way, no way in Hades he was going to cancel their planned holiday trip. And he was not about to ruin that trip cramming even one more trivial fact about the Late Church Fathers into his aching head.

So on December 19, a snowy Saturday morning, they loaded up their VW Vanagon and headed home for the holidays. It was an odd-numbered year and, according to an evolving tradition, the couple was supposed to spend that Christmas with Miriam's folks in Kansas City. But this was not only an odd year, said Miriam, but an odd Christmas, an *exceptional* Christmas if ever there was one: It was the last Christmas at home for Nathan's kid brother Philip, who had been accepted into Piedmont College in the north Georgia mountains. And neither Nathan nor Miriam would have spent the holiday anywhere on earth other than with Philip and the McKees in Frederick, Maryland.

The radio in the Vanagon was shot, so they began singing Christmas carols when they hit the Mass Pike and ended up caroling more often than not during the seven-hour trip south to Maryland. And when they were not caroling they were talking about Philip. How wonderful it all was. All his life Philip had battled a speech impediment compounded by a severe learning disability. He spent three years in first grade and had been in special education (of one type or another) for the balance of his school years. It never got the better of him. After fifteen difficult years, at the age of twenty, he had done it. He had beaten the disability. He not only graduated from high school—defying the expectations of many people who should have known better— but he would be matriculating at Piedmont College the following Fall.

To celebrate the achievement, in particular, and Philip, in general, Nathan and two of his childhood buddies had promised to take Philip, an incurable fan of Spiderman, on a rappelling adventure on the great cliffs of Skyler Heights, just across the Maryland state line in West Virginia.

December 20 was the appointed day. Nathan and Philip were up before the sun preparing their gear. Their mother, true to her conviction that breakfast was the most important meal of the day, insisted; so they had eggs, bacon, toast, juice, and cereal with the family before heading to the hills.

"You're in good hands, Philip," she said, standing there pulling the lapels of her terry cloth robe together against the chill as her sons packed the rappelling gear into the back of the Vanagon. "I wouldn't trust you with anyone else but Nathan."

A few miles down the road, Nathan said, "Well, buddy, here we go. Rapelling is as close to *'does whatever a spider can'* as we two-legged landlubbers can get."

"Not to be sappy or anything, Nathan," said Philip, "but you've always been my favorite superhero. I'd take you over Peter Parker any day of the week."

Nathan nodded. He knew it was true. So many times he had come to Philip's rescue when bullies made a sport of picking on the slightly built, "slow" kid, whom they called "retarded." Retarded. And now he was going to college. And most of those bums had probably not made it halfway through Frederick High School.

"Well, not to be sappy or anything," said Nathan, "but same to you. You've got more courage in your little toe than I have in my whole body, little buddy."

They had a lot of catching up to do, so they talked nonstop during the twenty-mile trip southwest on U.S. 340 from Frederick to Harpers Ferry National Historical Park at the junction of two rivers (the Potomac and the Shenandoah) and three states (Maryland, West Virginia, and Virginia). Nathan delivered a none-too-serious lecture on the keys to college success, complete with some obviously apocryphal lore about his own wild and woolly college days, which, they both knew, were anything but.

It was mild for December, and by the time they pulled into the gravel parking area, the thermometer clipped to Nathan's duffel bag read fifty-two degrees Farenheit. When they got out of the car, Philip said: "It feels like nothing, this weather. It's not hot or cold, or warm or cool."

Nathan paused, turned around and smelled the air, felt it on his face and neck, and found Philip's statement was true—though Nathan himself would have never thought to put it that way. "You're absolutely right. It does feel like … nothing."

They unloaded the gear and, by turns, saddled each other with a duffel bag. "Neither hot nor cold," Nathan said, as they made their way down the footpath leading to Skyler Heights. "It's like we're one with nature today."

They arrived at the designated meeting place—the entrance to the Thomas Jefferson Path, so called because local legend had it that Thomas Jefferson himself had trod the self-same footpath to the top of the mountain back in 1783 and called the land "Via Liberty" or "Via Freedom" or some such. Nathan and his friends referred to the path simply as *The T.J.* Nathan and Philip were at the T.J. at 7:30 a.m., half an hour ahead of Bradley Coleman and Spunky Harrison.

"Whoa," Philip said, squinting up at the twelve-hundred-foot stone face of Skyler Heights, which jutted up like a dagger into the soft blue sky.

"Whoa is me," said Nathan. "Let's scope out our stairway to heaven here." He was giddy. "Boston schmoston," he said.

"This is where life is." He surveyed the mountainside for the best place for the team to make their ascent. "Oh, that," said Nathan, looking up at the rock. "'T ain't nothing but a little old rock. And trust me, the slide down's a lot easier than the trudge up. You'll take some physics in college," he added with a wink. "What goes up must come down."

"Yeah," Philip said. "That's what scares me."

"Not to worry, my boy," Nathan said. "Take gravity, that great force that keeps us from floating out into space. It can be harnessed. That's why Spiderman there," he pointed to the iron-on image of Spiderman on Philip's T-shirt, "could scale skyscrapers. That's why planes make safe landings rather than crash-landings."

"Spiderman wasn't real," noted Philip, "and planes, they do make crash-landings sometimes."

"They do indeed, my dear boy. But the weather, as you said, feels like nothing. So we don't have to fear any wind shears today. Besides, crash landings are almost always due to—"

"Pilot error."

"—pilot error." Nathan cupped his hands over his mouth and made a static sound. "Ladies and gentleman, this is your friendly captain speaking, and on behalf of your flight crew, I'd like to welcome you to Flight Rappel 101. We're beginning our initial ascent onto Skyler Heights. We'll be cruising at an altitude of twelve hundred feet, and radar shows there's no turbulence, only blue skies as far as the eye can see. So relax and enjoy your flight, and, as always, thank you for flying the friendly skies."

"Over and out, Captain." Philip smiled. "So you're telling me that Mom was right: I'm in good hands."

"The *best* hands," said Nathan, clenching his fists. "Well, old Spunky might have something to say about that—if he and Brad ever get here. Spunky is a real-life Spiderman. So, let's just say that your fate rests in four *very* good hands and two *excellent* hands."

"I feel better," said Philip, though he was anything but steady on his feet.

Nathan took Philip's uneasiness as a simple case of the first-time jitters. "Just think," he said. "If crazy old John Brown, who was arrested in the arsenal just over yon river bluff, had known how to rappel he might not have had to *lie a-moulderin' in the grave.*"

"I get it," Philip said, smiling. He sang the lesser-known third verse of the hymn "John Brown's Body" (sung to the tune of "The Battle Hymn of the Republic"): "John Brown's body is a-climbing up the rock ..."

Nathan joined him on the refrain, "His neck goes marching on. Glory, glory, hallelujah ..."

"Old John Brown," Philip said, when they had finished singing, "would have mouldered in the grave sooner or later."

"Certainly by now, at any rate," Nathan said. "We'll all lie a-mouldering some day, but maybe not with rope burns on our necks. The rappel ropes will attach to our rumps."

Philip agreed. "Hey, Nathan ..."

"Yep?"

"I read that book you sent me: *The Absolute Beginner's Guide to Rappelling.* Every word of it." A note of triumph played in his voice. "I've got it memorized by heart."

"Man, oh man, that's great!" Nathan said. He recalled how, not long ago, Philip could hardly read the captions in his Spiderman comic books. "Have I told you lately how proud I am of you?"

"About twenty minutes ago."

"Well, let me say it again: You're the man!"

Brad Coleman and Everett "Spunky" Harrison arrived at the site at 8:15 a.m., having been delayed at the ranger station where they signed in and bought climbing permits for the foursome. The reason for the delay, as Brad explained, was that Spunky, ever true to his name, spent ten minutes charming the telephone number out of the pretty deputy park ranger.

"Yee haw!" Spunky shouted as he got out of the same old blue Chevy van he had been driving since their high school days. "Seems like old times! Geared up, boys?" Brad and Nathan were journeyman climbers; Spunky was a master, literally: He was a certified rappel master. He boasted, as he led the way across Sandy Hook Road and along a Civil War military byway toward the imposing cliff face of Skyler Heights, that he had, just last month, single-handedly (no pun intended) transformed a company (nay, a legion) of acrophobic freshman ROTC cadets at West Virginia State into fearless mountain-tamers.

"Old times, all right," said Nathan with a wink. "You haven't lost a step, Spunk. Hey, Brad, you didn't tell us … Did Spunky get her number—the deputy ranger's?"

Before Bradley Coleman could answer, Spunky had pulled the slip of paper out of his shorts pocket and kissed it. "Two numbers and one address."

Brad laughed. "They're probably all for the lecher-holics anonymous hotline. You should have heard some of the lines he cast, Nathan. What was the one about not feeding the bears, Spunky?"

"Sour grapes," said Spunky. "I don't see you with any numbers in your pocket."

Nathan laughed. "I'm sure there was a little envy in that lecher-holics anonymous remark."

"Maybe a little," Brad conceded. "She was cute."

"Cute," said Spunky, "is what you call your little sister. She was a fox."

"That, too," said Brad. "Now, in the spirit of fraternity, how about handing over those numbers, Spunky. One for me and one for Philip. Nathan's spoken for, and your little black book is thicker than our family Bible."

Spunky led the way, and an hour later they were ready to rappel. Spunky and Nathan had hand-drilled a ten-millimeter anchor into the smooth rock on a plateau some sixty feet up the cliff face. "This should do for starters," Spunky said. "We'll go twice again as high after Philip, our distinguished master of ceremonies, gets a feel for it."

Brad Coleman had remained on the ground as bottom belayer. His job was to control the bottom end of the rope to slow or halt the descent by applying down force to it in case things started moving too quickly.

Up above, Spunky said, "Since Philip here's a freshman— and congratulations on Piedmont, man—let's start with what the pros call a 'buddy rappel.' What that means, Philip, is that you're going for a piggy-back ride down Skyler Depths on the back of that big old piggy there you call your brother—"

"Watch it," said Nathan, patting his gut. "I know I've put on a few pounds, but—"

"It was a joke, Nathan," said Spunky. "Now, Philip, all you have to do is strap in, hang on, and enjoy the ride. The illustrious Brad the Bottom Belayer, and yours truly—you can call me Peter Parker—will take care of the rest. So just relax and leave the driving to us."

"You're in rare form, Spunk," Nathan said.

"Why, thank you, Nathan," said Spunky. "I *soitenly* am. Well, that should just about do it." He gave the knot that fastened the rope to the anchor a final yank.

Nathan and Philip put on their headgear and gloves while Spunky inspected the integrity of the knots and anchorage. He positioned the rope pad at the edge of the cliff to prevent the rope from making direct contact with the rock, which could create friction stress on the rope.

That done, Spunky rose to his feet and shook the rock dust from his palms. "Let's put her to the test," he said. He and Nathan then prepared to do a dead hang test to put the rope and anchor knots through their paces. Spunky informed them: "I think we're good to go. Even though it might appear to the callow that we are deviating from standard safety protocol, which mandates a three-man static-load test—not to worry. See." He patted his gut. "I make at least two of the svelte Sir Philip there, and Nathan, well he makes at least three—"

"Watch it," Nathan warned.

Spunky and Nathan backed to the edge of the cliff, eased down, and put both the lead and the back up ropes to a dead-hang test.

"We're there," Spunky said when he and Nathan had climbed back onto the plateau. The dead-hang test was a complete success. "There's nothing to it, kid," Spunky told Philip in a pretty fair impression of W. C. Fields's *my little chickadee bit.* "*Look out, here comes the Spiderman,*" he sang. Then, after a final check of both ropes, the knots, and the anchor point, he said, "We're according to Hoyle."

Nathan was winded. He doubled over with his hands on his knees and took in as much air as he could. Then he stood upright and patted his hand over his heart.

"You sure you're up for this, Nathan?" asked Spunky.

"Yes," Nathan said. "I'm fine." There was a prickly edge to his voice.

"Whoa," Spunky said. "Lighten up, my friend."

"I need to lighten up," said Nathan, "by about twenty-five pounds." Nathan turned to Philip. "You all right, buddy? You look a little pale."

"No, no. I'm fine," Philip said, his voice quavering just a little. "Nathan, were you scared your first time out?"

"To death," Nathan lied. "Listen," Nathan said, turning his head aside and lowering his voice to a whisper, so as not to be overheard, "if you want to just watch this first rappel, that's fine. You can be our top-dog belayer."

"No," Philip said.

"If you're sure," Nathan told him. He placed a hand on Philip's shoulder and looked him in the eye. Philip winked and smiled at his heroic big brother, and off they went.

Spunky attached the snaplock of Philip's seat harness to Nathan's seat harness and ran it through the sling rope and cinched it for additional support.

Nathan said, "Now, we're attached at the hip, Philip. *Literally.*" Nathan and Philip backed slowly toward the edge of the cliff face in lockstep. "On rappel!" Nathan shouted.

"Rappel on!" Spunky shouted in reply. He released some slack on the rope.

"On belay!" Brad hollered from the ground.

"Ready … Set … Go," Nathan said, as they began their descent, very slowly, along the steep pitch of the cliff face.

"L," Spunky called down to Nathan.

Nathan placed the soles of his feet flat against the cliff face and straightened his legs. Then he tried to bend at the waist to bring his back parallel to the cliff face, to establish the prone "L" position. Together, Nathan and Philip and their gear weighed nearly four hundred pounds, and Nathan, having practically lived in a carrel in the seminary library in Boston for eighteen months, was in the worst physical shape of his life.

He strained; he felt muscle fatigue burning in his arms and shoulders, in the small of his back. Again, he tried straightening his legs by pushing the balls of his feet as hard as he could against the cliff face and pulling down on the rope with both hands.

He could manage only a "C" position. "Dammit!" he shouted.

"What's wrong?" said Philip.

"Nothing. Nothing is wrong!" Nathan shouted, his tone sharp.

Spunky, who was lying belly-down with his head hanging over the cliff edge about ten feet above them, cautioned: "Careful. *Easy* does it."

"Argh," Nathan growled. He flexed his knees so they swung in close to the cliff face, then, with all his might, he kicked out while pulling down on the rope. He and Philip swung out a full eight feet from the cliff face. Nathan wanted to come back into the face with his feet flat to get some momentum. It was his only hope of making the L, but despite Brad's best effort to steady the rope from below the rope rotated a half turn left and Nathan and Philip hit the wall right-side first.

"Easy, Nathan," said Spunky. And now *his* voice had an edge to it. "*Easy!*"

Philip was squirming now, literally hanging on to Nathan for dear life. He practically had Nathan in a chokehold, and Nathan lost his grip on the hand brake. In the second or two it took Nathan to get ahold of the brake and apply enough down force on the rope to stop them, they free-fell twenty feet.

"We're gonna die," said Philip.

"Of embarrassment maybe," muttered Nathan.

They hung there suspended some forty feet above the ground, flat against the cliff face. Nathan again tried to establish the "L."

Spunky Harrison had been so preoccupied monitoring the situation on the cliff face that he had not given a moment's thought to anything else, such as the anchors. So it was only after he was on his feet and had turned around to grab his seat harness so he could do a rescue drop to get Nathan and Philip safely down that he caught sight of the anchors. "Oh, God!" he said, gritting his teeth till they almost broke.

Nathan's repeated attempts to establish the "L," and Philip's squirming around, had jigged both the lead rope and the back-up rope laterally about fourteen inches—off the rope cushion. Both the ropes, the lifelines, were wedged down into a sharp-edged fissure on the cliff edge. Spunky knelt down and inspected the two eleven-millimeter climbing ropes. The stress on both was evident; the nylon gilding on the rope surface was friction-frayed. It looked as though it had been sawed halfway through with a jigsaw.

Spunky fell facedown, hung his head over the cliff edge, and issued a frantic order: "Descend posthaste!"

Before Nathan had the chance to release his hand-brake and begin the descent, a sound like a small-caliber rifle shot rang through the dry December air, and the climbing ropes snapped.

Nathan and Philip plunged forty feet down. The lock connecting their seat harnesses prevented them from separating during the fall. Nathan pulled hard to his left, pulled with all his might and with all his will, to keep from hitting the earth square on his back. They hit the hardpan earth with a devastating impact. Nathan's left leg struck the ground first; the femur cracked and splintered, which folded his body to the left, thus depriving Philip of any cushion from the hard earth. Philip landed slightly to the right of Nathan and had nothing, not a limb, not a brother, not a seat-harness, not a loving Lord, to break his fall.

They were airlifted to Frederick Memorial Hospital where two hours later, Philip Andrew McKee, age twenty years, two months, and twelve days, was pronounced dead of multiple massive internal injuries.

In the Emergency Room, each time Nathan regained consciousness, if only for a moment, he asked anyone within earshot: "If I had landed flat on my back, and Philip had landed flat on me, what would have happened?"

"I don't know," they said, wagging their heads. "Nobody knows."

"God knows," Nathan said. And he convinced himself that he knew, too, or at least had a pretty good idea: He, Nathan, would have died; Philip would have survived to ask the question. And would to God it *had* ended that way. *If only*, he reminded himself without mercy, without grace, if only he had not flexed his knee and tried to break his own fall, he would have broken his brother Philip's fall.

Greater love hath no man than this, that a man lay down his life for his friends. Over and over, the words of Jesus assaulted him.

Nathan, whose own injuries included multiple contusions, compound fractures of his right tibia and left femur, a dislocated left hip, several cracked ribs, a collapsed right lung, fractured faith, and a broken heart, had not wept that day as he lay in the Emergency Room at Frederick Memorial. Nor did he weep at Philip's memorial service, which he attended in a wheelchair, having checked himself out of Frederick Memorial on Christmas Eve—against the passionate protests of his parents, his wife, and every doctor, nurse, and orderly at Frederick Memorial Hospital. He was in shock, they whispered, on that bitterly cold, bitterly gray Christmas Day as Nathan sat expressionless in his wheelchair, which he had instructed Miriam to park well to the right of the funeral canopy.

On December 26, the day after Philip's Christmas Day interment, Miriam drove and Nathan rode, silently, back to Boston. There were final exams to prepare for. During his twelve-week convalescence, Nathan immersed himself in academics like never before. He never spoke of Philip or the "accident" and tuned her out whenever Miriam did.

In his youth, life had been as black and white as a 1950s sit-com: *God was in His heaven, all was right with the world.* For every problem under the sun, there was a solution. And if the visible world *appeared* chaotic it was only because we saw it through a dark glass, too dark to see the radical underlying order of divine providence.

Then one day in December the dark glass broke—shattered into countless little shards and crystals. And not only was all *not* well with the world, but God, it seemed, was not in his heaven.

And even if he were: He was not the God who Nathan thought he had known. A god who would allow such a thing, which was beneath the dignity of the best humans, must be called something other than LOVE.

Though for all he blamed God for the tragedy, Nathan blamed himself more.

Miriam once told Nathan, a year or so after the tragedy, that she suspected that his internal injuries—his guilty conscience, his broken heart—were as fatal to his soul as Philip's internal injuries had been to his body. If she hoped her words would open a dialogue, she was disappointed. He said merely, "I couldn't agree with you more."

Now, nearly seven years later, as he lay in the graveyard behind the Historic First Church of Tynbee, Tennessee, Nathan wept. He wept for Philip, and he wept for their mother, who had died a few months after the tragedy—unofficially of a broken heart, and he wept for himself, more dead in so many ways than they were. And he wept for Ryne O'Casey and wondered:

Am I breaking my own fall—again?

Coming Soon

RYNE O'CASEY HAD AN EERIE FEELING that his time was running out. No one had told him that. No one had to. He knew good and well that, unless some miracle happened, he was a goner, as they say. His clothes were getting baggier; his friends, fewer; his mother, angrier: all signs that AIDS was winning and he was losing. His chances of beating AIDS were about as good as Hobgoblin's chances of beating Spiderman—which meant, roughly speaking, that he had no chance at all.

Unless some miracle happened.

The Reverend Sister Miranda Stryker was a miracle-working faith healer. "You supply the faith, hawny child," she said, "and Docka Load Jesus gonna be fateful and just to render you a miracle." Ryne figured he could supply the faith; now about rendering that miracle, Doctor Lord Jesus? *Why not?*

Ryne was sure Sister Stryker would be willing to give it a shot. She was a good woman, after all (like Ryne's own mother). And not a day went by that she did not deliver some regular-looking person from the evil clutches of cigarettes or cancer or blindness or laziness. Ryne had seen it with his own eyes on his TV screen. She and Doctor Lord Jesus working together just might be his last—his *only*—hope.

By the time he shut off the TV at 1:25 a.m., Ryne O'Casey knew what he had to do. He lay in his bed under his dog Samson, a sheet, a blanket, and a blue-and-red afghan his mom had crocheted the previous winter (which was supposed to have a big red Spiderman on it but Spiderman turned out looking more like a red tomahawk, so they decided if nothing else it might bring the Atlanta Braves some good luck). His mom always said it was layers that keep you warm, but even under all those layers Ryne was still freezing. He clamped his chin down against his chest to trap what little warmth there was.

Minor Wonder number 60: Why do you feel colder as your temperature gets hotter? He would have to try to remember that one until tomorrow; he was too cold to crawl out from under the covers and write it down.

Then he got the shakes. Not just *body* shakes. *Mind* shakes. His mind went haywire like that sometimes and he could not do anything about it but lie there until it ran itself out. His mom called it "giddy." She said that was how Samson felt sometimes when he got weirded out and took off through the house like a wild thing with Ryne's mom hot on his tail until at last she managed to corner the beast with a broom and shoo him out of the house telling him not to bother coming back until he got the devil out of his system.

Ryne's mind was giddy: He thought about his mom's going wild that day on the town square; about T.K. Kirby's just missing that Dale Murphy home run ball; about Sister Stryker's getting what she called "the goody jones" on and socking the daylights out of people.

Ryne had already decided that the best day of his life was the day the TV came. But, when it came right down to it, he would have to say that the most *exciting* day of his life had been that very day. Who cared that his dad had to use every last dime of the Super Nintendo and Dollywood money to bail his mom out of jail? It was well worth it. He knew that no Nintendo game and no ride at Dollywood—not even the Twist and Shout Scrambler—could match the scene that Esther Jean O'Casey, his own mom, made that day when she beat the dickens out of that little preacher man who sounded like Gomer Pyle, then got cuffed and stuffed down into the backseat of a police cruiser, with its blue lights flashing and sirens squealing, and hauled off to jail.

Then his thoughts returned to what his mom called morbid things. Time was running out. It was the bottom of the ninth in the seventh game of the World Series—three runs down, two outs, bases loaded, full count. It was now or never. Sister Miranda Stryker, he thought, might just might deliver a home run pitch that the Lord Jesus could rip out of the park.

It would help if he could get to the ballpark first. He doubted that either Sister Stryker or Doctor Lord Jesus made house calls—even in right serious cases like his. If worse came to worst he would call the toll-free number and talk to one of the prayer counselors who were standing by twenty-four hours a day. Maybe they could get the Sister on the phone for a ... *phony healing*. Ryne smiled. In his condition he had better shoot for the real thing. Odds were the counselor would tell him that if he wanted to be healed he had to find a way to get to one of the crusades.

Faith healing might be a longshot; but Ryne knew it was his *only* shot, and like his dad always said, if your only shot is a long shot, you had better set your sights and fire away. The healing might not even take; sometimes it didn't. But it might. And that was a *might* better than all the pills he had taken over the past year. Sister Stryker herself had said, "Now I myse'f ain't God, now honey child. Listen to me. *Listen to me*: I myself cain't *heel* a frisky little old dog, child. God, Jay Hova Rappa his self, through the power of Load Jesus's name, is the only God that healeth thee."

Sister Stryker was not God. She made that perfectly clear. She even pointed out that sometimes it was not even God's will to heal people, which seemed a little strange to Ryne, but since Ryne was not God either he just let it be and trusted that God knew what he was up to. One thing was sure: You would never know whether it was or was not his will to heal you unless you gave it a chance.

Maybe it was not God's will to heal him even if he did get to Sister Stryker. That very night Sister Stryker had said: "Sometimes God heals you without *healing* you; heals those around you without healing you; heals your body without healing your soul; heals your soul without healing your body. Blessed, child, be the name of the Load. Can I get a witness?" Then Elder Butts hit a lick on the organ and stood up and screamed, "Tell it Sister!"

Ryne had not seen Sister Stryker smack the AIDS out of anyone—but he had only been watching for a few days. He was willing to be her guinea pig in experimenting with knocking AIDS out of people. He *had* seen the Sister knock the cancer and cigarettes out of people with the palm heal attack, and she even kicked the walker out from under this old man and he took off hobbling around the stage like Quasimodo screaming bloody murder. He was hobbling so badly even after he got the walker kicked out from under him that Ryne grimaced to think how bad off he was before Sister Stryker got a hold of him. Though he figured hobbling beat the tar out of having to use a walker to get around.

Ryne understood what Sister Stryker meant when she said that God did not always want to heal people who were sick— *sort of*. She said suffering and sickness sometimes brought out the very best in people. She said that sickness could either draw you to God or drive you away from him. Ryne had a good idea he knew what she meant. He had always said his prayers—every night when he got in bed; every day before he ate breakfast, lunch, and dinner; and sometimes even before he ate snacks. He prayed that God would help him remember things he wanted to tell his mom and dad, forgive him when he said cuss words or hateful things to people, and protect him when he was scared out of his wits by the likes of Beastie, the Whitfields' Doberman Pinscher, who was in the habit of hunkering down and baring his teeth at Ryne every time he saw him. He had even prayed—prayed right hard—just last week as he and his dad were whizzing this way and that on the Twist and Shout Scrambler at Dollywood that the man who put the thing together hadn't missed a screw that would come loose and send them twisting and shouting across the parking lot.

He was praying more and more now that he was getting sicker and sicker. He prayed that God would warm him when he got the chills, cool him off when he burnt up with fevers and night sweats, and let him know that everything would be all right when he got scared.

So maybe that was what Sister Stryker meant when she said sickness could draw you to God and make you a better person.

That very night on Sister Stryker's show, "Believe & Receive," after she delivered her sermon about the Ten Lepers, and as people were making their way up to the stage to be healed, the man who looked like a heavier version of Dr. J came on and invited everyone to "join the Reverend Sister Stryker in Nashville, Tennessee, for three blessed harvest days to reap God's richest spiritual blessings. Jay Hova is going to make a special guest appearance." Ryne accepted the invitation, and it hit him as never before just how urgent it was that he find a way to get to Sister Stryker.

She was coming to Tennessee, coming soon!

He had to find a way to talk his parents into taking him to the Nashville Arena for The Greater Tennessee Crusade on

September 24, 25, and 26. When he had mentioned it to his mother the week before, she got a funny look on her face and said, "Now Ryne, I don't know about all that kind of thing," which usually meant NO. Then she started talking about Some Young Moon and things took a turn for the weird.

Ryne kept at it—"Please-please-please, Mom; pretty please with whipped cream and a cherry on top; you look like you've shed some of those unsightly pounds, Mom. Have you? And come to find out, Dolly Parton lives there in Nashville (I was wrong about Hollywood), so we could drop by and sit a spell with her while we're in the neighborhood; so come on, please, Mom," and finally she started smiling and hugged him and said she would discuss it with his dad and get back to him about it, which again usually meant NO.

But what did *they* have to lose? And wasn't his mom always saying that she needed to get away from it all for a while since she could not even recall the last time she had been on a real vacation? The worst that could happen, Ryne thought, was that it would be his last vacation—or his first trip to Nashville, depending on how things turned out.

Ryne had written in his sketchpad with a red marker: "***Remember to tell Mom that Jay Hova is going to be making a special guest appearance in Nashville. I think he's a singer or something. Call prayer counselor and ask if Sister Stryker has anything to do with Some Young Moon."

If Ryne was going to get to Nashville, his mom was the key. If he sold her on the idea, she would personally see to it that she annoyed the fool out of his dad, who would end up taking them to Nashville to hush her up, if nothing else. It was the same strategy she used to get him to take them to Dollywood. *Mom,* he heard himself telling her, *how about you and me and Dad going out to Nashville to see Dolly Parton and Kenny Rogers? They're gonna do "Islands in the Stream" just for you, Mom, on*

September 24 at the Nashville Arena. And guess what? Loretta Lynn and Tammy Wynette and George Jones are going to be there, too, for a big Grand Ole Opry special. Jay Hova's going to be there, too. And I think he sings real nice, like you like.

Maybe.

Or: *Mom, you know how you ruined that trip to Dollywood and the Super Nintendo by beating the stink of that preacherman and getting locked up in prison, well I'd be willing to forget all about it, on one condition: You carry me over to Nashville on … No.* Sister Stryker—not to mention God—would not cotton to any lying to get to a crusade.

Ryne prayed. "Please, God, help me talk Mom and Dad into carrying me out to Nashville in September. I would really like to go and reap your richest spiritual blessings. It might help Mom and Dad, too. They seem real worried. Thank you, God. Amen."

Ryne hoped God had noticed that he had not forgotten to use his helping words in his prayer. He could hear his mom's voice: "It wouldn't have done us kids to talk the way kids talk anymore. Nothing rattled Mother's slats like somebody not having the decency to say please and thank you. Mother kept us fresh kids in line by saying she'd cut a hickory switch yay big and break us over like a shotgun and apply to our fannies something not to say please and thank you for. Yes, Ryne, I'll have you know that many a time mother broke me and Leroy and Mary over the rail of the front porch, which she called her wailing wall, and flat tore up our hindparts for disrespecting her the way kids do nowadays. And husbands, too, for that matter," she would add, winking at Olie.

Ryne always got a kick out of the story, which he had heard many a time, sometimes many times a day before he got too sick to get in much trouble. He pictured his gray-headed old Miz Ida Bea rolling herself down the porch steps and across the front yard to cut a hickory switch, then chasing his mom and Uncle

Leroy and Aunt Mary Fern around the yard in her wheelchair to *wear out their hindparts.*

It was hard to picture.

Though one time, according to Ryne's mom, the car broke down on the way to Sunday service, a good mile or two from the church, and while Olie and Esther were under the hood trying to get it cranked, old Miz Ida Bea somehow stole around to the trunk, got her chair out, and took off in it down the highway, and by the time they got to the church she was already seated on her pew with the hymn book open on her lap.

Please, God; thank you, God.

Ryne wished he was a member of Sister Stryker's Church, wished they were going to one of her crusades in the morning instead of back to Hysterical First, which is what his friend Terrence Ford called Ryne's church (and Ryne always said, "At least we don't go to First Whiskypalian"). Sister Stryker's *church* was different. The service was held in a basketball stadium—not an ancient shack that always smelled kind of funny—and you didn't have to get done up in your Sunday go-to-meeting clothes. For that matter, you did not even have to get dressed at all or even leave your own bedroom. *Where else could you go to church in Spiderman PJs without even getting out of your bed?*

All kinds of people attended Sister Stryker's Church. Long-haired people who looked like Jesus with big bushy beards, old people who rolled around in wheelchairs like Miz Ida Bea did when she was alive and cutting hickory switches to tear up his mom's hindparts, young people in shorts and T-shirts, and others who were blind and retarded and had cancer and drank too much.

But maybe the best thing of all about Sister Stryker's church was that all the people there seemed so happy and so friendly, not like some of the people at Historic First who gave Ryne the evil eye and wished he would just disappear—and their wish was going to come true, and soon, if Ryne could not talk his parents into the Nashville crusade.

Maybe things were different now that the people of the church had given him the TV set. *Maybe*. But when his mother finally got released from prison and announced to Ryne and Olie that her beating that man up was living proof that she had been away from church too long, "so you-all best rustle up your Sunday best so I can press them, and we'll head over to the meeting in the morning," Ryne felt a sense of awful dread. He was sure his dad did, too, if you could read anything from the sigh he made.

If he went to Sister Stryker and ended up not getting healed, that was one thing. He knew for sure that he would not get healed at the Historic First Church in Tynbee, Tennessee.

Ryne wondered how he would die. With AIDS the only thing you knew for sure was that you *were* going to die: Everybody with AIDS dies. Of course, everybody without AIDS dies, too, he thought, but when you have AIDS you can be pretty sure that it will get you before anything else—especially old age—does. AIDS made everything your enemy—inside your body and out, including people who had once liked you and mussed your hair and tweaked your cheeks when you went to church, people who had wanted their children to be your friend.

The trouble with AIDS was that you never knew precisely *which* enemy would get you and how. Like an earthquake, there were tremors and rumblings, but not even the best seismologist could predict with any degree of certainty when the quake would occur. As they always said about the megaquake rumbling along the San Andreas Fault that would one day plunge southern California into the Pacific: *It was only a matter of time.*

Ryne remembered when he used to play hide-and-seek and tag. There would come that moment when you knew you were caught, especially if you were hiding in, say, a corner of the cellar and had no escape route. The shadows fell, the footsteps approached, the heartbeat quickened. "There you are!" someone would holler, and you would scream, too. It felt that way with AIDS: You were trying to hide in a corner; you knew you were about to get caught; you could see its shadow, hear its footfall, but there was nowhere to go, nothing to do, but sit there sweating, heart pounding, and wait for it to get you.

If you got hit by a bus or killed in a car wreck—that was it. You were dead. You didn't have time to lie around in your bed, the way he was then, thinking about where and when death would get you. The bus drove into you, flattened you on the street, and that was all she wrote. You might have seen the bus coming, but not for long; otherwise, you would have gotten out of its way. With AIDS, you saw it coming from a long way off, but you couldn't get clear of its path.

At least if you did get hit by a bus, Ryne thought, you never got the chance to get really sick with fevers and all the "opportunistic diseases" he got. But then you never got the chance to find out how much people love you and … don't love you, either. It didn't really make that much difference, Ryne decided, when he thought hard about it. He remembered hearing his dad say, "There's not a person on this planet who's living now that the same could be said of him a hundred years from now," and he always felt better when he thought about it that way.

It was not as if Ryne were the only person on earth who was going—wherever people went when they died. Would tonight be the night? Was he wrong to think that he would see it coming? Maybe it would come from some other direction, like a runaway bus barrelling out of control. Take that preacher in the parade in Tynbee that very day: he might have been looking all around in case anyone—probably a black person—came running out from behind a tree to whomp him one. And then when he scanned to the other side of Oak Street—POW!—it was not a black man at all but a big old white woman in a flowered dress and flip-flops bearing down on him like a Mack truck on a runaway ramp.

Ryne nibbled the pad of his finger. The katydids and crickets had gone to sleep. The wind outside rustled the leaves of the big live oak that he used to think was alive. His mom always shut the window and locked it before she kissed him good night and headed across the hall to her room. He always opened it back up, sometimes for warmth, sometimes for cold, always because he did not feel so alone. He had never feared a killer breaking in to the house and getting them; he had always feared what was under the bed, in the closet, living in the attic, stowing away in the cellar making the floorboards creak. And if something did come out from under the bed, he did not want to be locked in the bedroom with it.

A light breeze blew the Spiderman curtains in over him like angels floating on a cloud. *Are you listening, God? Is this a sign?*

His mom and dad never talked about the dying part. So Ryne was not sure they even knew, really knew, that he was dying. At least, of course, they did not want to believe it. The only person Ryne knew personally who had died was his mom's mother, Miz Ida Bea, who died at Avery County Hospital at the age of seventy-three. She had suffered a stroke or two and was in a coma, so she just started gurgling and her blood pressure dropped and his mom started crying, and they whisked Ryne out of the room, and a few minutes later they said she had gone to be with the Lord. So Ryne, who was five at the time, was surprised when, a few minutes later, a man from the funeral parlor wheeled her out of the hospital room and took her down a special elevator at the far end of the hall. His mom told him then that it was Miz Ida Bea's *soul* that went yonder to be with Jesus; her body, on the other hand, was going to the Shelby & Son Funeral Parlor where they would see her the next day before they laid her to rest.

On second thought, Ryne figured his parents had to know that he was dying. They just did not want to let him know they knew. That explained why when he came upon his mom when she was crying, she would wipe her eyes and sniffle a few times and say her hay fever was acting up from all the pollen in the air or that her eyes were watering from the onions she was chopping for her stew (if she happened to be crying in the kitchen). He always wanted to talk to her about it at those times. Once he even asked her if she was crying because she was sad that he was sick, but she said, "Well, of course I'm sad about that, honey, but this pollen is just fouling my sinus up something fierce."

He had wanted to say there was not much pollen in the air in January, and if there were enough January pollen to foul up someone's sinuses something fierce, it would have rated a MAJOR WONDER on his list, but before he had the chance she changed the subject and went on to what she referred to as *happy things*.

His mom was on edge lately. Ryne was not sure what had set her off up in Tynbee that day, though according to his dad it had something to do with how much she loved him, but her outburst came as little surprise to Ryne. He was used to seeing her lose her temper at times and get somebody told—on average, Ryne calculated, twice a week, though he had never seen her hit anybody, much less waylay a preacher from his blind side. *Was the end approaching?* His mom was crying more; his dad was talking less; his body was getting weaker; his preacher was coming to the house for a visit (to administer last rites?). All that put together led Ryne to wonder if he was on the last leg of his journey.

He *would* make it to Nashville in September for the miracle crusade—one way or another. It was an appointment he had to keep.

Ryne tried cheering himself up, even though he was feeling about as low that night as he had ever felt. If he were going back to school the following month—which he wasn't and probably never would again—he would have some kind of paper to write on how he had spent his summer vacation. "Once upon a time we were on our way down to Dollywood, but we got stuck in a traffic jam in Tynbee where there was this big rigamarole going on. And my mom loved me so much that she ended up beating the stink out of a preacher who did not even do anything to me at a parade." Or: "My mom, all-pro linebacker Esther Jean O'Casey, of the Tynbee Torpedos, standing five-feet-four-inches high and weighing in at a whopping two hundred and twenty-five pounds, busted through the offensive line and sacked Gomer Pyle, the scrawny little quarterback for the Mayberry Midgets, from his blind side. Gomer ended up in the hospital, and Mom ended up in prison, where they did blood tests to see if she had been using steroids."

And my dad … Well, not much exciting to write about. He mostly just went to work and came home and ate supper, then read his Bible and listened to the radio in the living room. Most nights, he fell asleep in his chair with his Bible in his lap and his head bobbing around. Ryne and his mom would hoist him up out of the chair and lead him back to bed. Since the TV set came, Ryne's dad had been spending some time in Ryne's room after supper watching it with them—probably because he did not feel that he was expected to say anything.

Then the wind died down and the loudest sound in the world filled his room: complete silence. Even Samson, who was under the covers with him, quit snoring. There was no such thing as silence, Ryne decided, wondering if deaf people heard the silence, if blind people saw the darkness. He sure heard it, and saw it, the silence and the darkness: And he didn't like it one bit. Silence and darkness ranked right up there with candied yams and blaming sadness on pollen on his list of least favorite things in the universe.

His fever was rising yet again. It always started with a chill, a little shiver that raced up your back and made your arms pull up and your head twitch, like the ones you got when your mom almost side-swiped the car next to you when she was trying to tune in her hillbilly station on the car radio. His mom always said it was the Holy Ghost moving that caused those chills. But Ryne and his dad would tell her they did not think the Holy Ghost was the kind of ghost that haunted houses or scared people, and she would say, "Well, there's some people that needs to have the daylights scared out of them."

Maybe that preacher-man in the parade was one of those people.

Ryne was getting colder. He pulled the sheet up tight and bundled it under his chin and lifted it briefly every so often to blow a blast of hot air in. He would not yield to the temptation to reach down and pull the spare quilt from under the bed. That was another one of those things, like donating bad blood without knowing it, that was supposed to make things better but ended up making them worse: You have a fever but you are cold; bundling up seems like the thing to do; you do it; your temperature goes up; your body gets colder; your mom comes in; your mom goes ballistic; your mom yanks the quilt off of you; you fly way up in the air; your mom says, "Ryne, if I've told you once I've told you a thousand times: This is not the way to go about breaking your fever down. I'm of a good mind to lay holt to a hickory and wear you out." Then, soft and sweet: "How are you feeling, angel hair? I'll fetch you some Tylenols and juice now from yonder in the kitchen. But Lord is my witness, honey, if I come back in here and find you under that quilt I'll skin your hide. Then think how cold you will be."

The little shiver became a seismic tremor. His skin was hot, but inside he felt as cold as ice. The shakes. Soon, he knew, it would become a category-three earthquake, at least, measuring seven or maybe even eight on the Richter scale, if it got really bad like it did sometimes. He pictured his insides as tectonic plates shifting around at a fault line and his skin, like the earth's crust, quaking. His homebound teacher, Miss Blakely, had brought him an article she clipped from the *Knoxville News-Sentinel* that said there was a faultline under Tennessee that seismologists were predicting might be the scene of a major earthquake someday. *It was only a matter of time.* Ryne hoped the faultline did not run right under his bedroom, for the way he was shaking he was liable to set off the quake. He smiled through chattering teeth as he pictured the seismologists at Georgia Tech sitting around the seismograph watching the recording pen bobble up and down and saying, "What the heck? The epicenter is in Tynbee, Tennessee? Oh no, boys, this must be the BIG ONE!"

He knew he shouldn't do it—it was the worst thing you could do when you were chilling from a fever—but he was so cold that he did it anyway. He reached down with his right arm, rummaged through the pile of comic books, and pulled the heavy patch quilt Miz Ida Bea had made from under the bed. He draped it over his body then battened down the edges using his forearms and heels as spikes, making a mummy of himself. But he was still cold. Colder than he had ever been—though every time he got chilled he thought that.

He thought about calling his mom in, but decided not to; after all that had happened at the parade that day she was bound to be worn out. Besides, she would go ballistic for sure if she saw him bundled up under the afghan and quilt like that.

He squeezed his eyes shut and cried. He was cold and scared and sometimes, like now, he didn't care if anyone ever again mentioned how strong and courageous and champlike he was. Because it made you feel like a weak, cowardly loser when you did not feel strong and courageous and champlike and you wanted to break down and be scared and call your mom in for comfort.

"Now I lay me down to sleep, I pray the Lord my soul to keep, if I should die before I wake, I pray the Lord my soul to take. Dear God, please bless Mama and Daddy and Samson and Kaitlyn and Elder Gosset and all the people at the church and let that man at the parade Mama knocked down be okay. In Jesus' name I pray, Amen."

And P.S., Lord, please let me get warm.

Can Any Good Thing Come out of Tynbee?

W HEN MIRIAM FOUND HIM lying facedown in the deep dew-slick weeds on the ballfield behind the church, Nathan was sound asleep. He lay so still and so silent in the glow of the Coleman lantern that she took him for dead. In a sense, she thought, as she led him home from the graveyard and tucked him into bed, he *had* died out there in the graveyard behind the Historic First Church—died, if not for good, certainly for the better. She just knew it. Knew it was about Philip's death and Nathan's guilt.

WHEN THE PHONE RANG at a few minutes before midnight, Nathan was lying in bed with a heating pad on his hip and an icepack on his head.

Miriam entered the bedroom, put a hand on his shoulder, and whispered, "Nathan."

"Yes."

"I hate to wake you."

"You didn't."

"You should be asleep."

"So you could wake me?"

"Yes," she said. "Elder Bailey is on the phone. I told him that you weren't feeling good and had retired—"

"I wish."

"—for the *evening*, but he said it couldn't wait. It's an emergency."

Nathan limped down the hall as quickly as he could to the kitchen, the only room in the parsonage with a phone jack. "Hello."

"Elder Bailey here. I regret disturbing you, McKee," he said with a tone that screamed otherwise. He was the only member of the congregation who didn't call Nathan "Preacher." Nathan pictured him in a shady backroom somewhere with those snake eyes and that long shriveled face fluted with deep vertical lines, a face that, from a distance, looked five times higher than it was wide—especially when he had on his black porkpie hat. There was probably a damp, frayed toothpick poking through his cracked blue lips, too. "A right serious matter has come up that demands immediate action on the part of the officers of the church."

"Yes," Nathan said.

"As I expect you've heard by now, McKee, a woman of our congregation by the name of Esther Jean O'Casey went berserk today and attacked an evangelist who was visiting our community. I say *attacked*; she very nearly killed him."

"She did?"

"Yessir, she did. Now I know it's right hard to picture."

"Sort of," said Nathan. He pictured Esther running across the stage at a Billy Graham crusade and smacking Bev Shea around in the middle of "How Great Thou Art."

"This Esther has hurt the witness of our church, McKee," said Elder Bailey, "that's what she's done—"

"That took some doing," Nathan mumbled.

"And it behooves us leaders of the church to administer *church discipline* to the offensive party, in accordance with the constitution and bylaws of the Historic First Church. We must do what we can, all that we can, to salvage the reputation of our church."

"We must," Nathan said. *Just not the way you're thinking we must.* Nathan wondered if the insanity defense would work because if, as Elder Bailey said, Esther truly *went berserk*, it was not business of the church to mete out discipline to the sick— though the Historic First Church did have a precedent for it: the O'Caseys themselves.

"Truth to tell, McKee, I'm right surprised you haven't caught wind of this. Our preachers in the past have always made a point to keep current on goings-on in the community. Course none of them was a *inter-'em* either."

Interim, Nathan thought: *They'll inter 'em, all right. The 'em in question being Esther O'Casey and I day after tomorrow if I don't do something very decisive.* "Okay, help me out here. What set Esther off?"

"Hormones, I reckon," the elder said. "Must be genetic. Her mother, Ida *Bea*, was the same way. Forever foaming at the mouth. Forever spoiling for a fight. You can't just go off on somebody every time they say something you don't want to hear, McKee. And that's what happened as far as I can tell. A group of folks passing through was exercising their first amendment rights of free speech and assembly this afternoon here in Tynbee, on the town square. Well, in so doing, somebody said something that didn't set well with *big old* Esther O'Casey, and it brought her hormones to a boil, and she took it upon herself to 'bridge them rights. Didn't matter one whit that Judge Horace Lester had granted them permission to assemble, no-sir. Esther's a law unto herself. She couldn't abide some of the things that man of the cloth was preaching, so she took matters into her own big mitts, stampeded across town common like a spooked mastodon, and beat him to a bloody pulp."

"My goodness," Nathan said.

"That's right," Elder Bailey said. "Are you with me here? Now it's a right serious offense for anybody, even a normal-size person, to go attacking a man of God while he's proclaiming the gospel he was called to preach."

"You don't say," said Nathan.

"But, as I'm sure you know, McKee, Esther's not exactly what you'd call a normal-size person. She's right big of flank *and* hock. She's a big old woman."

"That she is."

"That body's a lethal weapon as sure as a loaded gun."

"It could be," Nathan said. Esther was a big old woman. *To whom much is given much will be required.*

Elder Bailey went on about the scene Esther made on the Tynbee town square. Nathan's mind wandered. He recalled how, as a bookish fifth-grader, he had finally got up the courage to stand up to the school bully who had taken Philip's lunch money.

Now is the time to muster the courage to stand up to a bully of another sort, the time to stop making a virtue of neutrality. For all his good intentions and nonpartisan politics, mainly in the interest of saving his own hide or at least his interim job, Nathan was still attempting to break his own fall.

Nathan said, "What did the evangelist say?"

"Young man," Elder Bailey said, having worked himself into a frenzy, "I don't care if Reverend Everett Hulsey said her dead mother was a woman of the night. That wouldn't be a good enough excuse for Esther O'Casey doing what she did."

"Hwooo," Nathan exhaled. *Don't lose your cool.* "In the first place, Elder Bailey, *a man of God* would probably say no such thing. And, second, I can tell you this for sure, if anybody called my dead mother a woman of the night I would be apt as not to beat the devil out of him."

"I'm not saying Reverend Hulsey said *that* to Esther, McKee. He don't even know her or Ida Bea, neither one. My point was,

Esther O'Casey's a loose cannon and had no business firing off on that preacher the way she did. And we can take necessary action according to the church bylaws either with you or without you, McKee."

"That's nice to know," said Nathan. "So, tell me, Elder, what do you propose to do? Or, rather, what disciplinary measures do the church bylaws prescribe for such an offense?" For all he knew Esther could be required to wear scarlet letters—maybe BOW for *Big Old Woman*—on her person thenceforth, world without end.

"This is clear grounds for disfellowshipping Esther Jean O'Casey from the congregation of the Historic First Church for a period of not less than one year."

"You *can't* be serious. This is absurd. It is not as if she committed the unpardonable sin, or did I miss the part about Esther's blaspheming the Holy Spirit?"

"She come mighty close."

"She did not."

"Why—"

"The woman is on a razor's edge, Elder Bailey," Nathan said. "Sure she is. Who wouldn't be in her situation? Esther O'Casey's laboring under a burden of grief that you and I can hardly begin to relate to. She, of all people, needs our love and support, *not* our condemnation. We need to proceed with caution here. We need to hear from witnesses, find out what really happened and—"

"Well, McKee, I've just a few things to say, then I'll hush up and go on," Elder Bailey said at the end of a long, fateful silence. "It's clear you're not with us on this, and that means you're again' us. I'll take this up at the Board of Elders' meeting tomorrow, first thing. Meantime, on the power vested in me as the Chairman of the Board of Elders and according to the *Constitution and Bylaws* of the Historic First Church of Tynbee,

Tennessee, I hereby relieve you of your duties as interim pastor of said church until further, official notice of the Board."

"You're firing me?" Nathan said. "Because I urged restraint and wish to consult witnesses?"

"What further need have we of witnesses?" Elder Bailey shouted, and Nathan knew that he had to know that was the same question the High Priest Caiaphas had asked when Jesus was delivered to him on charges of blasphemy. Elder Bailey said, "I've told you the truth here."

"Yeah, well, what is *truth*?" Nathan asked, then gently hung up the phone. He leaned heavily against the kitchen wall and felt the pain shoot like flames in his hip. His knees buckled.

"Steady there, Nathan," said Miriam. "You're okay," Nathan could not tell whether it was a statement or a question.

"I am?" he said. And he could not tell whether that was a statement or a question, either. He eased down into the baby's high chair, which was set against the wall.

"Nathan," Miriam said, "one of these days you're going to bust that thing. It wasn't made for grown-ups."

"Really?" Nathan said, without sarcasm and without getting out of it.

"Oh, never mind," she said, rolling her eyes. "What was all that about? What's the urgent situation?"

"We're going to get run off."

Miriam said, "What does that mean?"

"It means we had better head down to the Piggly Wiggly and get some boxes," Nathan said. He thought: *I am about to be run off, probably by a vote of seventy-one nays to seventy-three ayes.*

Being run off. Imagine that. Run off: The term people in Tynbee, Tennessee used for relieving a pastor of his duties. Mountain folks had various uses for the term. When a woman cut off her sorry two-timing old wine-bibbing husband from bed or board, she was said to have run him off. When some old yahoo fired buckshot into the air on a Saturday night to shoo off stray animals that became a nuisance, he was said to have run them off. When the soil was so saturated that it could not absorb the rain, the tributaries that formed were called runoff.

The term fit what was about to happen when they impeached him, Nathan decided. *Let's see: Count One, I'm a sorry old two-timer; Count Two, I'm a stray who's become a nuisance; and Count Three, I will never be absorbed into the social or—good Lord!—spiritual soil of Tynbee, Tennessee. Ever.* It was that simple. *To every thing there is a season, and a time to every purpose under the heaven:* a time to be dragged in ... and a time to be run off.

I wish to enter a plea of guilty on all charges.

Miriam was philosophical about it at first. "Everything happens for a purpose," she said. She shrugged her shoulders and smiled, a bogus little smile as solid as water. A moment later she was theological about it. She pinched her chin between her thumb and index finger and said: "Oh well, like Paul said, 'we know that in all things God works for the good to them that love him and are called according to his purpose.'" She tapped her index finger against the tip of her nose, and finally, as usual, Miriam McKee became practical about it.

"Wait a minute, Nathan, we have no place to go," she said, as though the fact had just that instant dawned on her. "So they can't just up and fire you—us!—without due cause. You *have* a contract." Her philosophy was provocative, her theology sincere, but at heart Miriam Alice McKee was a pragmatist—a believer that in *what works is good.* She stood up and planted her palms flat on the tabletop and reminded Nathan, "According to the terms of your contract, Reverend McKee, you'll serve as interim pastor of the Historic First Church until October fifteenth. And that is *that!*"

The prosecution rested her case. *Then* she wanted the facts, the evidence. "By the way, Nathan, what happened? What's all this nonsense about anyway?"

"Mm. It seems Esther—Esther O'Casey—went wild and beat up a visiting evangelist, or as his royal heinie put it, 'a man of the cloth,' at a camp meeting in Tynbee this afternoon."

"Wait a minute," she said. "Wait, one, minute. Where did this camp meeting take place?"

"On the town square, I think he said. Why?"

"Because when I went to pick up milk this afternoon, I couldn't get to the Piggly Wiggly because the roads were blocked."

"Yeah," said Nathan. "So."

"So that was no ordinary camp meeting revival, Nathan. It was a KKK march."

"The Ku Klux Klan."

"None other."

"I see," he said. "I see."

"A man of the cloth," said Miriam. "A man of the cloth ... sheet."

"Right, and I wonder what, or who, brought them to Tynbee."

"I have a few ideas," she said, nibbling on her bottom lip. "And Esther is who she is. Who could blame her? Her little boy's dying, she has no support from her church family—"

"No support from her pastor," added Nathan.

"I wasn't going to say it."

"You didn't have to."

"Glad to hear it," Miriam said. "So let me get this straight, Nathan. Esther beat the Klan preacher up, and Elder Bailey wants *you* to do something about it."

"No, he wants *us* to do something about it. Translation: The Board of Elders will shackle Esther and lead her to the gallows and fasten the noose around her neck, and after giving her a good old public condemnation, I'll kick the floorboard out from under her and give her the grand sendoff."

"Excommunication?"

"Disfellowship, he called it. Same thing, I guess."

"Call Elder Gosset," Miriam said. "He won't abide any such nonsense."

A few minutes later, Nathan was on the phone with Elder Travis T. Gosset, the nemesis of Elder Luther Bailey. "Elder Gosset, I suppose you got wind of Esther O'Casey's run-in with the Klan today up town in Tynbee." He looked over at Miriam. His use of the Tynbee vernacular was not lost on her. She had told him recently that she had to get him out of Tynbee before he started dipping snuff and wearing bib-and-apron overalls and saying *yee-haw*!

Miriam whispered, "You sound like Huck Finn."

"Yes, I have," said Elder Gosset. "Luther and the Klan go back a ways. I heard about it from Lenora, my daughter. She called and said Kaitlyn, her daughter and my granddaughter, saw the whole thing. Then, this evening, Martha Jeeves called and told Lula that Esther had pretty well worn out the Klan's so-called preacher." Elder Gosset cleared his nose: "Sounded to me as if that fella got pretty much what he had coming; the very idea of coming to a town where a little boy's got AIDS and praising God for it."

"I know," Nathan said. "I agree. Well, Elder Bailey called a little while ago demanding that we take immediate action against Esther to salvage the church's reputation."

"He called me too. Good thing I was in the shower," said Elder Gosset. "Well, first off: A reputation such as we've got is not a thing to be salvaged. Second, Elder Bailey calling you don't surprise me none. The Ayatollah of Appalachia strikes again. I reckon he wants to restore Historic First's reputation for shooting their wounded. See, Preacher, Luther Bailey's not exactly a champion of the underdog—because he's not one. Never has been."

"Does he own the Historic First Church? *A church of God?* Maybe it's time for a separation of church and state here in Tynbee. How much power does he really have, Elder Gosset?"

"Way too much, by all accounts save his own," Elder Gosset said with a sigh. "So much so that he's about three sheets to the wind with it. I'll give you an example. Luther's about as tight as a fat heifer's hide. A few years back, he proposed that the church start charging a ten-dollar return-check fee for bounced tithe-and-offering checks. The proposal passed by a narrow margin, but after that no one ever bounced a tithe check. Because the names of those who did were going to be posted on the bulletin board in the vestibule. Now, that right there should tell you quite a bit about the man."

"Quite a bit," Nathan said.

"Now, technically, Preacher McKee, Luther has no special privilege, but the problem is this: He owns more than half of the members of the church. Here's a parable on the power of Luther Bailey: Doodle Corley and his wife, Wanda, voted for giving the TV to Ryne at the business meeting last Sunday night. Well, Wanda calls up Lula Monday evening crying because Luther Bailey came by and told Doodle that unless they could come up with the back rent they owed him by the end of the month—and, Preacher, they've been into him deep for years—he would be forced to evict them. Now, all of his tenants owe him money. So everybody knows he made his list and checked it twice. And Doodle and Shirley weren't the only ones who acted naughty in voting their conscience. Preacher, don't think I don't feel somewhat responsible. I was the one who insisted that a written vote be taken. That's vintage Luther Bailey for you—flexing his muscles in case others of his hostages decide to go against him."

"I see," said Nathan. "But he, Bailey, doesn't really have *any* special privileges under the Constitution and Bylaws of the church?"

"Preacher McKee, far as I know nobody's so much as ever seen the Constitution and Bylaws of the church Bailey's always making reference to. It must be written on Luther's heart or somewheres else on his person. But I know that, officially, the church has what they call a 'congregational polity.' All matters are to be decided by members' voting their will and their conscience. But like I said, Bailey's tenants know they have to let *his* conscience be their guide."

"It's time he produced the document. If it's just an oral tradition, well, that's going to be a problem. I suggested that we consult witnesses and not take action against Esther O'Casey until we investigated the circumstances surrounding the incident. I suggested, in my own way, that he was being a little rash."

"A little rash? A big itchy rash is more like it," Elder Gosset said.

"That he was rushing to judgment."

"The quicker to get there."

"As you can imagine, he didn't appreciate it. So he relieved me of my duties until further notice, which means, I guess, pending the Elders' meeting in the morning."

"That sorry son-of-a-bi—gun," said Elder Gosset. "He's got no authority to make a decision like that on his own, without at least consulting the other members of the Elder Board."

"But, like you said, he can do pretty much whatever he wants. If it went to a vote, he would win just as he did on the TV vote."

"Well, we're fixin' to see about all that." Elder Gosset's tone had turned sour. He was clearly perturbed. He told Nathan that Luther Bailey was no doubt using this situation to settle a score with Esther's mother, Miz Ida Bea Porterfield, who years ago had gotten him told in front of the whole church over the issue of whether they should allocate money for (a) renovating the fellowship hall, of which Miz Ida Bea told Luther Bailey during the morning worship service that for as much fellowshipping that went on in there the thing might as well be razed to the ground, or (b) purchasing a church bus to tote children to and from the church. "Of course, I reckon you've not seen a trace of the bus," said Elder Gosset. "The assembly hall got a fresh coat of paint and ceiling fans in place of the old lighting fixtures. Luther won, by a narrow margin; but Ida Bea was after him every day of his life for the rest of her life. God bless her."

"So … What should I do? Am I fired or—"

"No, you're not fired. Not officially. Not yet anyway." Elder Gosset explained the procedure: "There's a pulpit steering committee (and they've run us off the road a few times, but never mind all that). The pulpit steering committee is made up of the Board of Elders plus two ladies of the church. Their duty is to recommend the dismissal of a pastor, with cause, to the church as a whole. Then, all members eligible to vote do so, and on the basis of a simple majority the recommendation either carries or doesn't."

"What are the grounds for dismissing me? I merely suggested that he might be overreacting a little and—"

"No," Elder Gosset interrupted. "You merely suggested that you were the pastor and he was an elder. And for that he'll trump up some charge against you—Lord knows what he could come up with in his kangaroo court. He'll probably say you were derelict in your duties—"

"He could make that case," Nathan whispered.

"Well," said Elder Gosset, "you just take the day off from the pulpit. Miriam, too. But I want you there at the church service."

"We'll be there."

"See that you are," Elder Gosset said. He sighed. "I am awful sorry about this, Preacher. I wish I could say it was a fluke, this sort of rabble-rousing on Luther's part. But it's not. And, well, we'll do something to straighten it all out tomorrow."

"We'll do something," said Nathan.

Even if it's wrong.

Just As I Am

A CENTURY-OLD TRADITION at the Historic First Church prescribed the manner in which member children were to get saved. They were to go forward during the invitation on the Sunday following their twelfth birthday and make a public profession of faith in Christ Jesus and be baptized two Sundays hence. Ryne O'Casey was only ten years old. But in Ryne years, as he calculated them since he got AIDS, one year equaled about eight years for anybody else. Which meant that at ten he was really eighty. If he lived to see twelve, he would be ninety-six years old. On good days he thought it was possible; on most days—not-so-good days and just plain old bad days—he knew better.

The Reverend Sister Miranda Stryker always warned near the end of her show: "Woe to you, child, if you hear the voice of the Lord and hearken not unto it. If you have ears to hear, you better lo unto my voice."

Ryne took the fact that they were going back to church, after laying out for so many months, as a sign. If there are better and worse days on which to give your heart to Jesus, the Sunday morning on which Ryne went forward at the Historic First Church, at ten years old, might have been of either variety—depending on how you looked at it.

ESTHER WAS SERVING OLIE AND RYNE what she called their Sunday go-to-meeting breakfast—scrambled eggs with mild cheddar cheese, homemade buttermilk biscuits baked butter-in, crispy blackened bacon, and Ryne's least favorite, sugared grits.

Olie removed the Sunday newspaper from the plastic delivery bag, looked at the front page, and said, "Oh my." He did his best to flip the paper over before Esther, who was serving Ryne some eggs, could see it.

"What is it, Olie?"

Ryne had seen it and, bless his heart, couldn't help himself. His head was bowed and he was giggling for all he was worth.

"What's going on?" asked Esther.

Olie said, "Just some old news."

"Some old news what?"

Olie was giggling, too, by then. He said, "Let's just say I think you best set a spell before you read the paper this morning, Mother." He turned the newspaper to the front page.

"Lord of mercy!" shouted Esther. She looked down at the scrambled eggs she had spooned into Ryne's glass of orange juice. "Roll a glory!"

There she was on the front page of *The Avery County Banner/Herald* under the headline **LOCAL WOMAN BATTERS SUPREMIST PREACHER**. The picture of Esther Jean O'Casey was not flattering by any stretch. She was shown in her faded zinnia sundress straddling the Klan preacher she had clotheslined at the intersection of Main and Oak Streets in the shadows of the Tynbee City Hall. Her meaty hands on the lapels of his leisure suit that looked ash gray on the page (though Esther remembered was a medium brown), she had him raised a good ten inches off the pavement, and his eyes beady as a possum's were fixed on her. Esther squealed. "Ah. Just look at my face, will you?" Esther said. "I look like one of them poor people that lives in a 'sylum somewhere. I look like I'm on something."

"You *were* on something, Es'," Olie said—"that little old fella there who looks scared clean out of his wits." Using his toast like a dustpan, Olie swept his scrambled eggs onto it and shoved it into his mouth.

Ryne looked at the picture. "You look like Buddha, Mom," he told her. "Or a sumo wrestler, the way they look when they squat down with their hands on their thighs and stomp around."

"Oh, Ryne, go ahead on," she said. She looked at the picture again. There was a resemblance. "It's my hair." She had pinned her long hair up in a bun that morning to keep the stringy stuff from going haywire on the rides at Dollywood. And the way gravity was drawing her full cheeks and round eyes down as she hovered over the preacher did, she had to admit, put you in mind of a Sumo man.

Olie said, "I was thinking more along the lines of the WWF. Haystacks Calhoun if you had a been wearin' overalls."

"Haystacks Calhoun," she said. She preferred to think she looked a little more like Mama Cass. She clucked her tongue. "Well, at least I was dressed more decent than Buddha or them Chinese Sumo people. Besides, it was just the angle the camera was at. They didn't exactly say, 'Cheese!'" *Haystacks Calhoun.*

Ryne said, "Listen to this: 'It might be a long time before independent preacher Reverend Everett Hulsey, 42, of Ozark Peak, Arkansas, says "Praise God for AIDS" again, at least without bracing himself first. At a white supremist rally in Tynbee on Saturday morning, Esther Jean O'Casey, 41, of Tynbee, bolted from the crowd of spectators that had gathered to watch the marchers parade around the corner at Main and Oak Streets on their way to the town square and waylaid Hulsey, who was to deliver a message … Said one man who witnessed the event, "It was like as if she'd been fired from a cannon. She was moving at a good clip for a woman of her size, ran right on by us and bowled that little feller over like she was pickin' up a spare."

Another witness said she was "like a big old carnival balloon that the air's been let out of it.""''"

"I'd say them people saw it firsthand all right," Olie said.

"If I knowed who that was said those awful things, I'd bowl *him* over," Esther said. "And the person who wrote that article, too, for telling all of Avery County my age. 'A woman of her size.' Well, I am a big woman, but what does that have to do with the price of eggs in China? I'm surprised they didn't give my weight while they was at it. 'A big old carnival balloon that the air's been let out of it,'" she mocked.

Esther went back to the sink and began wringing nothing but her hands in the warm dishwater. "I'll never live this down," she mourned. She looked out at the clearing sky and heard Ryne and Olie still giggling. "If it wouldn't make us late for church this morning, I'd skin and cure both your hides right here in this kitchen." She adjusted her cotton duster and said, in a sad voice, "Imagine the rigamarole. Now everybody in creation is going to know about me being middle-aged and cutting that big old shine up in town."

Ryne drained the last of the gritty sugar milk from the bowl of *Cap'n Crunch* he had eaten instead of eggs. "Why would anybody praise God for AIDS?" he asked.

Esther, who had turned back to the sink and was watching a squirrel stealing the stale bread she had put in the feeder for her little birds, started to speak her piece about it. But she heard Olie tell him, "For the same reason some people take a tommy gun into McDonald's and blow people away while they're lunching on a Big Mac, son. There's something about human nature makes people take out their anger on other people. Take a cat; she'll stalk a mouse and play with it, slap it around, and maybe even end up killing it or at least maiming it. But not because she's mean. Curious maybe, but not just plain mean. Little people, no matter how rotten they are, feel a little bigger if they can put somebody else down. You know, the runt in every litter is usually the one acting up to draw attention to hisself."

Ryne nodded slowly, as if pondering the difference between curiosity and meanness. Esther called to the squirrel through the window screen: "Go on now, you greedy little dickens. Leave some for them chicks or I'll make shoes of you." The squirrel raised up on its hind legs, glanced up at her through the screen, and nibbled on the bread it was rotating in its front paws the way Olie sometimes ate corn on the cob. "Squirrels can be pretty mean, too, Ryne," she said. "That thing's all the time chasing away my little robins and blue jays and even other squirrels. Squirrels' inhumanity to squirrels." She chuckled at herself. "The little pig."

"Did God really cause AIDS?" Ryne asked.

"Some people say he did; some people say he wouldn't. What I want to know is: How do they know?" Esther said. "Mother always said it was funny how when people went to speaking for the Lord they always happened to agree with what they said he was sayin'."

Ryne put his cereal bowl in the sink. "But it says in there in the Bible that God sent Moses to deliver plagues on the Egyptians. Is AIDS a plague?"

"Well, that is true, Ryne," she said. "But I imagine it was only because them Egyptians must have done something to deserve them locusts and such."

"But there were probably babies there in Egypt, too," Ryne said, "and little kids and old people who didn't have nothing to do with Pharaoh keeping the children of Israel in bondage."

"Jesus didn't care one bit for the ways of them Pharaoh-sees either, I can tell you that," Esther said. "So they must have been a pretty sorry bunch. Preacher McKee was saying something about that very thing the other day when you-all was off whooping it up at Dollywood." *Was it the preacher who had said it, or she?*

She couldn't remember and didn't imagine that it made much difference either way.

Olie said, "Those are good questions, Ryne-o. Deep questions of great theological importance. Maybe you could ask the preacher about it after the service lets out this morning. I can't see God sending a plague on you, son, that's for sure. Way I figure, God made the world good and we fouled it up—and now we blame God for all the bad and take the credit for all the good. I reckon we just have to keep the faith that God knows what he's doing, and in the end everything's going to turn out right."

Just then it struck Esther that Ryne had not been baptized and, barring some miraculous healing touch of Jesus, he would not live to see his twelfth birthday. She was not going to lose hope. The grief books people gave her and Olie—as *gifts*—had a word for her hoping Jesus would do a sign and wonder and heal Ryne: They called it *denial*. Esther had a word for it, too: *faith*. She had a word for those who wrote such books, too: *blasphemers*. Denial had nothing to do with it. Nobody was denying anything (except the people who wrote such books— they denied Jesus his right to perform a miracle of healing and his followers the right to have faith that he might do just that). Esther was certainly not *denying* that Ryne was dying. Unless you were blind, you could see that, even if you didn't want to—and she surely did not, but she saw it plain as day all the same. But she was not about to *deny* that God could perform a miracle if he took a notion to. That would not only be *denial*, she thought, but sacrilege.

Esther had known of the Lord to do miracles before, like the time one Sunday she and Olie slipped and slid thirty-some miles over the Smokies from Sylva, North Carolina, in a blizzard with the fuel needle hanging practically out Olie's door, and her praying *Please Lord Jesus don't let us get stranded up here in the snow with all them bears ... even if, as Olie has just told me, they're hibernating, then please don't let them things wake*

*up and come out, and you just breathe on this car and blow
us on back home to Tynbee.* Lord Jesus had come through: The
car ran out of gas just as they were turning into the driveway
out front. If she was not about to get her hopes up about Ryne's
being healed of AIDS, she knew that hope was about the only
thing they had.

And hope was not denial.

And faith was not foolishness.

Hope and denial were still on Esther's mind as Olie headed
the old gray Nova north on 112 toward the church. "I expect
they'll ex-commemorate me for that harangue I made up yonder
in town yesterday," Esther said.

"Well, if they was to, Es'," Olie told her, "you'd be the prettiest
person ever to be excommunicated."

"Well, Olie, aren't you sweet," Esther said, her heart warm.
"Or either you're just trying to make up for saying I looked like
Buddha in that newspaper picture?"

"I believe it was your son there dragged old Buddha into all
this." Olie winked at Ryne in the rearview mirror.

"Well Buddha's some better than Haystacks Calhoun," she
said.

Then she turned the rearview mirror on herself and tried to
finger curl the stringy forelocks of her hair. "My hair's a mess,"
she said. "Mary Barry's lost her touch, and I'm half thinking she
might be hitting the bottle pretty regular again. You know, she
swore off drink for a while. There I go spreading gossip again.
I'm beginning to wonder if there's any hope for me. Lord Jesus,
please forgive me." Back at her hair: "I sure do wish Santa
Claus would bring me one of them Hair-dini thing-a-majigs for
Christmas."

"I bet he will," Ryne said, "if you're real nice."

Esther smoothed the lap of what she called her *lemony
chiffon* dress, which she had picked up at Wal-Mart with a pair
of matching high heels and pocket book back before times got

so hard. Her mother always said that yellow was Esther's color, and Esther, seeing it shimmer in the morning sun against the pale skin of her arms, was inclined to agree. You really had no choice, Esther thought, when it came to agreeing with Miz Ida Bea, which is what everyone, including Esther's father, called her. You ended up agreeing with Miz Ida Bea whether you wanted to or not. Olie used to say of his mother-in-law: "That Miz Ida Bea's the onliest one I ever knew that you could get blessed out for either agreeing with her or not agreeing with her." People would agree to what she was saying, even when they knew good and well in their heart of hearts she was dead wrong, just to keep from getting her ire up. And sometimes even then she would catch you redhanded trying to get one over on her and shake you down until the truth came jingling out.

Esther missed her mother something fierce, especially it seemed when they were going to the church-house. Miz Ida Bea had been a fixture there on the middle pew, the widows' pew, for so long that it would have seemed less like something was missing if the baptistry had disappeared instead of Miz Ida Bea. Near the end of her life, one of the ushers would roll her down the center aisle, stopping at nearly every row on the way so she could shake hands and greet her friends and tease her enemies, and park her in the center aisle at the end of the widows' pew. Sometimes, when Holy Ghost moved her, Miz Ida Bea would raise her frail right hand—she always clutched her pocketbook with her left when she was in the church—and say, "Amen," or "Hallelujah," or (if she happened to disagree) "Keep on a-readin'."

Esther wiped the tears from her eyes with her kerchief and had just finished blowing her nose when Ryne said, "Mom, Dad?" He waited until he was sure he had their attention before he went on. "Remember that lady-preacher, Sister Miranda Stryker, that I was telling y'all about? You know, the one I've been watching on TV late at night?"

Olie nodded. "I've seen of her. She's the one sort of puts you in mind of Bertha Snowden, only with flashier clothes."

"Yeah," Ryne said. "Kind of. She's colored just like Mrs. Snowden. She sings all those songs you like, Mom, like 'Up From the Grave He Arose' and 'I'll Fly Away.' Sounds a lot like Dolly Parton. Anyway, she preaches real good and does healings like I was telling you. Like just last night she healed a man with a tumor on his spine. And after he got up—because people always fall down on the ground when she sends the Holy Ghost into them, to get the demons out, I guess—well, anyway, when they picked him up, he could bend over and touch his toes. She kept having him do that over and over until he finally said, 'Ooh, my back' and took off running down into the crowd with his hands up in the air screaming, 'Ooh, aah, Jesus!'"

Esther looked out the window. She felt Olie glancing over at her to get a read on her reaction. She ignored him. She studied a little group of slaughter-hogs huddled by the chicken-wire fence bounding Cora Pike's barnyard from Route 112. *Maybe*, she thought. "Well, Jesus *did* heal people, Ryne. That much is a fact, I imagine." She kept her eyes trained on the pigs. "Like that time Jesus cast them devils out of that poor man Leauge'n who lived naked in the graveyard and vanished them into a herd of swine. Talk about bad pork. My Lord."

Esther wondered: *Was it a sign, them passing those pigs just when Ryne was talking about healings? Then she thought to herself: But Sister Stryker is no Jesus, thank you very much, and Ryne was no League'n either, possessed with all them devils and prancing around in his birthday suit out in a graveyard. O me of little faith, she thought, if I had the faith of a mustard seed ...* It was not for her to say, Esther decided. God could do whatever he took a notion to do, and that was the bottom line.

"Well, Ryne, your mother has a point," Olie said, as the car crunched across the gravel parking lot beside the church. "Do you think all that healing and stuff is for real?"

"I can't see Sister Stryker making up things like that, Dad," Ryne said. He picked up his *Children's Picture-Story Bible* and leaned forward, resting his chin on the top of the front seat. "She's coming to that brand-spanking new Nashville Arena in September for a Greater Tennessee Crusade for Healing and Renewal, 'three great days of the outpouring of God's richest spiritual blessings.' Do you think we could go out there and see her? Everybody's going to be there. Elder Butts—"

"Watch your mouth, Ryne," Esther said.

"Elder *Bottoms* and Jay Hova, too," Ryne added. "I think he sings or plays an instrument."

"Jay Hova," Esther said, wondering if your last name was Hova whether it would constitute an act of blasphemy to name your son Jay—like those baseball players named Jesus?

"I think," Olie said, "they mean that the Lord's going to be there at the meeting—Jehovah."

"Maybe," Esther said, still studying the issue of blasphemy.

Olie said, "Mother, what do you say in the matter?"

Esther said, "Don't press me, now Olie. I'm thinking it over." Then she shrugged her shoulders as if Holy Ghost had moved her. "We're late enough as it is," she said. "And I think Sister Strykers would agree that the first business of healing is my heart and me getting forgiveness for showing out yesterday. Besides, we've got a whole month to see about that, but only about a minute to make the call to worship, so let's get a move on."

As she got out of the car, the high heel of Esther's right shoe burrowed into the gravel, and when she applied her full weight to it, the heel snapped off like a twig. "Lord of mercy," she said, and ended up banging her head on the roof of the car as she sat back down in the passenger seat. "The devil does things like this. I imagine it could've been the Lord, serving me right."

Ryne suggested that, since they had no glue, they just pop off the other heel so at least Esther's shoes would match. "It's either that, hop-along, or go barefooted," he said.

"Well, I suppose with a little elbow-grease we could make a pair of flats out of these," Esther said. "I loved these shoes. Mother always said there's nothing as sad as shoes."

Olie tried to snap off the left heel with his bare hands. It wouldn't budge. At last he said, "Ankle grease is more like what it'll take to get the job done. Do to this one what you did to the other one."

"It's not like I did it on purpose," Esther said.

"I'm not saying you did, Es'."

"I guess just standing my big fat Haystacks Calhoun self on top of it," she said, as she stood up and, with one hand on the roof of the car and the other on Olie's shoulder, put all her weight on the heel and ground her foot into the gravel, "should be about enough to cast iron."

The whole operation took about five minutes.

NATHAN AND MIRIAM MCKEE entered the sanctuary of the Historic First Church through the vestibule at five minutes before eleven and sat on the back row on the right side of the church. "I don't see Elder Bailey," Miriam whispered.

By long tradition, and as a matter of principle, the church refused to get pew cushions lest—as Nathan heard it—the congregation be lulled into a soul-damning complacency. As Nathan worked his way into the straight-back pew, he decided the pews had failed in their mission. In fact, Nathan thought, if the sanctuary of the Historic First Church was furnished with every medieval torture device ever built and every last congregant was forced to heed the sermon while spinning madly in a whirligig suspended from the rafters, you would be hard pressed to find one soul among their number that would be damned by anything *other than* complacency. (And the business meetings would hardly be any more nauseating.) The hardwood pews, after all, did not touch the heart.

Nathan surveyed the congregation. A few stragglers filed in and made their way down the aisles to their appointed places. Those already seated exchanged pleasantries and shifted about while looking at their bulletins—most of them unaware that there had been a change of plans. No one seemed to notice that Miriam and Nathan were not on the podium but on the back row, or, if they did, they did not show it—or again, maybe they were, despite the hardwood pews, simply too complacent to care. It was 11:05 a.m. and there was still no sign of Elder Bailey. "He wouldn't miss this to save his soul," Nathan whispered to Miriam, "if he could get those terms. I bet he's back in the office fashioning the slip knot in the noose they're going to hang me with."

"Hang you? I doubt you could get *those* terms, my dear," said Miriam, squeezing his hand. "Stoning maybe. My money has him out behind the church taking up stones. That's the Old Testament way."

"Amen."

Sue Ella Bailey, the elder's wife, was not there in her appointed place behind the organ. For where Luther was, the locals said, there was Sue Ella in the midst. A few of the congregants murmured about the absence of music; no one murmured, in Nathan's earshot, about the absence of the preacher.

Elder Gosset rose from his seat on the front row and took the side aisle back to Nathan. He leaned down and whispered: "Preacher McKee, I don't have the foggiest notion where Luther is. He didn't make the Elder's meeting this morning. But these people are gathered here for church, so let's just proceed as usual. Just slip out the front door and come in through the back and deliver your message—if you have one prepared, or just lead us in prayer if you don't."

Miriam squeezed Nathan's hand. "By all means," Nathan said. He looked at Miriam and cocked his head toward the piano. "Show time." Nathan had a sermon, all right, a sermon he thought would probably merit a letter grade of D, by Miriam's criteria. It was called "And a Little Child Shall Lead Them." The sermon notes were in his Bible, where he stuffed them somewhere in the book of Isaiah the previous night before he staggered out to the graveyard.

Nathan went to his office and put on his *casket,* as the minister's robe—a cassock—was called by a woman he overheard gossiping about a former pastor who was so big around he looked like a big tube of sausage when he was preaching in the thing (originally scarlet, it had faded over its hundred and some years odd years to an ashen rose). Miriam was playing "Higher Ground."

Buster Jeeves—who had been leading the congregation in song ever since the choir director, Ernie Laurel, got caught making out with the high school guidance counselor behind the Frozen Custard—waved his meaty arms without regard for pitch or tempo. Ah, but the man had soul. Nathan joined in on the third stanza:

My heart has no desire to stay
Where doubts arise and fears dismay;
Though some may dwell where those abound,
My prayer, my aim, is higher ground.
Lord, lift me up and let me stand,
By faith, on heaven's table land,
A higher plane than I have found;
Lord, plant my feet on higher ground.

"Excuse me," he said. The cassock had to go. The big thing represented everything that was wrong with the Historic First Church—namely, its history. It was more a poncho than a cassock, and Miriam said when he was preaching in it she always expected the Cisco Kid to come riding up. *Here goes.* If he was an enema preacher, as one of the church members had referred to his "interim" pastor, well, Nathan could stir up a big old mess. And a sure fire way to start was by casting off the cassock and all the tradition behind it. The thing was made of some type of heavy burlap material like a feedsack and reeked to high heaven. Miriam said it was a spiritual stink. Nathan said it was a physical stink: A century of windsucking mountain preachers had worn the thing while shouting down the glory. Nathan and Miriam had once smuggled the thing out of the church and taken liquid detergent to it, but in the end it smelled the same and Miriam quipped he would have to bear it as his heavy burden, 'neath a load of filth and shame.

They told him the thing was a mantle of biblical proportions, passed down from the venerable Reverend Isaiah RagsdaleDancy, the church's founding father, to each successive minister.

I hereby defrock myself, he thought. Nathan turned his back to the congregation and, tradition be cussed, slipped it over his head, careful not to profane the hallowed poncho (though he pictured himself dousing it with gasoline, while Miriam lit the match, and sending it to the final resting place where all such garments go). He folded it, then limped over and draped it rather ceremoniously over the back of the minister's chair. Someone else could return it to the utility closet so that it could be passed on to Nathan's hapless successor (probably within the week), who would be unaware that the church had run off enough pastors to fill a good sized chapter of *Foxe's Book of Martyrs* and every last one of them had worn that thing.

When he turned back around, he looked down at Miriam behind the piano. She winked at him and shrugged her shoulders and, in her eye, there just might have been a tear, though the fixtures in the Historic First Church generated "more heat than light" and Nathan's eyes were strained from sermon preparation and the experience in the graveyard.

A few of the congregants slapped their hands against their mouths and gasped in real or, more likely, mock horror, as though their pastor had taken off not merely the vestment but his undergarments as well and stood there for all the world naked. A few of the more composed members remarked: "How dare he shed the vestments in this holy place," or: "Well, it's about time we got shut of that thing."

Feeling a new sense of freedom, Nathan addressed the congregation: "Let us pray. Dear Heavenly Father, only and mighty God, in the name of Jesus Thy well loved Son, Savior of the world—even of us—we pray." The prayer that followed lasted a full seven minutes, which set a new record for "longest prayer" in the long history of the Historic First Church of Tynbee, Tennessee.

RYNE WAS HAPPY the family had slipped into the back pew without making a bigger scene than was absolutely necessary. His mom, as usual, made a fairly big scene as she repeatedly tried to hush Ryne and his dad (who were not saying a word): "Shhh. Let's be quiet now. We're late, and I don't imagine these good people—or the other ones either, for that matter—came here to listen to us carry on." Ryne was wedged in between his parents and slumped stoop-shouldered to avoid the glaring eyes of church members whose names he used to know and to keep as much of his body off the cold hard pew as possible.

He remembered the time back when Miz Ida Bea was alive when the church took up the matter of getting cushions to put on the pews like most churches have. Miz Ida Bea told them she wanted no part of that: It was unbiblical, for one thing, and un-Christian, for another. The way she figured it, the more you suffered in this life, the more apt you would be to long for consolation in the life to come. Then Elder Bailey said, "That's easy to say for one who sits in a wheelchair with two bed pillows under her bum." Miz Ida Bea went off on him then, told him that for one thing it took a bum to know one and for another he had a nasty mouth and for yet another there was no comparison between his bony sin-sick self having to sit on a straight-back oaken pew to get the fear of God put in him and her having a bad hip.

Unfortunately, Miz Ida Bea had won that round.

The fever and chills of the night before had left Ryne weak, and he leaned against his mom's arm to ease his aching back. He could not tell whether he or his mom was the target of the dartlike glances he felt shooting at them. Maybe they were both bullseyes: He, because he had AIDS; she, because she loved him enough to beat the fire and brimstone out of that preacher who was praising God for it. He hoped they were aimed at him. It was all his fault, anyway, not *hers*. If he had never been born, none of this would have ever happened. He was the one born with hemophilia; and he was the one who had caught AIDS; and he was the one she beat up that preacher in the parade for; and he was the one they had to give all that TV money for. Maybe that was what they were really mad about. Or maybe it was because they were afraid they would catch AIDS from him. He knew that was why Tray Bullock was no longer allowed to play with him— that and the fact that Ryne played with the Snowden children, who were colored. *Bottom line: It was not his mom and dad's fault. They didn't do anything to deserve this.*

Please, Lord, let us go to Nashville. The people in Sister Stryker's congregation at the Nashville Arena would not stare at him and his mom the way they were staring at them that Sunday morning in their own church—*Hysterical First*.

Ryne just knew that his mom and Sister Stryker would hit it off big time when they met at the September crusade in Nashville. *Please, Lord.* Even though Sister Stryker was colored and a preacher and his mom was white and just a mom, they had a lot in common. For one thing, they both liked talking about the Holy Ghost. Sister Stryker was always talking about how, on the Day of Penny-Cost, when all the disciples were sitting around the house weeping and wailing and gnashing their teeth because they did not yet know what Jesus wanted them to do, the Holy Ghost came rolling in on a hurricane wind and sat down on them—pinned them down like his mom had done that preacher—and shook them all up but good and set their cloven tongues on fire, and then they all started talking funny the way Sister Stryker sometimes talked: "Ah heal-y a shum-bah-la-ha. Hee-hee la ha-ba-da gran' *pooh*-ba!" Sister Stryker was something else, all right. She reminded him of what his mom would be like if she had been born colored and called to preach and wore flashy clothes and could heal people.

His mom and the Sister both talked a lot about things their mothers used to tell them when they were kids, too, and believed that without God you were pretty much headed up a creek without a paddle. They were both short and fat and loud and liked wearing bright-colored clothes.

Ryne wondered how Sister Stryker would have dealt with that preacher his mom walloped who was calling colored people the N-word. She would not have liked it one bit. He could picture the two of them, arms interlocked, taking off after that man like a WWF tag team and bushwhacking him.

If he could only get them together. *God was going to help him.*

Ryne scanned the pictures in his *Children's Picture-Story Bible*: Noah like a school crossing guard ushering giraffes, elephants, and squirrels two-by-two up the ramp into the ark; Moses waiting patiently while God engraved the Ten Commandments on the stone tablets; David slinging the stone at the mighty Philistine giant Goliath.

Preacher McKee cleared his throat and began delivering his message. Ryne expected it to be dull and—not to be mean—

kind of boring. But, surprise! It wasn't boring at all. It was about one of the miraculous healings Jesus did that Ryne had not heard Sister Stryker preach about. By the time it was over Ryne decided that the major difference (but, of course, not the only difference) between the service at the Historic First Church that morning and Sister Stryker's services was that the sermon was about … Ryne.

NATHAN STOOD BEHIND THE PULPIT without the cassock or even a sport coat. He had not even worn a tie, not because he was trying to antagonize anyone (as if he had to try) but because he had simply forgotten to in his mad rush to bathe and get ready so as not to be late for his excommunication. *Well, go all the way,* he thought as he rolled up his sleeves and got down to business.

"As we again go to the Almighty in prayer," he said, "are there prayer requests?"

"Wish we had a preacher who took his calling seriously," a woman cried out.

"Yes, amen," he responded. "Are there others?"

"Marybeth Adams is in a bad way," someone said, "her cancer's getting the best of her."

"We'll take Marybeth to the Lord in prayer," Nathan said, jotting a note on the back of his church bulletin. "Other concerns or praises?"

"Pray for Reverend Everett Hulsey, who was assaulted while preaching in Tynbee yes'day afternoon."

"We will *indeed* pray for him," Nathan assured the congregation.

Nathan prayed for another five minutes. He prayed for a preacher who took his calling seriously, for poor cancer-ridden Marybeth Adams who was in a bad way, for Reverend Everett Hulsey—"that the Lord might restore him not only to bodily health but to spiritual health" as well. The latter request was stated so sincerely, so skillfully, that the prayer continued without incident.

Nathan paused for a moment and, in his mind, heard Miriam's familiar voice saying, *Quit playing tag with God, Nathan.*

Nathan bowed his head, prayed. "We are blind, O Lord, let us see. We are deaf, O Lord, let us hear. We are mean, O Lord, let us be kind. We are divided, O Lord, let us be one. We are greedy, O Lord, let us give. We hate, O Lord, let us love. We are infidels, O Lord, let us believe. We are evil, O Lord, let us be good. We are goats, O Lord, let us be Thy sheep. And may God richly bless each and every one of us, in Jesus' name and for our sake. Amen."

Nathan read passages from Isaiah, Chapter eleven, about the glorious time when such harmony will prevail that "the infant will play near the hole of the cobra, and the young child put his hand into the viper's nest" without harm, and from John, Chapter 9, about Jesus's healing of the man blind from birth:

> *And as Jesus passed by, he saw a man which was blind from his birth. And his disciples asked him, saying, Master, who did sin, this man, or his parents, that he was born blind? Jesus answered, Neither hath this man sinned, nor his parents: but that the works of God should be made manifest in him. I must work the works of him that sent me, while it is day: the night cometh, when no man can work. As long as I am in the world, I am the light of the world. When he had thus spoken, he spat on the ground, and made clay of the spittle, and he anointed the eyes of the blind man with the clay, And said unto him, Go, wash in the pool of Siloam, (which is by interpretation, Sent.) He went his way therefore, and washed, and came seeing.*

Nathan cleared his throat. "I want us all to take note that Ryne O'Casey and his parents, Esther and Olie, whom you all know, are here in church with us this morning."

Those seated down near the front, who had not seen or heard the O'Casey's making their triumphal if late entry, craned their necks to see the O'Caseys with their own eyes. Nathan raised his right hand. "Shhh," he said. "Listen. As many of you know, Ryne was born with a rare blood disease called hemophilia, which means that his blood does not clot normally, the way yours and mine—"

"Is there a message in this, Preacher?" an annoyed man asked.

"Yes, there is. A very important message, if you'll just bear with me." Nathan answered him softly in hopes of turning away his wrath. A few more of the congregants addressed him, and Nathan felt his own wrath bubbling. "This is not a business meeting. It's a worship service, so I'll thank all of you not to interrupt me when I'm preaching so long as I'm the pastor of this church."

"Which might not be so long," a woman said, "if you keep on like this."

"Might not be long at all," Nathan said without malice or sarcasm, then added: "if *you* keep on like that."

After a moment more of murmuring, order was restored.

Nathan continued. "Ryne has AIDS. A-I-D-S: Acquired Immune Deficiency Syndrome. AIDS is to us what leprosy was to the people living in Jesus' day: the most dreaded of all diseases. Now why did Ryne get AIDS? 'Because he's a sinner,' some of you will say, are saying to yourselves right now. 'Because his parents, Olie and Esther, are sinners.' Well, who's not? But is that why Ryne got AIDS? Let us ask ourselves: Are you and I really in a position to make that kind of judgment?"

A long pause for reflection. "Why do I and many of you wear glasses? Because of sin? Why do some of us have heart trouble?

Because of sin? And what about gallstones and hangnails and irregularity? Because of sin? Maybe. But the fact is, we live in a fallen world. Bad things do happen to good people, and good things happen to bad people. Innocent people get killed by drunk drivers, by axe murderers and serial killers, and by freak accidents. People, like our dear sister Marybeth Adams, get cancer. We are fallen and we live in a fallen world, and God is the *only one* with the power to pick us back up, to lift us out of our fallen condition. If he were here with us this morning, who would Jesus be sitting with? Who did he sit with in his own day? He, the Great Physician, came to heal whom? Those who are not sick, he said, don't need a doctor. Jesus would be with the prostitutes—"

"I've heard enough of this," someone said with a gasp.

"Hush now, sister. Let's hear the preacher out," someone responded.

"Bear with me, please," said Nathan. "It's in the Bible. Jesus sought out those who needed him. Of course, everyone needed him. But he sought out those who needed him and knew they needed him. He had little patience for those who needed him but didn't know, or wouldn't bring themselves to admit, that they needed him. He was for the children, the sick ones, the outcasts, the tax collectors—not the best and healthiest of us but the worst and sickest of us. And thank God for it—all day and every night."

Nathan paused, lowered his head, squinted to dam up the tears in his eyes. "I don't know why some people get sick and others don't. I don't know why my baby brother struggled all his life with a learning disability and ended up dying at twenty years old. I just don't … know. Things just happen in our fallen world. And it is what we do, and whom we seek, after those things happen that shows what we are made of, and to give God a chance to show us what he is made of—the God who did not just sit idly by and watch the suffering in the world but took part in it and became suffering for us. The Apostle Paul didn't really understand why, after he had prayed and prayed, that God, in his infinite wisdom, chose not to remove his thorn in the flesh. But the Lord told Paul: 'My grace is sufficient for thee: For my strength is made perfect in weakness. Most gladly therefore will I rather glory in my infirmities, that the power of Christ may rest upon me ... for when I am weak, then am I strong.'"

"For whatever reason Ryne got AIDS, Jesus is saying to us: Don't miss the point. Don't go hunting for the sin that caused it, for it is an opportunity *that the works of God should be made manifest in him*. Make no mistake: God will hold us responsible for the way we treat Ryne and Olie and Esther O'Casey. On the day of judgment when we stand to give an account of ourselves to Jesus, God forbid that Jesus will have cause to say to us, 'Depart from me, ye cursed, into everlasting fire, prepared for the devil and his angels: For I was sick and ye visited me not. Verily I say unto you, Inasmuch as ye did it not to one of the least of these, ye did it not to *me*.'"

A great hush had fallen over the congregation. For once, there was no murmuring, no fussing, and not a single hateful outburst from either side of the center aisle. The only sound Nathan could hear from the pulpit was a sniffle here, a nose blowing there.

"In closing," Nathan said, "let us remember what Jesus said after he had healed the man blind from birth: 'For judgment I am come into this world, that they which see not might see; and that they which see might be made blind. And some of the Pharisees which were with him heard these words, and said unto him, Are we blind also? Jesus said unto them, If ye were blind, ye should have no sin: But now ye say, We see; therefore your sin remaineth.'"

Nathan closed his sermon: "Are we not, all of us, sick?"

WOW! RYNE THOUGHT. Maybe practice did make perfect, after all. Maybe Preacher McKee had been practicing preaching really hard since Ryne and his parents quit going to church. Though Preacher McKee had not stomped around the stage singing and dancing, goody-jonesing and wise-cracking as he delivered the message, he had raised his voice when he said certain things and did not speak any Greek and, for once, you had a feeling that he really believed what he was saying.

With Miriam at the piano, Buster Jeeves led the congregation in a spirited rendition of the invitation hymn: "Power in the Blood." Ryne thought that all they needed was Elder Butts jamming away on the organ to add the finishing touch. Mister Jeeves was doing his part, waving his arms way up high like Lord Jesus or Jaws one was after him.

Between the third and fourth stanzas, while the piano played softly, Preacher McKee, whom Ryne could not see, said, "This is the last verse, and then we're going to close. Every head bowed, every eye closed, just the piano, please, softly, and Buster singing. If anyone needs to make a public profession of faith in Jesus, rededicate their life to Christ, join this church. Anything at all. Come now. Don't delay."

When Buster sang, "There is power, power, wonder-working power, in the blood of the Lamb," Ryne's eyes filled with tears. He recalled the previous night when he lay in bed knowing that his time was running out. He could not afford to delay. What if tonight was the night ... *and if I die before I wake, I pray the Lord my soul to take.* He tugged gently on the sleeve of his mom's pretty yellow dress. She leaned down and said, "What is it, angel hair?" and he whispered in her ear, "I need to go forward and talk to the preacher. Do you think I could?"

Esther nudged Olie's shoulder and, when he had quit praying and opened his eyes, she made a shooing motion toward the center aisle. The three of them walked together down to the front of the church toward Nathan, who was standing before the altar.

Esther said, "Preacher McKee, Ryne here wants to talk to you. He's young yet, but I think he's ready to give his heart to Jesus."

Nathan smiled. It was years since he had heard those words. They are not seminary words. Nathan instructed Buster Jeeves to lead the congregation in another hymn, "Just As I Am." Then he led Ryne and Esther and Olie O'Casey out of the sanctuary and down the hall to his office and shut the door behind them. There was a single folding metal chair in Nathan's office (his desk chair). He lifted Ryne and set him gently in the chair, then knelt before it and said, "God bless you, Ryne."

Olie and Esther stood in front of the bookcase, hand in hand.

Nathan took Ryne's hands in his own, and said, "I'm sorry I haven't—"

"God bless *you*, Preacher McKee," Esther said, cutting him off.

Ryne, who was still crying, told the preacher that for some time he had wanted to come forward and be baptized, but then they stopped coming to church. He had been praying they would come back at least one more time so that he could be baptized before he died.

Esther said, "Sweet Jesus. Lord of mercy on my soul." Then she started gasping and huffing and dropped to her knees and started praying softly, almost to herself.

Olie said, "Like Esther said, Preacher, I know it's early. Ryne here's only ten, and by an ancient tradition of the church children are to go forward and get saved and baptized soon after their twelfth birthday. Under the circumstances, though, could you make an exception?"

"Yes," Nathan said. "Of course. It's a matter between Ryne and Jesus and has nothing to do with the Constitution and Bylaws or some silly tradition." He leaned forward and placed his hands on Ryne's shoulders and, through tear-filled eyes, looked into Ryne's small face. "Ryne O'Casey, do you believe that Jesus is the Christ, the Son of the living God?"

"Yes. I sure do," he said. He nodded his head. "I believe it more than I believe anything in the whole world."

Esther raised her trembling hands in the air, then clasped her hands together with a loud, startling clap. "Thank you, sweet Jesus!" she said. She took off her glasses and dabbed her damp eyes with her kerchief. And for once Ryne did not have to ask her what she was crying about and, for once, she did not have to invent some unlikely story about pollen or onions.

Ryne raised his hand as he had done years before when he was pledging his Cub Scout honor and said: "And I want to be baptized."

A few minutes later the four of them were back in the sanctuary where something close to a prayer meeting had broken out. Miriam was playing the soothing refrain of "Softly and Tenderly." A dozen or so people were kneeling before the altar praying, and some were even weeping as people weep only in times of repentance—but Nathan was not about to chance it. He took Ryne by the hand and led him (but not Esther and Olie) up onto the pulpit and said, "Ladies and gentlemen, may I have your attention for just one moment. I have some wonderful news to share with you." Nathan winced, anticipating the heckling.

No one said a word. "Ryne O'Casey just gave his heart to Jesus," he told them.

There was silence at first. Then someone started clapping— and in short order nearly all of the congregants on both sides of the church joined in. "Count it all joy, Ryne!" someone shouted.

Not everyone in the church was approving, of course, and a few outraged dissenters even stormed out, trying to make a scene in so doing, but no one seemed to notice or care.

Ryne stood on his tiptoes and pulled the microphone down. "I just want to say thank you to all of you for giving me that TV set. It sure was nice." His cheeks were damp and, as he spoke, he got choked up. "I, I hope some day before it's too late … that I'll be able to pay you back for it and let you know how much it means to me. Thank you-all."

No one on either side of the sanctuary said so much as a word and, softly and tenderly, the worship service seemed ready to come to a close.

Just about ready to close.

The Mean Man Brought Down

A T 11:55 A.M., AS NATHAN (with Ryne still beside him on the pulpit) was pronouncing the benediction to close the Sunday morning service, Elder Luther Bailey and his wife, Sue Ella, entered the sanctuary through the back door. The Baileys walked slowly down beside the choir loft, as Nathan prayed that the Lord would make his face to shine upon them all.

Elder Bailey shuffled like a man twice his age (and he was nearly seventy years old), as he staggered up the steps to the pulpit. His face was pale as ash and when he got close Nathan thought, *Lord, you are not making your face to shine upon him.* The old man shooed Nathan and Ryne from the lectern and with trembling hands tried to adjust the microphone.

"Sit down, everyone," he said.

And everyone, including Nathan and Ryne, did as they were told.

Elder Bailey wore a black three-piece suit that hung loose on his wasted body. It was the kind of suit old men get buried in. The pin stripes were far enough apart to run a golf ball through. He leaned against the lectern for support. The papery skin of his neck wimpled above his collar like the work of a careless seamstress.

Ryne was sitting on Nathan's lap, and Nathan hugged him close. The events of the previous night—facing the Skyler Heights tragedy and the big 'T'" Tragedy his denial had made of it; his guilt and his sorrow; his anger over Esther O'Casey's KKK episode—had drained Nathan. Drained him of everything but, perhaps, he thought, the desire not to break his own fall at someone else's expense.

He skimmed through *Children's Picture-Story Bible*, which Ryne had brought forward with him, slowly turning the pages. Whispers filled the church like static as Elder Bailey addressed the congregation.

"I am hereby calling a emergency general session of this here church." He paused, as if to allow the wonder to grow or maybe just to catch his breath, which seemed to be leaking out of him. "As the Chairman of the Board of Elders of this here Historic First Church it sometimes falls on me to make hard decisions. But," he added, "such is the burden of a leader." He paused again, and this time it was definitely to catch his breath. "Last evening, I made the hard decision to relieve our interim pastor of his *interim* duties. Pending the official decision of a full council of the Board of Elders, which will convene in emergency session immediately following this service—"

"I beg your pardon!" said Buster Jeeves, who had stood up down near the front.

"Hold your peace, Jeeves," Elder Bailey told him. "This is not an open floor meeting. You don't even know what I'm fixing to say, so just sit down and hush up. That goes for all of you."

It was a feeble command. And on this morning, Nathan knew, there was more bark than bite in old Elder Bailey. He hunched over so far that his chest was flat against the Bible on the lectern. "Do you believe in osmosis of the heart?" Nathan whispered in Ryne's ear.

"You mean," said Ryne, "like what if the Bible verses you

were reading in your message passed from your Bible up there into Elder Bailey's heart?"

"Exactly," Nathan said.

"Cool," Ryne whispered.

Elder Bailey continued. "Now I'm aware that this is a right serious matter, and I intend to tell you on what grounds I made this decision, in no uncertain terms, if you'll just hear me out. Reason I'm so late this morning is because I spent the better part of a bitter night on my knees in prayer about this."

Ryne whispered: "Looks like he could have used the sleep more."

"I'll give you one minute to state your case," Buster Jeeves said. He was still on his feet.

An old woman on the right side of the widows' pew, said, "We come here for church, not for this. We've heard one message this morning, and I don't expect what you're about to say is a message."

Elder Bailey shuffled the papers he had brought in with him. Then, as if it were an accordion, he unfurled the paper and held up the front page of the Sunday edition of *The Avery County Banner/Herald*. "I suppose most of you seen this over breakfast this morning."

Nathan, who had gotten up late and not had his usual cup of coffee over the Sunday paper, shifted a bit trying to see the front page, but stopped when Ryne said, "It's mom going Sumo and beating the devil out of that preacher-man."

"Oh," Nathan said.

"LORD OF MERCY," ESTHER SAID. She was sitting between Olie and Miriam on the front pew. She had never been so humiliated in all her life. There in the pulpit, in the shaky hands of Elder Luther Bailey, displayed for all and sundry, as though the devil was in her, was the awful picture of Esther Jean O'Casey straddling that nasty little man she had run down "like a big old carnival balloon that the air's been let out of it." There she was, looking like Buddha doing Sumo with his hair wadded up in a bun (if the Buddha had had any hair, and Mary Barry had a shop he went to way back in China).

She made a noise like a whippoorwill and squeezed Olie's hand so hard that his knuckles cracked and his fingertips turned blue. She stamped her feet on the ground so hard Olie thought it was a good thing the heels were lying out in the parking lot or they might have shot somebody. Every eye in the church was fixed on her, she just knew it. She bowed her head and closed her eyes and sobbed in shame. "Lord, forgive me of my sins," she prayed.

"It's all right," Olie said. "Calm yourself, Es'."

Elder Bailey, who had paused only briefly, continued his speech, and two-by-two the eyes turned from Esther on the front row to Esther on the front page. "I spoke with our interim pastor by phone last evening after hearing an account of this outrageous incident, which took place on the town square yesterday afternoon. The preacher here shrank back from his duty to impose, along with the elders of the church, the prescribed discipline for this shameful act of public humiliation of a man of the cloth."

Ryne whispered: "You're the incredible shrinking preacher."

Elder Bailey went on as though he did not notice that Nathan was giggling and that half a dozen people had risen to their feet to be recognized. "Esther O'Casey," he said, "whose big picture you see here, brutally attacked a visiting evangelist to our community and has brought disgrace home to roost on our church. Now, I am going to recommend at the council meeting of the elders that we take measures to expel this woman from our midst and to relieve our interim pastor of his duties. She's not fit to take bread in fellowship with us around the Lord's table. And he's not fit to break it."

If it came as no surprise that Elder Gosset and Buster Jeeves and others rose to be heard, it was a big surprise for Esther and everyone else when Olie O'Casey, a mild-mannered, even-tempered, good-natured, soft-spoken man, stood up and shouted: "Buddy row, I'll not have you slandering my wife."

Olie marched up the stairs to the pulpit, saying, "I can take a lot of things. But I will not have you or anyone else talking ill of my kin. Now … "

"Olie," Esther said. She dried her eyes with the lemon-colored kerchief that matched her shoes. Nathan stood up, sat Ryne down in the minister's chair, and rushed over to the lectern to head off Olie, who was shouting, "You'll not talk about my wife, my friend."

Olie O'Casey approached Elder Bailey, who was bracing himself on the lectern, and stopping short, pointed to the chair reserved for the music director, which was on the side of the chancel opposite the minister's chair. "You best go sit a spell, Elder Bailey, before I have to work you over right here in the pulpit."

For a moment, the congregation held its collective breath while it looked as though Elder Bailey might be fool enough to say something. But when Olie O'Casey, red-faced and shaking, edged closer to him, he thought better of it and staggered over to the chair and collapsed onto it. Nathan, who had stopped dead in his tracks by the lectern, assured for the moment that no violence was forthcoming, limped back and leaned against the front rail of the choir loft to give Olie room to say his piece.

"What you've just heard, people, is part true and part fiction." He held up the front page of the newspaper that Elder Bailey had abandoned on the lectern. "This here's my wife, Esther. You-all know Esther. You'd have to look far and wide for a better woman, as most of you, when you're completely honest, would have to admit. And you-all know, too, about my son, Ryne. Some of you have been less than kind to Ryne. And you know who you are. And I'm disappointed in you."

Esther held the kerchief to her eyes with one hand and gripped Miriam's hand with the other. "Oh, my," she said. "My Olie."

Olie loosened his necktie and unbuttoned the top of his shirt to free his thick neck. He said, "Like Preacher McKee said, Ryne is sick unto death with AIDS." He paused and gritted his teeth, as though he were realizing that awful truth for the very first time. "How many of you-all know what it's like to have your young'n come down with a deadly disease? How many know what that does to you? Well, I'll tell you plain out what it does to you: It flat kills you, slowly, a little at a time. Every day another little piece of your heart just withers up and dies." Olie was weeping then. He paused and, in the pause, there was utter silence.

"Moms and Dads, look at your little children there beside you and ask yourself: 'How would I feel if something so bad was to happen to my child?' 'How would I feel if people didn't seem to care about him?' Well, I can tell you how it feels. It makes you mad and scared and lonely and hateful and bitter … and it makes you long for death yourself. Yesterday, we were heading down to Dollywood with some money our dear brother Elder Travis T. Gosset and our dear sister Lula give to us. We ended up gridlocked in traffic up town, and listened for about an hour to the hatemongering that was going on. Hard as it was, we held our peace. When that so-called preacher came down the road with a big streamer saying PRAISE GOD FOR AIDS!, what do you think, if it had been you in our place, what would you have done? I know you people, and I know how much you love your children, and I can't believe you wouldn't have done the same thing Esther did. So before you go casting stones—"

"Look! What's wrong with Elder Bailey?" Miriam whispered.

Esther looked up at the old man, who was doubled over

with his head below his knees. His frail hands were pawing at his chest. She stood up and called out, "Olie, Preacher McKee, help him!"

Just then Elder Luther Bailey folded in two and slid limply, as if in slow motion, head first down to the floor. Nearly everyone in the church rushed down front in what looked, Esther would later say, like the altar call at a Billy Graham Crusade when Billy says, "If you've come with others, they'll wait." Esther herself and Ryne, whom she had instructed to stay put, made it to the scene just as Olie and Preacher McKee were rolling Elder Bailey over and feeling for a pulse in his thin neck. His eyes rolled back in his head and Esther just knew he was dead.

He wasn't. "There's a pulse," Olie announced. He cradled the limp elder in his arms. "Somebody call for an ambulance. Quick!"

It was nearly twenty minutes before a team of three paramedics—two men and a woman—from the Avery County EMS came busting down the center aisle of the Historic First Church. They took Elder Bailey's vital signs and tried, without success, to revive him to consciousness with smelling salts. He was alive, but just barely, it seemed, as they wheeled him out of the church strapped to a gurney and loaded him and Sue Ella into the back of the ambulance and sped off with lights flashing and sirens screaming to the County Hospital.

Preacher McKee offered a short prayer on behalf of the fallen Elder, then dismissed the congregation. Then, by turns, and in concert, Nathan and Olie and Ryne told Esther over and over again that, no, it was not her fault that Elder Bailey had passed out up there on the pulpit. Esther's mood was dark. For though she had never cared much for Elder Bailey, nor he for her, and everyone knew it—not caring for someone and taking his life were two altogether different things. It was hard to follow what she was saying, even for Esther herself, as she sat in a heap on the pulpit stairs, sobbing and rambling on about how if hemophilia had not run in her family, then she would not have given it to Ryne. After all, it was women who passed it on, and he would not be sick with AIDS, but then again he would not be Ryne, either, she didn't imagine; and if he had not been either Ryne or sick, then what that preacher said at the parade would not have bothered her so much; and that would be a shame in its own right; and if what the preacher said had not bothered her so much, then she would not have attacked him, and if she had not attacked him, then Elder Bailey would not have gotten so worked up, and if he had not gotten so worked up, Olie would not have stormed up there and scared him to death, and he might still be alive today.

They all reminded her that he was, in fact, as far as they knew and last they had seen of him, still alive today. He had passed out, not away. Esther pulled herself together and said, "I'm awful proud to know that." She looked at Ryne, who was standing there with his picture Bible clutched in his small hand and looking down through tear-filled eyes at his little scuffed-up wingtips, and felt even more ashamed of herself. "Lord help me," she said, thinking again just how sad shoes could be. "I'm all the time thinking too much about Esther, just like mother used to say."

She hauled herself up onto her feet and hugged Ryne to her big belly. "Your mama's just a big mess, Ryne," she told him.

Then the five of them—Miriam had joined them—walked together down the center aisle and out to the Nova. Preacher McKee, who was heading over to the hospital, promised he would call as soon as he got word on Elder Bailey's condition.

Miriam tucked Esther into the passenger seat of the Nova and said, "I would have done exactly what you did, Esther. Any loving parent would have. Even Elder Bailey. He knows that." Esther nodded, not knowing whether the "He" who knew that was God or Elder Bailey, and squeezed the tiny woman's hand. Then Olie gunned the motor and honked the horn and they drove off.

Esther was silent on the way home. So was Olie. So was Ryne. But in the heavy silence Esther decided, and so did Olie, he would later tell her, that if Ryne wanted to go see Sister Stryker in Nashville, then go he would.

IT WAS SEVERAL HOURS LATER when Preacher McKee finally called with word on Elder Bailey. Esther was laid up in her bed (to which she had taken shortly after lunch) with a swimming head and a heavy heart; Ryne was in his room watching TV; Olie was out in the backyard breaking the Sabbath building Ryne a TV stand from scrap lumber. Ryne was the first to the phone in the kitchen. "O'Casey residence: This is Ryne," he said when he picked it up. By then, Esther and Olie had made their way in to the ringing phone and stood by the kitchen counter.

"I see," Ryne said. He whispered to his folks, "It's Preacher McKee." Then there was a long pause on Ryne's part as he listened to whatever it was Preacher McKee was telling him. Esther tried to read Ryne's expression. She grabbed Olie's hand and squeezed it.

Finally, Ryne said, "Okay, then, we'll be there … Thanks, Preacher McKee. Bye now."

"He's dead!" Esther said with a gasp, thinking that Ryne meant they would see Preacher McKee at Shelby & Son Funeral Parlor where Elder Bailey was going to be laid out.

"No, he's not," Ryne said.

"He's *not*?" Olie said.

"No."

"Well, what is it, Ryne?" Esther said. "For cryin' out loud, spit it out."

"Preacher McKee said they think he had a massive heart attack. They're running a bunch of tests on him, and the doctor's not sure exactly what's wrong with him, but they're going to keep him in there for a while."

"They do that sometimes, Ryne," Esther instructed. "For obsoletion."

"Observation," Olie corrected.

"For something neither me nor your Daddy here knows anything about."

"Preacher McKee said the doctor said it's right serious. He said they're having a special prayer meeting tonight at the church for Elder Bailey. He wants us there."

"Well, I reckon he needs all the prayer he can get," Esther said. Then, realizing that it had come out a bit more sarcastically than she had intended, she said: "I mean, being so sick and all." The truth be known, Esther reckoned that, whatever the condition of his body, his soul was in worse shape, and she had known for years that Luther Bailey had a bad heart.

It had been ages since the family attended a Sunday evening service at the church. Esther studied the matter and decided that they had attended a service the Sunday they laid her mother to rest, and somebody (quite possibly Elder Bailey himself) had made a remark that did not sit well with Esther, and that was that. They quit going on Sunday evenings. Esther's mother, Miz Ida Bea, had a knack for making you suspect you were headed straight for perdition if you missed a Sunday evening service. Now that the church feud had reached the boiling point, Esther thought it might be the other way around: The more services you attended, the harder it was to imagine that any such people were saved—including yourself if you counted yourself in their number.

Under the circumstances, Esther figured the least they could do was show up and pray for the man—before it was too late.

Not five minutes later, and though her head was still swimming, Esther donned her apron and stood at the counter in the kitchen slicing the chicken she had planned to fry for their Sunday supper into strips to make a chicken casserole to take over to Sue Ella Bailey. Poor woman never said anything ill about anybody, but she had suffered quite a bit of guilt by association with her husband over the years. To Sue Ella's credit, on her better days and the elder's worse days, she would say, "He means well, mostly, but … " She would always leave it at that, but everyone who heard it knew just what she meant—that meaning well and doing well were two different things altogether.

When Ryne had gone back to his room to watch the Braves and Olie had returned to his TV stand project in the backyard, Esther prayed, as she chopped tomatoes, celery, and onions for the casserole: "Lord, no since me trying to fool *you*. You know good and well that I don't care much for Luther Bailey, but (hard as it is for me to believe) *you* do. Help me love him, too, in spite of himself and the mean things he's done to Mother and Ryne. Forgive me for my sins, and they are many, as you well know. In Jesus' sweet name. Amen."

"I'M GOING TO GIVE IT TO YOU STRAIGHT, Mrs. Bailey," said Dr. Marilyn Wright, Chief of Cardiology at Avery County Hospital. "The condition of your husband's heart is atrocious." Sue Ella Bailey was with Nathan McKee, Elder Gosset, and a small, but solemn, assembly that had gathered in a tiny lounge off the hospital's emergency room. "His heart muscle has sustained critical damage, much of it long before his attack this morning. There's no surgical procedure to repair it; it will have to be replaced. He needs a new heart."

Nathan hitched his hand around Sue Ella Bailey's shoulder and ran his thumb over the sharp bones. She was pathetic, as she sat there trembling. Her eyes were impossibly large through the thick lenses of her bifocals, and they darted around the room. She picked at her dress with her twisted fingers and patted down the wisps of her thinning gray hair, which were dull under the harsh fluorescent light. In a high voice barely more than a whisper, or a chirp, she said, "A new heart, you say?"

"I'm afraid it's his *only* hope," Dr. Wright told her.

"A new heart is his only hope," Sue Ella Bailey said. "Yes. I see."

"We believe he is a good candidate for a new heart."

"Yes," Sue Ella Bailey said. "He is."

"So," Dr. Wright continued: "It's a blessing."

"Indeed," said Sue Ella.

"I mean," said Dr. Wright, clearing her throat, "technically, your husband is too old to qualify for a transplant, but the good news is that there's a team of physicians at UT-Knoxville researching heart transplantation with older people. We have already placed him on the transplant list and alerted several organ banks across the country that we need to procure a heart post-haste. It's *urgent.*"

"It is," Sue Ella Bailey said. Her face brightened. Gone was the look of shock that had registered so clearly on her face just moments before. So dramatic was the change in her demeanor that Nathan wondered if she had misunderstood Dr. Wright.

"What's the time frame?" Nathan asked. Now, he was the one who felt himself drooping, as though Sue Ella's burden had been laid on him. She felt better; he felt worse.

He had mixed feelings about the whole business. Elder Luther Bailey was not, in Nathan's estimation (for all it mattered), a good man. He was, in fact, mean spirited and hard hearted. But when it came down to the fundamental human crisis—life and death—the differences between any two men seemed slight compared to the final thing they had in common: mortality. Death plays no favorites.

Neither did Dr. Wright, Nathan assumed. She was a matronly woman with a loud voice and a somewhat gruff manner. "It is impossible to say with any degree of certainty. But, oh, off the record I'd say that without a transplant he's apt to be dead in a month's time. Though it could be an hour. It's just *that* critical."

"I know it is," Sue Ella said, still fingering a few stray wisps of her hair. "How long does it usually take to get a heart?" Again, Nathan was surprised by the strength, the equanimity, in her tone. *Was it apathy?* She asked the question so casually that she might have been asking about how long it would take to process the order for a new transmission for the Bailey's Cadillac Seville.

Dr. Wright shrugged. "I'll know more about that in a few minutes, Mrs. Bailey."

"I'd like to be with him for a while," Sue Ella said. "May I?"

"He was in quite a bit of pain," Dr. Wright said, clutching the patient chart against her chest. "He's had a shot of Demerol, so he's probably pretty dopey and disoriented. But, go ahead: He's all yours."

Sue Ella Bailey took hold of Nathan's hand and led him slowly out of the lounge, through the swinging doors marked "Authorized Personnel Only," down the sterile white corridor that smelled of iodine and cleaning solvents—smells Nathan would forever associate with the ER at Frederick Memorial where Philip died. Elder Luther Bailey was in the last curtained cubicle on the right. His half-open gray eyes were dull, unfocused. The corners of his mouth turned up, in what might have been a feeble smile or a pained grimace, when he saw his wife.

Nathan, who had stopped about three paces into the room, watched Sue Ella take his hand in hers. "You're going to be all *right*," she told him. "*All* right."

Nathan wondered if this were the answer to a prayer—not a malicious prayer, a loving prayer—that she had been praying for years.

In the harsh fluorescent light Elder Bailey, the "Ayatollah of Appalachia," looked broken and weak. Nathan was careful to avoid locking eyes with the man. *Seeing me would do little to comfort the man*, Nathan thought, *and seeing him is doing even less to comfort me.*

"Reckon you're *it*," croaked Elder Bailey. With his free hand, he pointed a bony index finger in Nathan's direction. Then the hand fell softly, as if in slow motion, onto his chest. "You ... " Then he groaned and could not finish.

"I'm *it*," Nathan whispered. *You're playing tag with God, Nathan*, Miriam had told him not long before: *What are you going to do when you're It?*

It.

Nathan looked down at the polished tile beneath his feet. A coronation, a passing of the mantle: *What*, he wondered, *what is happening here*? He was about to ask, somehow, what the elder meant, but Dr. Wright and a nurse entered the room and told him and Sue Ella that they were going to transfer Elder Bailey to the Cardiac Care Unit.

You're right about at least one thing, Dr. Wright, Nathan told himself, as he stepped aside and watched two burly orderlies lay Elder Bailey on a gurney to transport him to a private room in the CCU. *Whatever is going on within Elder Luther Bailey, the oldest elder of the Historic First Church of Tynbee, Tennessee; whatever is going on between him and me; whatever is going on here, right now, in the Emergency Room of the Avery County Hospital: It is* critical.

Nathan drove Sue Ella back to the church to get her car. "I'm really very sorry, Mrs. Bailey. I—"

"Don't be," she told him. She folded her thin hands neatly on her purse in her lap. "*I'm* not. You of all people should know, Nathan, that the Lord's ways are not our ways."

Nathan nodded, and in that moment he might have been driving his mother through the streets of Frederick to pick up some groceries.

"He needs a new heart, *a change of heart*, more than he needs a heart transplant," Sue Ella said. "Maybe the good Lord will see fit to grant him both."

And all the people said, Amen.

A Lottery Ticket

RYNE O'CASEY WAS, for the first time in months, at least as happy as he was sick. The very day on which he went forward and gave his heart to Jesus in, of all places, the Historic First Church, the very day on which Elder Bailey had his massive heart attack in, of all places, the Historic First Church, Ryne's mom and dad came into his room and agreed to take him to Sister Stryker's crusade in Nashville on *one condition*—that he not get his hopes up too high.

Ryne shook on it. His main hope had been that they would agree to take him to Nashville to be a part of Sister Stryker's Greater Tennessee Crusade, whether he ended up getting healed or not. He knew that—no matter what else happened or did not happen—it would be amazing to be there with the throngs packed like sardines into the Nashville Arena.

Thank you, Jesus.

AFTER NATHAN DROPPED SUE ELLA BAILEY OFF at the church at three o'clock, he went straight home, got Peter Nathaniel out of his crib, and sat in the rocker by the sliding-glass patio doors and held his baby boy. He watched the wind *blowing where it listeth* in great gusts that shook the first leaves of Autumn from the sugar maples.They swirled around like big blood-red snowflakes. The baby was warm against his arm, sleeping softly, leading him. *And a little child shall lead them.*

Nathan could not help but wonder if Isaiah, who prophesied that "the mean man shall be brought down, and the mighty man shall be humbled, and the eyes of the lofty shall be humbled: But the LORD of hosts shall be exalted in judgment," had caught a glimpse of Tynbee, Tennessee, on that breezy Sunday morning in late August when Ryne O'Casey gave his heart to Jesus and Elder Luther Bailey was humbled and God tagged Nathan— you're *it*—on the pulpit of the Historic First Church.

You're playing tag with God, Nathan. What are you going to do when you're It?

If it was clear that there was nothing—not one single thing— Nathan could do to save Ryne O'Casey, and Nathan had serious doubts about whether Sister Miranda Stryker, the flamboyant faith healer, could do much for him either, it was clear that he could do a few things. He could baptize him Ryne in the name of the Father, and of the Son, and of the Holy Spirit. He could love him. He could defend him against the bullies, as he had done for Philip so many times. For all his guilt about breaking his own fall and not dying instead of Philip, Nathan at least knew this: He had never, not even once, backed down from one of Philip's bullies—even when he was outnumbered and outsized, scared to death, and bound to get the tar beaten out of him. He had loved Philip, and Nathan knew it, and when his time came, Philip knew it.

Would Ryne know, when his time ran out, that the man who was called to mediate Christ's love loved him—that Jesus loved him?

"WHY DON'T WE GO WITH THEM, Nathan?" Miriam asked.

They were in the single small bathroom in the parsonage

getting ready for the prayer service. Nathan had stepped out of the shower and was drying off. Miriam was at the sink brushing her teeth.

"To the crusade?" Nathan asked.

"In Nashville."

"They're going?"

"They sure are. I called to see how they were holding up after the service this morning, and Esther said Ryne *leapt for joy* when she and Olie told him they would take him to Nashville."

"Well, Miriam. I have misgivings—"

"Of course you do," she said. "Who doesn't?" She turned to face him with a mouth oozing with toothpaste foam and the toothbrush handle sticking out of her mouth.

"True, but Ryne is going to expect this faith healer to heal him," Nathan told her.

"Maybe she will."

"Odds are she won't," said Nathan. "Sometimes I wonder if they don't do more harm than good. I mean, terminally ill people have nothing but hope."

"That's all any of us has, Nathan."

"Well, sure, we're all terminally ill in an ultimate sense, Miriam. In the immediate sense, though, it's another story. Let's say she gets Ryne up on stage, which I think is very unlikely. But, for the sake of argument, let's say she does. She parades him around, lays hands on him, does some hocus pocus, and tells him that if only he has enough faith, God will heal him."

"That's how it usually starts," Miriam said. She was inspecting her teeth in the steamy mirror. "But then he comes home and he's still sick."

"Exactly. Then what?"

"Then, then we deal with it," Miriam said. "Esther said she and Olie cautioned Ryne about getting his hopes up. She said Ryne told her that Sister Stryker herself tells people that it is not always God's will to heal people."

"That's called hedging your bet, Mir'. It's the faith healer's disclaimer, I suppose," Nathan said. "It's the equivalent of the fine print on the back of a lottery ticket that puts you on notice that your chances of being struck twice by lightning during the Friday night drawing are better than your chances of winning the big game."

"Mmm," Miriam said. She was in that stage of female grooming that transferred lipstick from her top lip to her bottom lip. She raised a finger, which meant for him to hush until she could talk again and make a very important point. When her lipstick was to her liking, she turned and looked him dead in the eye and said, "Let's work with your lottery ticket analogy. If you knew for sure that you were going to get struck by lightning twice and drop dead during the Friday night lottery drawing *this week*, but there was a small chance—*any* chance—that if you bought a lottery ticket you would live, wouldn't you be tempted to buy it?"

"Well," Nathan said.

"And don't you even stand there, naked or not, and try to tell me you wouldn't. Because I know you, Daniel Nathan McKee, and I know how peevish you are. You wouldn't buy just one ticket, either. You would buy as many as you could afford with however much money you were able to beg, borrow, and steal."

"Well," Nathan said. "I guess if you put it *that* way—"

"Can you think of any other way to put it, considering Ryne's situation?"

"Hmm," he said. It was Nathan's turn at the sink. Miriam was standing in the doorway with her arms crossed watching him shave.

"Well?" she said.

"Well, in that case," he said, as he rinsed and toweled his face, "Nashville, here we come. If his hopes get dashed, I guess we'll just have to be there to put them back together—as best we can."

"We certainly will," Miriam said.

THE SUNDAY EVENING PRAYER SERVICE for Elder Luther
Bailey was not only well attended, but it was remarkably cordial
by the standards of the Historic First Church. The mood in the
sanctuary was somber and mournful—though Nathan would
not, if he were a betting man, have given short odds on how
many of the somber and mournful petitioners that night were
there for show (beholden as they were to "Filthy Luther") nor
on how many of them were praying for one outcome versus
another. The emergency session of the Board of Elders Luther
Bailey had called just minutes before his heart attack had of
course been postponed, so Nathan could have presided over
the prayer meeting pending an official decision. Elder Travis T.
Gosset told him so just moments before the service was to begin.
"Technically, Preacher, you're well within your rights to officiate.
You are still the pastor of this church, and, if I have anything to
do with it, you will be *long* after the postponed meeting."

"I'm not one for technicalities," Nathan told him, "in courts
or churches. I appreciate your support, Elder, but I think now is
the time for healing."

"Yeah, the devil is in the details, as they say." Elder Gosset
patted Nathan on the back—and it might have been the hearty
pat of his father's hand. "If it helps at all," he said, "I think you're
making the right call here."

Elder Gosset ended up leading the service. Though he had
suffered a lot of abuse over the years at the hands of Luther
Bailey and those who did his bidding, Elder Travis T. Gosset had
the respect of every member of the congregation. They might
not have cared for his convictions, but by God he had them
and integrity, too. He was a man of his word—and a Christian
gentleman, if not always a gentle man.

He was the anti-Luther.

Nathan and Miriam McKee sat with the O'Caseys on the back row of the church and listened as Elder Gosset updated the congregation on Elder Bailey's condition. "Let me begin by saying that Sue Ella asked me personally to send her sincere thanks to all of you for your prayers on Elder Bailey's behalf and for the food so many of you sent over this afternoon. She said to tell you that she loves all of you, her church family, very much."

There was a long pause. No one at the Historic First Church of Tynbee had ever in Nathan's hearing used that term—family— to describe their church body.

Nathan shrugged. *Were the congregants of the Historic First Church, after all, just brothers and sisters? Were their squabbles nothing more than a highland version of sibling rivalry?* Nathan knew that every man present—and every woman, too, for that matter—could recall standing out in the yard of his childhood home toe-to-toe with a brother and trading licks until at last their love and loyalty (or hunger and exhaustion) got the better of their anger and they helped each other back into the house to dress their wounds and get some victuals.

Elder Gosset stood there as a wise father might after witnessing a fistfight between his sons. His gray hair, which was usually slicked back with Vitalis, needed combing. He looked tired—battle weary even—and his voice was sorrowful. "Now, folks, let me bring you up to speed on Elder Bailey. He is in right critical condition. They've placed him in a room on the Cardiac Care Unit over't the County Hospital. He suffered a massive heart attack this morning right here, as most of you saw with your own eyes. The heart specialist, a doctor by the name of Wright, ran a number of tests and says Luther needs his heart replaced as soon as it can be arranged. Let us pray."

Elder Gosset closed his long, sincere prayer with the following petition: "Most gracious Lord, let us all—*all*— beginning with me, consider our need for a change of heart. In the name of Jesus, your beloved Son, our Friend, we pray. And all the people of the Lord said—"

The congregation lifted its voice in one accord. "Amen."

Elder Gossett leaned down close to the microphone. "Before we adjourn, I would like to invite whoever feels led, or just plain feels like it, to come down and join me in prayer here before the altar. If you don't want to, that's your business, and you can feel free to go on home."

Elder Gosset climbed down from the pulpit and knelt at the altar. Miriam made her way to the piano. And then, as if a floodgate had opened, the congregation flowed down to the front of church. Only the very old and the very stubborn on each side stayed put. But even they hung their heads, for all the world as if in prayer for Elder Luther Bailey who needed a new heart, for themselves who needed a new heart.

Nathan found a place beside the organ carrel, which was silent without Sue Ella Bailey's off-key playing, and knelt down to make his own peace with God. He cast off his seminary eloquence and prayed simply, "Lord Jesus, please help me. I've proved I cannot help myself."

EARLY THE NEXT MORNING Esther and Ryne went to Avery County Hospital to kill two birds with one stone. Ryne needed his monthly bloodwork and Esther wanted to pay her respects to Bertha Snowden, her lifelong friend, who had undergone some "private surgery," as she explained it to Ryne. When he asked what that meant, she said, "Now you don't have no need to know about all that."

They had waited for an hour in the laboratory waiting room for a five-minute visit, during which they drew five vials of blood from Ryne's arm, then Esther led Ryne up to the third floor. When they got to Miz Snowden's door, Esther said: "You wait right here, Ryne, in case Bertha's not decent—and I don't imagine she would be, poor woman, having been put through all that private surgery." Then she disappeared into Miz Snowden's room with a Tupperware container full of fresh-baked molasses cookies and a vase full of lavender camelia clippings she had worried over until she found just the ones she thought Miz Snowden might like best.

Ryne waited patiently outside Miz Snowden's door at the end of the corridor for what seemed like two hours—though his mom would later set him straight: "It wasn't no more than five minutes, Ryne," she said, then added, "though I don't imagine it could have been much less than that, either." Ryne fidgeted around in place for a long time. Then he began easing his way down the hall, which was bustling with people pushing shiny metal carts in and out of patient rooms while messages squawked over the P.A. system. Ryne was going from door to door, almost like he was trick-or-treating, reading the names and trying to determine whether they were in alphabetical order. He passed the nurses' station and kept going through some metal swinging doors and continued reading the nameplates. Halfway down the hall, he came across the typed nameplate for: "Bailey, Luther E."

"*Elder* Bailey?" he whispered aloud. Ryne glanced back toward the swinging doors and, when he was sure the coast was clear (of his mom), he gently nudged open the large wooden door and peeked in. There on the hospital bed was old Elder Bailey, with an IV in his arm and a green air tube stuck up his nose. He looked dead. D-E-A-D dead.

Ryne approached the bed very slowly and very carefully, a baby tiptoe step at a time. The poor man had given up the ghost. At the bedside, Ryne leaned over for a better look, to see if there was any sign of life and, if not, what death looked like before they fixed up your hair the way they had fixed up Miz Ida Bea's hair when they laid her out at Shelby & Son Funeral Parlor.

Was his chest moving? Was his heart beating? Did he have a pulse?

Closer still, until his ear was within inches of Elder Bailey's chest, and suddenly the old man let out a loud gurgling cough and his wet little eyes trained on Ryne.

"Ahh!" Ryne shouted. "You're alive."

"Not for long," Elder Bailey mumbled. His eyes were bugging out. It would be impossible to say who was more startled—Ryne O'Casey or Elder Luther Bailey—who emitted a weak squeal that sounded just like the electronic bleep used to cover up cuss words on the cable channels his mom told him not to watch. Each looked at the other, wide-eyed and open-mouthed, as if he had seen a ghost.

Elder Bailey was trying to say something else, but though his lips were moving no sound was coming out of his mouth.

Ryne began backing away from the bed. "I'm sorry, Elder Bailey. I didn't mean to scare you," he said, his voice quavering. "I just saw your name on the door, so I, uh, I thought I would stop in and tell you that I hope you get to feeling better real soon. Mom said they have a new—well, a used—heart for you. And they're gonna put it in, and fix you up good as new."

The old man said something—maybe: "Can't you see I'm dead already?"—but his voice was so weak it was impossible to tell for sure. He was crying.

"No, you're not," Ryne said. "I mean, if you said what I thought you did." He backed up another step or two toward the door. "And even if your new heart doesn't work, and I bet it will, then we'll carry you with us to Nashville and we'll get Sister Stryker to fix your old heart—I didn't mean old, like *old* old, but the heart you have now."

Elder Bailey fixed his eyes on Ryne, but did not really seem to see him. Tears were running down the sides of his wrinkled face. He was panting so hard his head was bobbing. Then he said something else that Ryne could not quite make out, but it sounded like, "Been dead for years."

Maybe it was the medicine they were giving him, Ryne thought, but Elder Bailey was making no sense at all. Ryne walked back over to the bed and put his hand on Elder Bailey's thin pajama-covered arm and said, "And, since I've already told everyone else, I wanted to say thank you forgiving me, I mean *for giving* me that TV and—"

Ryne stopped talking. The man's mouth opened wide and his cracked bluish lips were moving but, again, no sound came out—not even a mumble that Ryne could try to interpret later for his mom and replay in his bed late at night.

Ryne stood frozen in place staring at the man. He tried to move his feet, but they wouldn't budge. "I didn't mean to upset you."

Elder Bailey was wheezing and coughing.

If I don't get out of here, I am going to kill him, Ryne thought. The man's chest heaved. He lay there looking pitiful as a skinny baby. Ryne inched his way back, around the base of the IV machine and the corner of the vanity, toward the door, feeling behind him with his hands. He groped for the doorknob and tugged it open.

"Don't leave me now," Elder Bailey seemed to say, when Ryne had pulled the door completely open. He was crying again, harder this time, and Ryne stood paralyzed in the doorway.

"I won't," he said. "I'm not going anywhere. I'll just stand here by the door."

Just then his mom came upon him. "*There* you are," she said, heaving a big sigh of relief. She crossed her heart and said, "Lord of mercy, Ryne, I ought to tan your fanny but good for this. I've been from here to yonder looking for you, worried sick." Then she noticed the nameplate on the door. "Elder Bailey?" she said. "What on God's green earth is going on here, Ryne?"

She leaned over and stuck her head in the door. "Hey, Elder Bailey," she said. "You feeling all right?"

He was still crying. Esther slipped past Ryne and approached the bed. Ryne stayed in the doorway. "Elder Bailey? What's the matter?" He said nothing. He shook his head from side to side. "I'll fetch you a nurse," Esther said, with one hand on his forehead and the other on the call button.

Elder Bailey raised his hand. "It's not that," he said, and then said something else that sounded to Ryne like, "I'm already dead." His voice was weak and weary, and he was slurring. Esther very discreetly pressed the button, then said, "Okay, then," and let it slip back down by the bedrail.

Elder Bailey fell asleep then, bless his heart, just minutes before the nurses arrived to tend to him.

Been dead for years.

Not Without Honor

T-MINUS-ONE AND COUNTING DOWN. Something big was going to happen, Ryne just knew it: something really big.

If it was the most exciting month of Ryne's life, it was also the longest, but finally the big day—Friday, September 24—arrived. It was a cool, breezy Autumn day in the highlands, and the mountain range was golden one minute and charcoal gray the next as puffs of cottony clouds moved across the sky gentle as sheep. It was as if, Ryne said, the day could not decide whether it wanted to be sunny or cloudy—so it decided to be both.

"That's pretty much how life goes," said Ryne's dad, as he backed the Gossets' big old maroon Club Wagon twelve-passenger van out of the O'Casey's driveway. "Life is partly cloudy."

"Or partly sunny," said Ryne, "depending on how you look at it."

"Hear, hear," said Elder Gosset. "Partly sunny it is."

Elder Gosset was in the passenger seat beside Ryne's dad. Ryne's mom and Lula Gosset were in the second seat. Preacher McKee and his wife Miriam and their baby son, Peter Nathaniel, tucked into a carseat between them, were in the third seat. And T. K. Kirby and Ryne had the backseat, which was made for four, all to themselves. The van was huge, and they all had plenty of room to stretch out—even Ryne's mom, who often complained that the Nova was simply not a fat-friendly vehicle.

"I reckon we'll hit 40/75 in Knoxville," Ryne's dad said, and at length he assured them (and especially Ryne's mom) that it was not another of his infamous shortcuts, and Ryne and his mom breathed a sigh of relief when Elder Gosset confirmed that it was indeed the best way to get to Nashville. "I figure it'll take us near-about four hours if we make good time."

They had to stop a few times along the way so that Miriam could change the baby, who had become fussy, and Lula Gosset could stretch her arthritic legs, which tended to get stiff and achy. Their first stop was at a filling station in Oak Ridge, Tennessee, and Ryne's mom couldn't help but wonder aloud whether the Oak Ridge Boys still lived there in Oak Ridge. Everyone in the van except the baby told her, at least twice, that they might still live there, but it seemed doubtful. Ryne said the best kept secret about Oak Ridge was not the Oak Ridge Boys' street address, if they did happen to still live there, but rather that it was the "secret city" built as part of the Manhattan Project during World War II to develop atomic bombs.

When she heard this, Ryne's mom said, "Let's get on down the road, Olie. We're not making too good a time frittering around trying to get a glimpse of the Oak Ridge Boys. And besides, I don't imagine we need to be breathing in all these radiology fumes from those big old secret atomic bombs."

Elder Gosset cleared his throat, Miriam coughed, and Ryne just plain laughed out loud.

Ryne's mom did wonder aloud, though, whether those secret bombs had anything to do with why William Lee Golden, the gray-haired Oak Ridge Boy with the beard that hung to his knees, had gray hair and whether he once had golden hair. Ryne's dad said he reckoned William Lee Golden's gray hair might have more to do with age than radiation. And on they went, having a good time if not making good time, wending their way west through the rolling hills of middle Tennessee in Autumn.

It ended up taking closer to five hours, but for all Ryne cared it could have taken fifteen. He was having the time of his life. He and T. K. Kirby and Preacher McKee talked baseball trivia, trading cards, and mostly comic books. The three of them shared a passion for Spiderman, whom they dubbed the superlative superhero to set him apart from all the other noble but lesser specimens like Batman and Superman.

Nathan told them that his late younger brother, Philip, ranked right up there with Ryne for world's biggest Spiderman fan. They were the *superlative* fans of the *superlative* super-hero.

T. K. Kirby said, "It's t-time." He knelt on the seat facing the back of the van and pulled his duffel bag from the luggage in the cargo area. "You th-thought I was k-kidding about this." He reached into a side pocket of the duffel bag and pulled out a sealed issue of *Amazing Fantasy, Number 15*, dated August 15, 1962. Sure enough, it was in mint condition.

Ryne looked at it. He was speechless.

"It's m-m-my n-n-nest egg."

"Nest egg? Golden egg is more like it," Ryne said. *"Whoa!* This is amazing." He held the precious comic book with its side edges flat against his palms. He had seen the cover only in his price guides and trading magazines. It featured Spiderman with a thug called the First Burglar in a green Sunday-go-to-meeting suit slung over his arm and a caption that read: "Though the world may mock Peter Parker, the timid teenager … It will soon marvel at the awesome might of Spider-Man!" Ryne never dreamed he would get to hold it in his own two hands and see it face-to-face. He knew what it was worth—a fortune! Overstreet had it listed at forty-two thousand dollars (with a rating of Mint to Near Mint), though at auction it would bring a lot more. Ryne would have been less awestruck if it were the Holy Grail he held in his hands and not that Spiderman comic book.

T. K. Kirby authorized Ryne to remove the comic book from its protective plastic sheath and read it, but Ryne shook his head and said, "No way. I'm not going to be the one responsible for taking it from mint to near-mint. Don't ever take it out of its sleeve. Even a single fingerprint could cost you thousands."

Nathan refused the offer, too, most emphatically after Ryne appraised its true value. "That's worth more than all my earthly possessions," he said.

"Put together," added Miriam.

Nathan told Ryne that he had a cargo trunk full of comic books and trading cards that had belonged to his brother Philip. "I don't have the slighest idea exactly what's in there but the whole chest of buried treasure can be yours for a song."

"Which song?" Ryne asked.

"Oh, a few bars of the theme from Spiderman will do just fine," Nathan told him.

No sooner had the words left Preacher McKee's mouth than Ryne was singing, "Spiderman, Spiderman, does whatever a spider can … Look out! Here comes the Spiderman."

They all clapped, not so much because he had talent but because he had guts. T. K. Kirby stuck both index fingers in his mouth and let go a whistle so shrill the baby stopped fussing, and when the applause died down, Nathan said, "One steamer chest full of buried treasure due and payable to Master Ryne O'Casey directly upon our return from the country music capital of the world."

"So," Ryne asked, "just exactly whatever happened to poor old Philip?" The chatter in the van faded to silence. The roar of the big eight-cylinder engine seemed to quiet to a rumble, and even the baby, who had begun fussing again, hushed up to hear the story of his poor old uncle.

"Oh, it's kind of a long story, Ryne," Preacher McKee said.

"We're not even halfway there yet," Ryne told him. "You could at least tell us half the story on the way to Nashville, and the other half on the way back."

"Ryne," his mom said, clearing her throat. She turned and gave him one of her stern looks intended to let him know that she meant business. She tilted her head down so that she was eyeballing him over the rims of her glasses. It was the same look she had given him a few weeks before when they were on their way to see Bertha Snowden at County Hospital and Ryne kept trying to get her to explain what "private surgery" meant.

Ryne's mom cut her eyes over at Preacher McKee and said, "That child always could talk a blue streak." Then she turned back to Ryne. "Now, why don't you do us a few more bars of that Spiderman song or something, Ryne, or tell them about that new model car your assembling."

Again, Ryne did not bother telling her that the model car was really a Panzer tank. He *got* her drift, finally, and felt embarrassed. His dad had turned the radio on for the first time since they had left Tynbee, and Crystal Gayle was singing, "Don't It Make Your Brown Eyes Blue?" and all Ryne could think, as he slumped down in the seat, was don't it make my white face red? His mom was right. It was clear that Preacher McKee did not really want to go into it, and who could blame him? But, then again, it seemed like it might do him some good to talk about it. Besides, his mom always said talking things out always made *her* feel better.

We were having a good time, laughing and cutting up and carrying on, then I had to go and ruin it by bringing up something sad.

Ryne said, "I'm sorry, Preacher McKee. Never mind," and then he saw Miriam turn her head and give Preacher McKee a look that was not all that different from the look his mom had given Ryne, and Preacher McKee started, very slowly at first, explaining what had happened to poor old Philip.

Preacher McKee picked up momentum as he went along. He told them about Philip's learning disability and how other children sometimes picked on him and called him "retarded."

"I know how that f-feels," T. K. Kirby said. "They d-do it m-me, too. They used to c-call me p-porky p-pig and ask me to say, 'that's all f-folks!'"

Esther said, "Well, don't you cast your pearls before them swines, T. K.."

They all got a kick out of the pun, except Esther, who said she did not think there was anything funny about children teasing each other. Then she turned and looked T. K. in the eye and said, "You sure aren't retarded."

They all agreed. He sure wasn't.

"I don't know how many pearls you got, T. K.," Ryne added, "but don't go casting your *Amazing Fantasies* before them swines either. They wouldn't treat them with respect."

Preacher McKee related events from his and Philip's childhood years, which he said he had not thought about for years—at least six, which was about the time when the story took a tragic turn for the worse. He described the horrendous plummet from Skyler Heights that claimed Philip's life and how he had felt angry and guilty ever since and could not, until the previous month when he had all but had a nervous breakdown in the church graveyard, bring himself to think about the accident.

Ryne could not keep himself—did not try to keep himself—from crying. He said, "It's just one of those strange things, when you're trying to do a good thing and something bad happens. Like the person who donated the sick blood I got."

"You're wise beyond your years, Ryne," Preacher McKee told him. He finished his story with a tribute to Philip. He said,

"Philip squeezed more life into twenty years than most people live in eighty."

"Bless your heart," Ryne's mom said. "God bless your heart."

IT WAS 3:30 IN THE AFTERNOON when Olie pulled the Club Wagon into the parking lot of the Airport Motel 8, "conveniently located just five miles east of downtown Nashville and directly across Interstate 40 from the Nashville International Airport." Esther had called the week before and reserved three double rooms on the ground floor (because Lula Gosset, she told the clerk, could hardly be expected to climb up a flight of stairs; just climbing in and out of their big old van was trouble enough). After Elder Gosset checked them in, then they found their rooms, and Olie, T. K., and Preacher McKee unloaded their luggage from the back of the van.

Then, while the womenfolk set up housekeeping, the menfolk—and that included Ryne—piled back into the van and drove downtown to scope out the Nashville Arena, which Elder Gosset believed was not far from the banks of the Cumberland River. When they stopped at a Union 76 to gas up the van, Ryne and T. K. raided the brochure racks and picked up literature on every tourist attraction within a hundred-mile radius of Nashville.

The crusade was scheduled to begin at 7:30, and Ryne couldn't wait. Since there was no reserved seating for the service (the man who looked like a heavyset Dr. J said seating was on a "first come, first seated" basis), and it was already nearly four o'clock, Ryne proposed that he and T. K. be dropped off at the arena now so they could save a place in line while the others went back to the Motel 8 to pick up the women and the baby. He made his case: Not only did they need to be sure to get a seat in the handicap section on the lower level—on account of Lula's knees, and at a healing service there were bound to be thousands of handicapped people—but wouldn't it be a crying shame if the crusade sold out after they had driven all that way?

"You have argued your case well, Ryne," said Olie issuing his verdict. "But let's do it this way. Seeing as how we've not had supper, I say we go back to the Motel 8 and fetch the womenfolk, grab a quick bite to eat, and rush back down here to the service. We'll have time to spare."

Ryne was not sure about that. As the van made its way west on Hermitage Avenue toward the Nashville Arena complex at the corner of Broadway and Fifth Avenue, Ryne found it impossible to sit still. He fidgeted and squirmed and stared wide-eyed in hopes he would be the first to spot the twenty-two-story tower next to Adelphia Stadium, home of the Tennessee Titans.

"Whoa! Way cool," Ryne said. "There it is." Already the parking lot was filling with Greyhounds and church buses from every type of church Ryne had ever heard of from as far away as Columbus, Ohio. "Fine, Dad," Ryne conceded. "I guess we'll have to do it your way. But don't blame me if it sells out."

"We won't *let it* sell out, Ryne," Preacher McKee told him. "We'll do whatever it takes to get into the crusade."

IT WAS 4:58 P.M. TIME TO GO. It was Friday afternoon at rush hour, and the leading edge of the cold front coming in from the west brought torrential downpours, so traffic was extremely heavy, the going very slow. At least they beat the dinnertime crowd to Shoney's and got a seat for their party of eight and a half with no wait. Everyone except Ryne made several trips to the food bar (his mom made four, not including her first trip, which she informed Ryne did not count, because it was only for soup and a salad).

Ryne told them all he was too excited to eat, but the main reason was that he felt horrible.

Several times during the meal Ryne fought the urge to lay his head on the table. He simply could not risk it. If he laid his head on the table, his mom would surely cancel the trip to the crusade and rush him back to the motel and put him in bed. Sister Stryker was his only hope of getting healed, and he did not want to be laid up in bed at the Motel 8 when he needed to be laid out on the stage of the Nashville Arena.

They were only going to attend the first two sessions of the four-session Nashville crusade—Friday night, which was the opening session, and the Saturday morning session. After the morning service, which was to begin at ten the next morning, they would have about four hours for sightseeing before heading back home to Tynbee.

Preacher McKee had to get back to deliver the Sunday sermon, and they all kind of wanted to be there on Sunday afternoon when Elder Bailey was scheduled to have his heart-transplant surgery: A suitable heart was finally available—and none too soon. The elder's heart was, as Ryne's mom put it, *totaled.*

Ryne had wanted to attend all four services, of course, but two out of four wasn't bad. It just meant that he had to find a way to get to Sister Stryker *tonight* (he could not be sure that she even did healing miracles at the Saturday morning service, and the Prayer Counselor he called on the toll-free number said he *thought* she healed at every service but he didn't want to say for certain).

Uh-oh.

"You're peaked, Ryne," his mom said. She laid the back of her hand on his forehead (in sort of a reverse palm heal attack) and just made a serious face.

"I'm just excited, Mom," Ryne told her. That was a good part of the truth. The *whole* truth was that his stomach was burning, every muscle in his body ached, he was starting to chill, and the very sight of all that food on the table made him want to vomit.

All of the sudden Ryne started crying. He definitely did not want to do that, not in front of T. K. and Preacher and Miz McKee and Elder and Lula Gosset. "It's pollen, Mom," he told her, trying to smile. "It's all those onions in your salad."

Esther put her hand on her hip and gave him a look. Then she said, "I guess I had that one coming, Ryne."

Preacher McKee, who had not eaten much either, wiped his mouth with his folded napkin and laid it on his plate. Then he got up and said, "How's about you and I take a little walk, Ryne, while everybody else is finishing up?"

Thank God. Ryne was sure that his mom felt a fever and, knowing her, was on the verge of calling the crusade trip off and taking him back to the Motel 8 where she could nurse him back to health. What she did not seem to realize is that all that was a lost cause. There was not enough Tylenol and juice in the world to help him now. Doctor Lord Jesus was the only one who could possibly heal him. Ryne got up and placed his napkin on the plate of food his mom had fixed him, which he had barely touched, and walked hand-in-hand with Preacher McKee toward the exit.

They sat on a curb in the parking lot on the side of the restaurant that had no windows. "I figured you could use a break," said Preacher McKee.

Ryne nodded and shrugged his shoulders.

A long silence followed before Ryne, sure that his secret was safe with Preacher McKee, admitted, "I feel awful."

"I know you do. It's been a busy day, buddy," Preacher McKee said. "Truth is, I'm not feeling so good myself. Ever had a day when you can't seem to really wake up?"

"You mean, like, every day," Ryne said.

Preacher McKee hitched his arm around Ryne's shoulder and pulled him close, and Ryne melted against him and began crying again. Then a strange thing happened. Preacher McKee started crying, too, and Ryne wondered, but did not ask, whether he was crying about his brother Philip. He figured he was.

Neither could later say how long they sat there together on that curb crying, but it must have been a good long while, because when Ryne's mom came across them she said that she almost hadn't seen them. It was dusk.

"WE'LL DROP YOU OFF and then go find us a parking spot," Olie said. He weaved the van through the throngs of people and caravans of tour buses and church vans converging on the intersection of Broadway and Fifth. Olie pulled up close to the curb in front of the main entrance to the Nashville Arena. It was 6:40 p.m. To Ryne's great relief the crusade was not a sellout— yet. But he had little doubt that it would be before long. People were pouring into the arena and jamming into portals in search of a good seat. In under ten minutes, Olie and Elder Gosset joined them in the grand corridor of the Nashville Arena.

"Show time," Ryne said as he led the way to the nearest portal and asked directions to the handicap seating section on the ground level.

A short, stocky man with a black-and-white referee's shirt with "EVENT STAFF" printed on it broke the bad news—the floor-level handicap section was full. The good news, he said, was that each of the arena's four levels had a handicap-accessible section.

"Please," Ryne said, but the event staffer said he was sorry but the fire marshall, not he, made the rules. Lula Gosset even tapped her cane against the floor and made as if she were about to fall. But the event staffer simply shook his head and said he was sorry.

Nathan called the event staffer aside with a sideways nod of his head, and they took a little stroll down the portal toward the steps leading down to the arena floor. Ryne strained his ear, but could not make out, over the chatter of thousands and the organ music that was piping through the sound system, what Preacher McKee was telling the man. So he leaned against a cold sidewall of the portal and watched very closely for any clue about how the conversation was going. Preacher McKee talked nonstop to the man, who at the beginning of the conversation was shaking his head the whole time but was shaking it less as the preacher said more. Then the stocky man raised his right hand with two fingers sticking up like a peace sign. *For a moment, Ryne thought Preacher McKee might have resorted to threatening him so that he was trying to make peace? But no.*

Then Nathan was heading quickly back to them. "Okay, we're all set," he told them. "I practically had to twist his arm, but he authorized two of us to go down to the floor in front of the stage. Ryne and Olie, or Ryne and Esther."

"How about Ryne and *you*, Preacher McKee," Esther said.

"Yeah," Ryne said. "That sounds good, unless you want to go with me, Miz Gosset, and get Sister Stryker to heal your knees."

All eyes turned on Lula Gosset, who smiled and said, "You two go on ahead. Maybe I'll get this strong-strapping elder here to escort me down when she starts her healing."

Ryne wondered if Miz Gosset, too, thought that, after Ryne, who definitely needed a healing, Preacher McKee seemed to need a healing more than the rest of them (which was saying something, because her knees were, as Ryne's mom put it, twisted up something fierce). They all hugged Ryne and wished him well, and Esther again felt his forehead with the back of her hand and made a funny face. They arranged to meet Ryne and Nathan at the right side of the main door in the grand corridor when the service was over. Then they headed off to catch an elevator up to the second level.

The event staffer, now looking a little sheepish, directed Ryne and Nathan through a portal that led down to the handicap section right in front of the stage, where the orchestra pit would have been if Sister Stryker had an orchestra instead of the Jehovah's Jammers band. The man, who Preacher McKee now addressed as Ricky, said: "Tell Sheila that Blue-C-101 authorized your access to the area." Preacher McKee thanked him again, then he picked Ryne up and carried him down the stairs, where he relayed the cryptic code to Sheila, who smiled and brought out two padded folding chairs and set them up between two people in wheelchairs.

Ryne felt a sudden burst of energy, not unlike the buzz you get from too much sugar or red food dye number two when your mom let you drink Hawaiian Punch. He surveyed the whole arena, from the stage just six feet in front of him, to the huge crowd that extended all the way up to the nosebleed sections where you needed a telescope just to be able to see the arena floor, to the four-square scoreboard just overhead on which, he and Preacher McKee agreed, Spiderman would sit if he took a notion to attend a Nashville Kats game or a crusade. They looked all around but could not spot Esther and Olie and the rest of their party. They could have been anywhere in the huge arena, Ryne thought, though his mom should have been easy enough to spot and not just because she was four-by-heavy but because she was wearing a white dress with softball-size blood-red polka dots.

What an incredible unreality check!

It seemed so real, so impossibly real, that it had to be unreal. The atmosphere in the arena was charged like a gigantic force field. The droning buzz of the fifteen thousand congregants sounded like a fleet of F-16s on takeoff.

Gearing up! Cleared for takeoff! All systems go!

Ryne might have suspected it was all just a dream if he had not dreamed about the crusade every night for the past three weeks. But all those dreams, even the best of them, the most vivid of them, was nothing compared to this—the real thing in all its splendid glory. *No, I am awake all right, more awake than I have ever been, here with Preacher McKee, inches from the stage of the Nashville Arena amidst a sea of people who look so familiar, though I have never ever been to Nashville and never ever met a single one of them.*

At exactly 7:30 p.m. the house lights dimmed. Ryne and Preacher McKee rose to their feet, along with everyone else in the arena who was not in a wheelchair (and even some of them got up). They stood in silence before the stage, which was pitch dark except for the red lights on the front of Elder Butts's organ and the huge stack of amplifiers. The shrill hiss of feedback filled the air and then came the familiar voice of the ring announcer: "La-dies and gen-tle-man, child-ren *of* Gawd: Welcome to the Greater Tennessee Crusade for Healing and Renewal." Spotlights slashed wildly through the arena as the voice intoned, "Join me in welcoming to the stage the Reverrrend Sisterrr Miran-da Stry-kerrr!"

The audience went nuts. People whooped and whistled and screamed. They clapped their hands and stamped their feet. They waved their arms and shook their tambourines way up high in the air. Elder Butts was at the organ pounding out a funky rhythm and the band played on. Ryne made a megaphone with his cupped hands and, with all his breath, screamed, "All right! Bring *on* the Sister!"

He trained his eyes on the right side of the stage, from which Sister Stryker always made her glorious entrance, and was, he would later contend, the first to see her just before she bolted out onto the stage.

Sister Stryker shot across the stage as though she had been blasted out of a bazooka. She twirled around in tight little pirouettes like the Tazmanian Devil and spun across the stage. "Just look at her go, will you!" Ryne shouted, and Preacher McKee just stood there with his jaw hanging to his knees and took in the wild scene unfolding just a few feet in front of them.

Sister Miranda Stryker was in rare form that early Autumn night in Nashville. No: She was never better. She had on a purple sari with dazzling sequins and a forest green sash, and high on her head sat a purple turban with a green tassel that matched her pumps. The Sister was dripping gold, and on that magical Friday night in the Nashville Arena all that glittered *was* gold, and everything she touched turned to gold.

Sister Stryker got a goody jones on then. She clapped her hands nonstop—hand-over-hand—and led the congregation in rousing renditions of several camp-meeting praise songs. "This is the day—HALLELUJAH; this is the day—OF-THE-LOAD, -CHIL'; that the Load hath made, that the Load hath made; I will rejoice—AND-YOU-WILL,-TOO; I will rejoice—STOMP-YOUR-FEET,-Y'ALL; and be glad in it, and be glad in it. ooooOOOOHHHH this is the day …"

The songs went on for a full fifteen minutes before rising to a climactic crescendo with the organ going full blast, cymbals crashing, drums banging, and the bass bumping a funky rhythm. Then it stopped. But the audience didn't, and Sister Stryker kept saying, "Well praise his wonderful name!" and "Bless the Lord! O my soul," with Elder Butts, as usual, echoing her every word on the organ.

After reading the scripture passage her sermon was based on—John 7:53 through 8:11—the Sister directed them to set their blessed hides down, hush up their mouths, and open their hearts. She explained, "When I was a little old child, and yes, hard as it is for some of y'all to believe, I was a *little* old child at one time. Little old skinny child. Anyway, I was reading this here story about the woman taken in adultery, and I thought it meant she was caught being a grownup, you know, a *ad-ult.* I figured that an adulteress was a growed-up woman. Suddenly, my eyes be open, and everything came clear. So I went and ax my mama, I say 'Mama, what do it feel like being a adulteress?' Mama said, 'You fixin' to find out, young lady,' and child she proceeded to tear me up so bad that, listen child, she put the fear of *Gawd* in my heart by way of my fanny, and I think it was right then I knew I was called to do the Load's work."

Ryne was clapping; he could relate. "Tell it, Sister," he said, and he was sure that for just an instant—though it was a long instant as instants go—their eyes locked and she paused, which is something Sister Stryker never did.

"Anyway, y'all," She seemed momentarily to have lost her place. "Where was I? Anyway, y'all—Oh, yeah, well, anyway I had to find out the hard way," the Sister told them, back in herself then, somewhat. "When I was childish like that I came across another word as I was studying my Sunday School lesson one Saturday night. A – G – A – P - E. Ah – gah – pe. I knew it meant *love*, but when I went to my little old student dictionary and looked it up, it said the word 'agape' meant slack-jaw stunned with your mouth a-hanging wide open. Now I'm here to tell you, chil', that THAT is what God's unconditional love does to us *all* when it lays a-holt to your heart: It leaves us stunned with our mouths hanging wide-open because *Gawd's* agape love knows *no* bounds!"

Sister Stryker went on for about forty-five minutes explaining just what God's unconditional agape love was all about and how Jesus left everybody he met slack-jaw stunned with their mouth hanging wide open. It was the kind of love, she said, that Jesus had for the woman taken in adultery, for the IRS folk of his day, for people born blind and dumb and crippled up and bleeding. It meant compassion, fearlessness, tenderness, forgiveness, and a whole lot more—*no matter what*! She closed her sermon by urging all of them to practice loving everyone in the world unconditionally, with agape love—"and you just watch," she said, "how people who are hurting, bloodied and beaten up and bruised by the stones life hurls at 'em, so used to being condemned and scorned, embrace that agape love slack-jawed with their mouths a-hanging *wide* open."

Then, after she said a long prayer asking God to touch and bless everyone there in the Nashville Arena and everyone watching her show on TV, she invited all and sundry to come forward and profess Jesus as Lord and Savior and be healed.

Ryne was on his feet before the last word left her mouth. He grabbed Preacher McKee's hand and together they climbed up the stairs leading to the stage, and, just as he had dreamed it, Ryne was the first in line to be healed. The house lights dimmed again, and through the darkness two ushers approached them. "And just what can Lord Jesus do for you, my young man?" the older of the two asked.

"I have AIDS," Ryne told them. "I don't have long to live unless Doctor Lord Jesus decides to heal me."

The usher nodded and looked Preacher McKee in the eye. "Are you his father?"

"No," said Preacher McKee, "I'm just a friend who happens to be his pastor."

"Well, step right up the both of you," the man said in a voice like Uncle Remus', "and let's just see what Jeez wants to do about dis." He took Ryne by the hand and led them out to the center of the stage, where Sister Stryker was standing, her head bowed in prayer, in the bright white glow of a single spotlight. The man who sounded like Uncle Remus whispered a few words into her ear.

Sister Stryker opened her eyes and without turning said, "Come unto me, child." She knelt down in front of Ryne and he knew by the way she squinted just a little that she remembered as clearly as he when their eyes had locked and she got a little beside herself for a minute and lost her place. She got him in a bear hug, tight, so tight that Ryne thought at first it might be a new technique designed to squeeze the AIDS clean out of him. She spoke softly into his ear. "O Load, child," she said, "Jesus loves you. *Yes* he do! Oh how he loves you and me …" Then she was singing and the congregation joined in: *"Oh how he loves you and me. He gave his life, what more could he give. Oh, how he loves you and me."* Then she placed her palms against his cheeks and said: "He love you with that agape love, child. And I love you, too, little Rind."

Little Rind, who was not about to correct this holy woman who had a wicked right hook he had seen her use on many a demon, said, "Sister, can you and Jesus help me? I have AIDS, and I'm afraid I'm going to die soon."

"I know, honey," the Sister told him. "Yes, child, of course me and Jesus can help you, sugar. Now getting rid of that AIDS, it all be up to the Load."

Sister Stryker got back onto her feet and took ahold of Ryne's hand and quieted the crowd. "Hush up your mouths, y'all."

When they had hushed up their mouths, she spoke. "I would like to introduce you to Mister Rind, this fine young man here from a way up in the mountains of Tynbee, Tennessee, and this is his pastor, the Reverend Nathan McKee." The audience started going berserk then, and the Sister had to quiet them in order to go on. Sister Stryker asked Ryne, publicly this time, "What can the Lord do for you, Rind, if it be his will?"

Ryne pulled her down close and whispered in her ear. "It's Ryne, with an *e* on the end, not a *d*."

"Well, I beg your pardon, little Ryne honey," she whispered back. Then she told the crowd: "This is Ryne, y'all, not Rin*d*. I must be thinking about something else."

Then she held the microphone for Ryne. "I have AIDS," he said, "and my time is running out, and I know that if Doctor Lord Jesus wants to, he can heal me."

"Right you are, Ryne," Sister Stryker told him. "He gonna heal you one way or the other. Now blessed be the name of the Load."

At that, the audience went flat berserk. Sister Stryker did not even bother to tell them to hush, for, even if she had, it would have been of no use. They went wild, hog wild then, wilder than Ryne had ever seen them go on TV. Then it started, in various parts of the audience, a chant. "*We* love you, we *love* you, we love *you*." And before long, over and over, and at the tops of their lungs, shouting to high heaven, the fifteen thousand people in the Nashville Arena, two hundred miles from his home in Tynbee, expressed their agape love for Ryne O'Casey. He broke down weeping, and Preacher McKee and Sister Stryker and Elder Butts with him, as they stood there at center stage, hand in hand, as if to take their final bow.

"Oh, you-all sure-enough do me proud," Sister Stryker said, when at last the ovation ebbed. She mopped tears and sweat from her face with a shimmering silk kerchief with lavender and green paisleys. "Y'all do know a little something about agape love. Lord, there be nothing like it in all God's creation. Ha-le-a-hi-le-o hay-he-ho ha-le-o."

Then the Sister motioned for Preacher McKee to pick Ryne up. "My dear brother Preacher, Load Jesus has laid it on my heart that you, too, are going to get a blessing."

Nathan picked Ryne up and held him close. The two ushers moved in and stood behind them. Sister Stryker placed her soft damp palms on the sides of Ryne's head and threw her own head back so that she was staring straight at the scoreboard above and maybe beyond it into the very face of Jehovah Rapha. "Ah lee ah la-la da-ba-da me-lee," she shouted in that foreign language. Then she prayed. "Load Jesus, little Ryne here be in a right bad way. You will heal him, Load, we know that much. We don't know how you'll go about doing it and Load, no, we don't know just *when* you'll go about doing it. For that be your business alone and your ways are not our ways. But we know you have done it, are doing it now even as I speak, and will continue to heal this blessed little child of yours world without end, forever and ever and ever and ever. Amen."

Sister Stryker paused. The crowd in the Nashville Arena was so quiet that Ryne was sure he could hear people's feet shuffling around out in the grand corridor, could hear all those fifteen thousand hearts beating together in time. Then the Sister said, her voice rising as she went on, "O Load, you giveth and you taketh away, blessed be the name of the Load. We *all* got to go because it is appointed unto a man once't to die, but if it be thy will, Load, spare this child an untimely demise and don't make his mama feel the pain you felt, Lord, when we took your only child and *nailed him* to a tree—not because of anything he did, but because of all the things that we did and didn't do!"

"Load, please," she screamed, begged, pleaded, dealing with the Lord, as he had heard his own mom do so many nights. Tears and sweat made her black face shine like maple syrup on burnt pancakes. "Either way," she said, shaking her head, "He's your child first. Your onliest littlest son, too. Grant it, Load, that we all be together on that glorious yonder shore when the fullness of time shall come. Have mercy on us. Amen!"

Then, without opening her eyes, Sister Miranda Stryker delivered her palm heal attack, which landed square on Ryne's forehead. It started in the tips of his toes, a warm tingling sensation, like warm water on cold skin, and spiraled up all the way to the crown of his head. It reminded him of all those good times he had spent playing mummy with Terrence Ford, who used to mummify Ryne with old bed sheets they had snuck out of his mom's linen closet. Only this was better, so much better.

Sister Stryker's palm seemed to linger forever on Ryne's forehead, then slowly, very slowly, he and Preacher McKee were falling, falling backward, backward slowly, slowly down, and in that falling instant the world seemed to stop spinning right then and right there. They might have been falling from the highest heaven, might have been falling from a cliff forty feet up, might have been falling into the very hand of God.

And when, at last, they touched down, Nathan clutched Ryne tight against him—back to chest—and made no (*absolutely no*) attempt to break his fall. He shifted neither left nor right and let himself fall flat into the waiting arms of the ushers, who laid them gently down on the carpeted floor of the stage in the Nashville arena.

And they were healed.

The Healing

THE THIRD SUNDAY NIGHT IN OCTOBER was moonless and frosty. A bitter wind rustled the leaves of the mighty hardwoods and rattled the single-paned windows of the Historic First Church of Tynbee, Tennessee, where the congregation was assembling for the monthly business meeting. Interim Pastor Daniel Nathan McKee sat in his office warming his hands before the glow of the small space heater he had brought over from the parsonage.

It was the thirteenth—and, according to the terms of his contract, the last—such business meeting over which he was to preside. And as with the preceding twelve such meetings, so it was with the thirteenth business meeting: There was but one item of business on the agenda—whether to permit Ryne O'Casey, who had given his heart to Jesus the previous month, to be baptized by immersion in the church baptistry.

It was almost six o'clock—the appointed time, and Nathan was eager to get the meeting started. He switched off the heater and got up, gathered his Bible and the hand-carved hickory gavel. "They needn't bother voting on this issue," Nathan told the empty office. "Ryne O'Casey *will* be baptized, by *me*, in the baptistry of this church, if it's the last thing I ever do."

He stepped out in the drafty hallway, felt the chill, and for a moment considered the burlap cassock, which had been locked up in the metal utility closet since he had shed it like a molting snake the day Elder Bailey suffered his heart attack, the day Ryne O'Casey went forward. *Maybe just for warmth?*

No, he decided: You cannot fit new preachers in old cassocks. Then he was off, heading quickly toward the sanctuary, where Miriam and Sue Ella Bailey were playing their duet, "Sweet, Sweet Spirit."

A few minutes later, Nathan stood at the lectern and directed the congregation to be seated. The church was full, and with a few notable exceptions the congregants were in their respective positions on either side of the church. Luther's folks were on the left. But during the preceding month, he had come to view the longstanding opposition between the warring factions in the church as more a matter of politics than principles and passion (unless the principle was *what they are for, we are against* and the passion was for *a big old slapdown*). It cut both ways. There were saints and sinners, and there was love and hate, and good and evil, on both sides of the center aisle at the Historic First Church. And if they were not exactly distributed equally between the sides, they were there nonetheless.

Delegates from neighboring churches had not made a strong showing, thanks be to God. This was an internal affair, a family squabble, and, as the old saying went, airing the family's dirty laundry was something better done out back than out front. Three important family members were present—Ryne, Esther, and Olie O'Casey—and Nathan was glad for it because, in the event that the matter had to be settled by vote (every matter in the preceding twelve business meetings had gone to a vote), the O'Caseys just might provide the needed swing votes.

Nathan shook his head. *No.*

I am the swing vote, even if what I have to swing is a whip of cords to clean out my Father's house; even if the vote is unanimous, 147-0, in opposing Ryne's baptism, even if Ryne himself has changed his mind and votes against his own baptism, even if ... Ryne O'Casey will be baptized next Sunday, right back there in that rusty old baptismal pool, even if I have to dunk him in the water kicking and screaming.

Nathan banged the gavel to officially call the meeting to order. *Would it go out with a bang or a whimper?* he wondered, as he recognized Elder Gosset. "For what purpose does Elder Gosset rise?"

"Preacher McKee," Elder Gosset drawled, "I hereby enter a motion that we grant the petition of our dear friend and little brother in Christ, Ryne O'Casey, to be baptized by immersion in the church baptistry yonder at the conclusion of the worship service Sunday morning next."

"A motion has been entered," Nathan said. "Is there a second?"

At once, several dozen people on both sides of the center aisle rose to be recognized. Nathan felt his heart sink. *Not again,* he thought, *not over a sacrament. Folks, this debate is moot—a holy waste of your time and my energy.* He was the only officially ordained member of the congregation, and, though he didn't believe his clergy status accorded him any special privileges not shared by all believers, he would pretend to believe it, if need be: He would pull rank. *That was that.*

"The chair recognizes Mr. Jeeves?" he said.

Buster Jeeves shouted, "I second Elder Gosset's motion, *whole*heartedly."

"A motion has been duly entered and seconded," Nathan informed the congregation with the somewhat mercurial tone that was the province of prophets who knew the outcome before it came. "Before we turn our attention to other matters, let us take a referendum on the seconded motion under consideration, the motion to grant Ryne O'Casey's petition to be baptized in the baptistry of the Historic First Church of Tynbee, Tennessee, next Sunday morning after the worship service. All in favor let it be known by saying 'aye.'"

A chorus of ayes thundered throughout the sanctuary, the most emphatic of which came from the back row of the right side of the church (where Esther, Olie, and Ryne O'Casey were seated alongside T. K. Kirby). The windows rattled. T. K. Kirby's "aye-aye-aye-aye" was unmistakable (Esther said later it was like his hollering "aye" echoed into eternity or from eternity, like God himself was saying, Let it be done). And maybe tonight his stuttering "aye" had more to do with his love for Ryne O'Casey than with his speech defect.

"All opposed let it be known by saying 'no.'"

To the surprise of all, the chorus of no's was decidedly weak compared to the ayes. It was hardly a chorus at all. "In the opinion of the chair," Nathan said, "the ayes have it."

The no's, however few, were not going to take it sitting down. At least one wasn't. Jimmy Joe Cole, the usher, stood up. "I motion that a written vote be recorded, Mister Chair. Seeing as how this poses a serious health risk to us all."

No one, not a single person, rose and seconded Jimmy Joe's motion, but Nathan granted the motion anyway. "A motion has been entered and the chair, in the absence of a second, so orders: Let there be a recorded vote."

Nathan summoned the ushers to come forward. As he was charging them, the congregation let go a collective gasp. Nathan broke huddle and looked up, straight down the center aisle, and there in the door of the sanctuary, propped up in a wheelchair, was the ghastly—if not *ghostly*—figure of Elder Luther Bailey, with Sue Ella behind him in the shadows.

The pitiful old man looked, Esther would later remark, like death twice warmed over and she half thought, on first sight and until she was sure he wasn't toting a sickle, that he was the grim reaper. They had all heard that Elder Bailey was making a "satisfactory recovery" from his heart transplant surgery, but it couldn't be proved by looking at him. He was still quite ill and looked worse than he had on the day of his heart attack when they rolled him out of the church on a gurney. If he was wasted before his heart attack, he was positively skeletal now.

Sue Ella stooped down and whispered in his ear, and he said something to her that no one could hear, then she pushed him slowly down the center aisle to the altar and turned him around to face the congregation. "Ushers," he said, trying to raise his hand, "go back to your kinfolk and sit down." His voice was weak but stern.

The elder's breath seemed to catch in his throat. He coughed carefully and winced, then continued: "There's no need for a written vote on this matter. Bad off as I am, and without my hearing piece in, I could tell that the ayes had it—prob'ly by a hundred and thirty or more. It is finished, people. It is *finished*. And Ryne O'Casey will be baptized here next Sunday morning after the service."

It was finished, he had declared. The congregation sat silent and perfectly still for a long while before, a clap at a time, they broke into applause.

With a motion of his frail right hand, Elder Bailey summoned Nathan, who had sat down on the front pew. "Preacher McKee," he said, "I have an announcement to make, if I might."

"Of course," Nathan said. "You have the floor."

"People," he said, and everyone cocked their heads to hear, "I am resigning my post on the Board of Elders of this here church. Effective immediately." He paused. His eyes were damp. "I've done a lot of thinking over this past month, and a lot of praying, too, and I think it's time for some new *blood* here."

NATHAN LAY IN BED THAT NIGHT THINKING: *A chain is only as weak as its strongest link.* That's probably the spin Jesus of Nazareth would put on the old saying if he were telling a parable about the events that occurred in Tynbee, Tennessee, during the past several months. Jesus had such a remarkable way of turning things—not least the whole world—upside down. He would also say, perhaps, that *what goes around does not always come around—and should not.* But at the Historic First Church of Tynbee, Tennessee, thanks to the effective, fervent prayers of many members—on both sides of the aisle—the church was perhaps beginning to come around to a very new and startling discovery about the power of love, about the meaning of grace.

If they had not exactly beat their swords into plowshares, they were mending their ways, slowly and, Nathan hoped, surely. What had begun on that magical Autumn night in the Nashville Arena (and even before) was nothing short of a miracle.

It is finished.

Epilogue

LOOKING BACK from some months' distance on that blustery night in late September when Sister Miranda Stryker laid her hands on Ryne and prayed, prayed hard, in the halo glow of the spotlight in the Nashville Arena, Esther O'Casey said they all knew—she and Olie and Ryne—that Ryne had not been cured of AIDS.

But they also knew—without a doubt—that they had been *healed* of AIDS that night.

The chills and the fevers, the aches and infections and fatigue, never went away. But neither did that tingling sensation, like warm water on cold skin, that filled him in that graceful moment of agape love as he stood in the spotlight two hundred miles from his home. "We love you, we love you, we love you," his friends had assured him, expressing their agape love for Ryne O'Casey, whom they knew only as a child well loved of God who was, in Sister Miranda Stryker's words, *in a right bad way.*

When the end came, Ryne, weary from the hard fight, was far more ready to go than his mom and dad were to let him go. How they clung to him—Esther and Olie and the others who loved Ryne best: T. K. Kirby and Buster Jeeves; Elder and Lula Gosset; Uncle Heyward, still smelling to high heaven of drink but minding his manners; and Dr. Daniel Nathan and Miriam McKee. They kept vigil and wept and laughed and ate and prayed and wondered.

And on a bitter cold day in February, as the first golden light of morning gilded the eastern range, with a Spiderman comic book in his hand and the voice of Sister Miranda Stryker in his ears, Ryne O'Casey was healed.

About the Author

Scott Philip Stewart was reared in a Christian home with loving parents and a great many siblings (sixty, in fact, three of whom were biological and fifty-seven of whom were "fostered" by his family). Stewart quips that he was born with "a broken heart" ... but notes that after three tries his physicians finally managed to fix it. He holds degrees in religion, psychology, and human development (Ph.D., University of Georgia) and was for eight years a counselor in practice before returning to his first love—writing.

The Healing of Ryne O'Casey is Stewart's first novel and a story very close to his heart. While a student at Princeton Theological Seminary in 1986, word came that his two older brothers had been diagnosed with HIV. Stewart returned to Atlanta to be with his family and experienced, during the years that followed, joy and grace in the midst of the great pain and loss. His favorite verse of Scripture is, "My grace is sufficient for you," which he has found to be true despite the trials he has faced, the mistakes he has made, and at the very best and the worst of times. Stewart lives with his family in Atlanta, Georgia, and is at work on his second novel.